The Tatiana File

For Patricia

The Tatiana File

William Paterson

FISH EAGLE BOOKS

About the Author

William Paterson, a journalist and author, was born of Scottish-Cornish parentage in Durban and grew up with his sister in an old colonial clifftop house, surrounded by virgin bush, with views of the Umgeni River and the Indian Ocean. He was educated at Michaelhouse, then the Durban School of Art in Natal and the University of Westminster, London. Upon his return to South Africa he spent most of his working life in the media. He is now settled with his Irish wife Patricia in Co Wexford, Ireland, where he continues to write.

Acknowledgements

I am indebted to the many helpful people who provided invaluable insights, without which parts of this novel could not have been written: Bruce Botes General Manager of the Cathedral Peak Hotel, KwaZulu Natal, and Selby Mkhize, Ezemvelo Wildlife Ranger, concerning nocturnal fauna in that part of the Drakensberg Mountains; Gerald Buttigieg, Telkom Fundi and cofounder of the website Facts About Durban, for enlightening me on the limitations of the South African telephone system in 1949 or thereabouts, which was still emerging from the prewar 'nommer asseblief / number please' days; Michael Dempsey, Librarian, Wexford Public Library, for descriptions of Wexford quayscapes during early post-war II; Johan du Toit, owner of the 'Star of the West', Kimberley, for allowing the venue to be made part of the story; Torstein & Susan Strandenes-Ellis, bell ringers and musicians of note, for practical guidance on ringing the changes, and providing clarity on clock tower bell access; John Garahy, retired Irish solicitor and historian, who threw light on traceability of records of Wexford Poorhouse inmates' death records during the late thirties; Des Gunning, Former Curator of the James Joyce Centre in Dublin, for unearthing the 1948 exchanges in Dáil Éireann concerning a Russian debt; South African journalist Bridget Hilton-Barber, who enlightened me with fresh insights into the arrest, imprisonment, and harsh treatment of political detainees during the Apartheid years. Initially in solitary confinement, Bridget was held for three months without being charged. Her autobiography, *Student Comrade Prisoner Spy* records the personal effect of her opposing Apartheid, as a young white student at Rhodes University in the Eastern Cape of South Africa. Her paperback was published by Penguin-Random House; *The Deadly Ethnic Riot* by Donald L Horowitz offered much graphic detail; Leana McLean, Kantoorbestuurder, NG Kerk Stellenbosch Moedergemeente, for NGK marriage requirements; Gareth McCullagh, Diamond Grader, for guidance on gem stone assessing and grading; Shiona Moodley, Head, Department of Rock Art, National Museum, Bloemfontein, for constructive observations on overhangs utilised by the San people, their ancient rock paintings and stone engravings; Jane O'Connor, a former Attorney in the South African Civil Service, for detailed clarification of that country's legal processes during the Apartheid years; Kirkwood Paterson, for most of the Glossary; Michael Poole, Ferry Master, for insights on the operation of Wexford Harbour during the early years after 'The Emergency'; Insights gleaned from Matthew Graham's Manuscript titled 'Cold War in Southern Africa' [accepted by University of Sheffield on 14/06/2010]; Sabrina Slattery of Hazelwood Stables, Co Wexford for practical guidance on winter stabling; Jane Tatam of Amolibros, my editor, whose wide knowledge and considerable editing experience has helped to knock this novel into shape; Charl Wessels of Clarens Educational Tours for details of the NG Church clock tower; Brian Williams, local historian, for rescuing this manuscript from a web Black Hole; David A Williams, Airborne-qualified US Marine veteran, for an overview of the transition from the OSS, at that time.

Apologies to the spirits of T S Eliot and Vicki Baum for allusions to their writings in a railway sequence during Manie's wanderings.

The cover design is by Áine Bogan of Think Print & Design in Wexford, Ireland. The cover picture of an Orange Free State windpump was kindly provided by Andrew Clelland of Johannesburg and the source of the back cover portrait of the Czarevna Tatiana is acknowledged as Boasson and Eggler, St Petersburg.

Foreword

William Paterson is an unusual individual – someone who has an intimate knowledge of both South Africa's and Ireland's troubled histories with the insight both of a son of South Africa and of his new home in Ireland. His insight and discernment equip him to draw in this experience into his new novel, which is lively and erudite, fast-moving and filled with high adventure and pathos. *The Tatiana File* will make its mark in the steadily growing bookshelf of Irish-South African literature.

Today there are, for the first time in the linkage between Ireland and South Africa, more South Africans living in Ireland than Irish in South Africa. In the past, the Irish huddled masses yearning to breathe free did not leave Ireland in great numbers for the highveld or the scrubby thornbush of the Eastern Cape. Most followed their kinfolk across the Atlantic to New England, replacing a miserable rural life with a slum in Boston, Pennsylvania or New York. Only a few followed the route taken by Stout Diaz centuries before and ventured across the equator, south to the end of the African continent, where they made a home. As they said of the old Oregon Trail – the cowards never started and the weak died along the way.

To South Africa came the Irish missionaries of God, the Irish soldiers of the Queen and the adventurous, inquisitive and the foolhardy. A cohort of about 100,000 at its height, who concentrated in specific occupations, creating an impression of far greater impact than their numbers justified. They worked on the railways, which, more than gold, wars or mielies, helped to create a unified South Africa. The Irish were also in the old colonial mounted police forces and militia (the Cape Town Irish Rifles never fired a shot in battle). They founded such household stores as John Orrs, R H Henderson and William Cuthbert's – and the Irish were on the mines.

Mining was one of those professions which attracted the best and the worst. John MacBride, to be shot by the British in Dublin in 1916, and Arthur Griffith, the founder of the political movement Sinn Fein, were with other Irish lads out in the old Transvaal working on the Langlaagte mine. Others were across in Griqualand West at the diamond diggings, where illicit diamond buying, prominent in this novel, was the order of the day.

Meanwhile, back in Dublin, and stirred up by Griffith, Maud Gonne and W B Yeats pro-Boer excitement swept nationalist Ireland, as fervent as pro-Gaza sentiment today. And being Irish and to complicate matters, Irish Catholic soldiers in the Irish regiments in the British army out in South Africa served heroically as front-line spear-head forces – the Dublin Fusiliers, Connaught Rangers, 5th Royal Lancers – about 30,000 in total. The finest war memorial in Great Britain and Ireland is the triumphal arch at the top of Dublin's Grafton Street. The names of the dead from the slums of Dublin are engraved on that South African war memorial, a reminder that life is not always convenient for any nationalist narrative.

Belfast's Harland and Wolfe built Union Castle liners. There were Irish mission stations in the Karoo and Zululand; a host of Irish-South African newspaper founders and editors;

and the extraordinary phenomenon in the 1920s of the newly created Irish Free State and General Hertzog's South Africa hunting as a pack, in a 'Fellowship of disaffection', to undermine and destroy the British dominion system and, by extension, the British Empire.

And then arrived formal, structured and illogical apartheid. And slowly but surely a curtain came down between South Africa and the new post-World War II Western world. Soon, Irish governments were happy to airbrush away their old link with which southern Africa had dated back to the 1780s. They cautiously encouraged the Irish Anti-Apartheid Movement, which flourished in intellectual Dublin, and introduced some symbolic sanctions. Slowly but surely the gate slammed shut. Such is the Irish diasporic background to this extraordinary saga penned by William Paterson, no stranger to either region; one a small green island with five million inhabitants and the other a large arid sub-continent with 65 million people. A salt-of-the-earth, honest, Afrikaner police detective, who could as easily have come from the peat bogs of Ireland; a mysterious young Irish woman found dead atop the train from godforsaken De Aar; the beginnings of forced removals; and lush subtropical and exotic Durban, where the track ends. And bookended between the wide expanses of South Africa is a nuanced Ireland of the late 1940s; poor, under-developed and confined within the structures laid down by the church. There is Wexford, where the Normans first landed in 1169; the timeless White's Hotel in Wexford, where closing time meant the front door was shut but the spirit still flowed; and the working-class Liberties area of Dublin, where grinding poverty was assuaged by robust talk and sharp observation.

It is an accepted maxim that imperial Russian jewels are best avoided; bringing doom as they did, and no doubt still do to their current possessors. This is Paterson's fast-moving chase after them, with the story's equally exotic end beside a small koppie in the Orange Free State, a million miles away from the avarice brought by diamonds and the greed of men a continent away.

Donal P. McCracken FLS, FRHistS, Emeritus Professor
of History: University of KwaZulu-Natal
Irish books include: *Irish Heritage in South Africa,*
MacBride's Brigade: Irish Commandos in the Boer War,
Ireland & South Africa and the Anglo-Boer War, Teddy
Luther's War, General Nicholson and Irish Threatening Letters.
Editor of *Southern African-Irish Studies*
Named South African Genealogist of the Year

Main Characters

Manie Marais – Bloemfontein detective

Rentia Myburgh – Clarens paleo-archaeologist and Curator of the little Clarens Museum

Nerene Marais – Manie's musical sister in De Aar

Jannie van Niekerk – Manie and Nerene's cousin. He and his family have a farm near Wamakersdrift.

Mavis April – Manie's mixed-race housekeeper

Sophia Vitali-Kluczynska ("Zosha") – Polish émigré lepidopterist at the Durban Museum

"Izambane" – nickname of Manie's stalwart Zulu assistant, Lungelo Myeni

"Biscuit" – Portsmouth Detective George Baker, married to Judy

Theresa O'Brien – Irish postgrad student, seconded to "Zosha"

Anne Butler – Tern ornithologist. Dwells on Forth Mountain

"Mazawatee" – Anne Butler's mother

John Scantlebury Blankenheimer – Packard Car representative. An American

Fiachra Brennan – Detective Inspector at The Faythe Garda Station

Aleksander Turetsky – Polish refugee

The Potgieters – Pretentious Rhodesian couple

Adam & Alexandria – A couple from Manicaland, friends of Anne Butler

Contents

Preface

Our novel is set in a notional 1949, but strays, in places, to compress a string of events, factual and otherwise. Except for a few people, now long gone, any resemblance to persons living is unintentional; and the characters in these pages are figments of my imagination. There is, however, a close echo of events in South Africa, its landscapes, history and prehistory. Some Russian and Irish passages parallel actuality even more closely, but you won't be able to find that little graveyard in The Faythe, or the Phoenix in Bloemfontein, or the Ou Waenhuis in Clarens, although the NG Kerk clock tower does exist there, near Architect Gerhardt Moerdyk's Manse.

As a young son of a proudly Scottish father, I struggled to read the Robert Burns' poetry he offered for my study, hindered mostly by the poet's, often impenetrable Scots. For the sake of clarity, then, when you read passages where Afrikaners converse, no attempt has been made to imitate the veld-drenched accents of Afrikaners speaking English. In fact, you will just have to imagine that they are speaking in their mother tongue, where they do, despite being captured here in English. The same applies to the Zulus. Manie Marais is pronounced '<u>Mar</u>-knee Mar-<u>air</u>' and Rentia Myburgh '<u>Rensh</u>-ia <u>May-bearg</u>, the 'g' gutturally.

Prologue

'There was blood everywhere. We had to bayonet the children after shooting the adults. The servants screamed the loudest when they realised what was about to happen, but the Tsar and Tsarina just stared straight at us. The Tzarevnas clutched each other and howled when they realised that their fate was sealed.

'It was Yakov Yurovsky who gave the order to start the killings – on the instructions of the Ural Regional Soviet. That's what he said, but I don't believe it…it must have come from Lenin himself.

'When they were dead, they were stripped of their clothes and Yurovsky took charge of the gemstones found in the linings of Tzarevna Tatiana's dress. Then the bodies were thrown onto a cart that night and secretly taken up to the Koptyaki forest, where they were disfigured with hand grenades…then the body parts were buried. I don't know why, but the little children were buried separately.'

Chapter One

The girl's body was wedged between the second and third carriage canopies. It was spotted first by Detective-Sergeant Manie Marais, who was at the Bloemfontein railway station awaiting the arrival of his spinster sister aboard the train from DeAar.

The day remained hot, as only a Free State late afternoon can be, until a few moments later, there was the crash and tinkle of windows being blown shut all over the town by the sudden arrival of the hot dry highveld wind, which had dust-devilled its way across the Reddersburg livestock and mielie fields half an hour earlier, bringing a fog of fine dust and whirling paper.

It was early October, and no rain had fallen since April. The winter was well over, yet the few clouds that did form would drift away to the Maluti mountains in Lesotho. Most white office workers had gone home behind Naval Hill or had headed for sundowners at the Ramblers Club, a sports club and watering hole reserved for whites, as were all other Bloemfontein amenities. A few would have wandered off to the Mazelspoort riverbank to sip sundowners beneath the weeping willows, and, in time, to watch the usual evening train clatter across the bridge on its way to Brandfort, its lights twinkling. The all-enveloping dust soon arrived there too, exasperating the stargazers, yattering about exo-planets, who had gathered at the observatory. Viewings would be ruined for much of the night.

It was also the time for Sotho labourers to queue for their buses in Power Street, near the abattoir and the 'winkels vir naturelle', which would transport them back to a squatter settlement called Kromdraai, with its unlit, stinking and littered paths, well away from the manicured lawns and streetlights of town.

Manie was torn between greeting his sister and responding to the sight of the body. Fortunately, he spotted a railway policeman alighting and rushed to enlist his help in stopping travellers from leaving the platform; after which he raced to the station master's office to make calls summoning a police photographer, the police doctor and an ambulance. Then he returned to the platform, to hurriedly embrace his sister, asking her to wait inside the station buildings along with all the other alighted passengers so that he and the police might interview everyone from the second and third carriages.

'Yuss!' complained his sister. 'What kind of welcome is this? We've brought the Vrystaat dust too!'

In time, he left it to the railway policeman to complete the interviews, and returned to the railway carriages, armed with a ladder to supervise the police photographer and examine the body in situ.

The girl was slim and clad in light bush-bashing clothes of cotton blouse and khaki slacks. Her socks were still there, but her shoes or boots were gone and had to be found later by a constable pacing along the track all the way to Wurasoord station, near Reddersburg. The dead girl was aged about twenty-five or so, slim, with wide cheekbones – almost Slavic, or Malaysian, he thought. Her mouth was generously lipsticked but locked in a rictus smile of pain. He searched about for other belongings, but there were none.

Apologising to his sister, still sitting in the waiting room with her luggage, he arranged for a taxi to drive her to his house, then discussed the reports garnered by the railway policeman, who said that quite a few passengers had noticed a thump on the roof, as the train drew out of Wurasoord platform, near Reddersburg (the railway bypassed the dorp itself).

'Well, at least we can speculate that the body fell from the Wurasoord railway footbridge. It's a start,' he thought. 'My God, that poor girl! Slowly dying in the burning heat on the railway carriage roof; and what in heaven was she doing there? The only settlement nearby was a mission station. He sighed at the prospect of having to motor to that forlorn spot and decided to put it off until the Monday.

Spectators were kept at bay, except for the engine driver and stoker and stationmaster who pointed out that the delay was disrupting other services all the way down the line, in both directions. Inevitably, a reporter from *Die Volksblad* arrived just before a cub reporter from *The Friend*, managing to get through the barrier accompanied by a photographer lugging his Graflex.

'No bloody photographs!' shouted Manie.

'But he's taking photographs!'

'He's the police photographer, you bloody dummkopf – now bugger off, the lot of you, and take your Weegeeman with you, before I arrest all of you. You'll get a police statement well before your deadline tonight… . You can phone me at home and here's the number,' he said handing out cards to both journalists but not the photographers.

The light had faded before the passengers, holed up in the station waiting-room were allowed to leave and before the police doctor had completed his examination. Only then was the girl lowered onto a stretcher and taken away to the police morgue, and only then was the dust-coated train released to proceed.

Manie was tired of the palaver and was looking forward to catching up with his sister. He hoped that she wouldn't like the idea of dining out on the first night after all – even though he had booked for dinner at the Bloemfontein Hotel where they put on a good spread. He felt burdened by the thought of having to prepare a statement for the papers. Inevitably the report would find its way through the local press thence to the Press Association and Reuters – and heaven knows where that would land up. He would have to offer his sister a drink and then disappear to write the press statement.

Marais' wife, Emma, had died several years ago and he missed her terribly, particularly so, with both their sons having moved away, one to the Eastern Cape to farm fruit in Kirkwood, the other to Nottingham Road in Natal, with families and concerns of their own. Thus, it was comforting to have a close womanly relation in the house, with whom he got on very well, to supplement the motherly presence of his Coloured housekeeper, Mavis – who, probably, understood him better than anyone else. 'Coloured', is a curious South African nomenclature for a mixed-race person. She was permitted to live in rooms, attached, but separated from the rest of the house, and was not obliged to be out of Bloemfontein by the nightly nine o'clock siren, which would wail from the town's power station chimneys.

As he entered the house he heard music, and discovered his sister on the veranda, the French doors flung open, reclining on a wicker couch. She was holding a drink, which she held up in greeting and said, 'SHhhh!' At that moment the record changer, the latest thing, plopped the last disc onto the turntable. Then sounded the opening bars of the last movement of Liszt's First Piano Concerto, with its bewitched exchange between the triangle, the plucked strings and the piano.

Manie quietly poured himself an Opsaal brandy and ginger ale, then stretched down beside her.

They remained silent long after the triumphal ending, until Manie said,

'Nerene, I am so pleased to see you but I am sorry that events made a "gemors" of my welcome. I had planned to take you out to dinner but now I must write a report immediately after supper –otherwise I will be in trouble with the newspapers – you know what they're like.'

'I am relieved we are not going out – in fact I am going to crash immediately after supper.'

The detective's house was at the end of a short cul-de-sac which petered out into scrub at the foot of Naval Hill, a feature on the edge of the town, in a terrain where hills and koppies were few and far between, in a land where mirage-haunted roads ran straight from horizon to horizon.

The only other house in in their Kruis Street cul-de-sac was owned by an Eskenazi Jew, Cecil Bing and his Dutch artist wife, Beatrix. Cecil was a sub-editor at *The Friend* newspaper, which fought a noble but losing battle against the Afrikaans language newspaper, *Die Volksblad*. He whiled away his leisure hours writing occasional articles for overseas newspapers under a nom-de-plume and sailing his dinghy with their daughter Hannah on a farm dam. His wife stayed at home, made koeksisters, tended her flowerbeds with the garden boy, and painted large canvases with a great deal of art-school-trained talent. She pursued a form of stylised realism in portraying the deprived Sotho people all around her, their faces undernourished and exophthalmic. Manie professed to know 'nothing about art' but was drawn to her pictures. Hannah was in her first year, reading History. All were avid readers and competed in discovering unexpected novels at the modest municipal Library. Hannah's current discovery was *The Naked Moment* set in Reykjavik, of all places.

The Bings were cordial neighbours, and Manie had developed a friendship with Cecil, on the understanding that they possessed different views on religion and politics. Thus, on some Sundays, while the world was still bedewed, it would find them setting off to jog up and over Naval Hill, even while distant church bells sounded, barely disturbing the zebras which merely lifted their heads and left off grazing as they passed. The men's exertions would end with a plunge in the municipal swimming pool at the southern foot of the hill.

At breakfast the next morning, Manie and his sister had just commenced to spoon up helpings of maas, sweetened with sugar and a squeeze of lemon, when the phone rang. It was Corporal van Heerden who said, 'That body that came in late yesterday, in the morgue…'

'Ja, well?'

'The pathologist is grumbling about having to come in on Saturday, but he's here now and insists that you come down to the station immediately – we've discovered something in her clothing.'

'I wish you'd called me after breakfast. Okay, I'll get down there,' he said, putting down the receiver and, returning to the patio, said, 'Sussie, I have to go down to the police station immediately. Tell Mavis I'll have breakfast when I get back. It shouldn't take too long, but not my idea of a free weekend that I had set aside to spend with you.'

Down at the station, the pathologist and his assistant were sitting in Marais' office, smoking cigarettes.

'Before we go through, I want you to look at these,' the pathologist said, nodding to five unusually large gems the size of big walnut shells on the desk, one bright purple. 'We found them in the lining of her bush trousers. In one of the pockets was this train ticket and a small notepad crammed with sundry notes about figures and images – take this example, "Schaaplaats Therianthropes part-human, part-animal / altered state / eland and a rhebuck hunt. Fossil footprints * Hoekfontein / Clocolan 14 dancing. 6 infibulated / palettes /7 steenbok 1 eland /Mfecane refuge" and then there's this which she has underlined twice: "Ndedema. Cathedral Peak. <u>Falling antelope</u> <u>Bethlehem</u> also <u>Clarens</u> cave. Compare SA engravings rock art Blackstairs Leinster?" and on the next page "<u>Doda Yegolide</u>" doubly underlined – obviously very important – and a lot of gibberish. See, pages, and pages.'

'The train ticket is made out to Miss Theresa O'Brien, 3B Coupe, 2nd Class for the train from Durban to Bloemfontein, thirty-five days ago, and those gemstones. She had no wallet, so no other means of identification. The purse contained a £10 note and there's another £80 hidden in her brassiere, which has a small sachet to hide such things – oh, and loose change in her purse comprising a florin – look how it's twisted right out of shape, funny, that – three shillings, a sixpence, and three tickeys. We noticed that the lining of her trousers had been cut close to the other gemstones, and then clumsily restitched, as if some gems had been removed. One more thing – this tiny shaped stone. It's been flaked and chipped away as if to form a cutting tool.'

'I know what that is – you find a lot of them on farms near Kathu, about three hours away in the Northern Cape. They were left behind by the Stone Age people forty thousand –

maybe a million – years or so ago. I saw a collection of them in the McGregor Museum at Kimberley when I was visiting. Interesting that she was holding on to one. Kathu…that's a long way away. What was she doing wandering around there – or perhaps a friend just gave it to her, as a keepsake?'

'What about the shoes?'

'We found them on the line near Reddersburg. Strange they came off. They're hiking boots, mightily scuffed – lots of wear – they were bought from Cuthbert's in Durban, according to the labels. But why were they found further down the track? And where are her socks? But something else, her clothes were both labelled, Hikers' Haven, Wexford.'

'Wexford? Where the hell's that?'

'Buggered if I know. Have you got an atlas? Or try the newspaper or the library.'

'Well, there's nothing we can do until Monday, so I'll make out a list in front of you and then lock them in the safe for the weekend. As for the post-mortem, I'll leave you to that sickening prospect and see you on Monday morning. That is, unless you find something else untoward – if so, feel free to phone me at home over the weekend.'

He was on the point of leaving the police station when he was called back by Corporal van Heerden, explaining that the station commander had left him in charge for an hour, during which he had to deal with a family of Indians who were caught travelling through the Orange Free State without a permit. The corporal appealed to him for his help as he was the most senior person present.

'Where are they?'

'Their car's outside. I had to lock them into a spare cell. They've two young children with them, sir.'

Arriving at the cell, he saw a frightened family sitting on the floor. The parents looked prosperous enough, the wife swathed in a sari, he in a suit. There was a grandmother, similarly, clad in a nine-yard sari, and a boy and a girl aged about five or six. One of them, the boy, cried when Manie appeared.

'What the hell do you think you're doing, travelling to the Free State without registration…where are your identification papers?'

'Your policeman took them, sir. Sir, it is an emergency. We live in Ladysmith and got a call from our Cape Town cousins in the Bo-Kaap, in Dorp Street, sir, to say that our grandfather was dying and that we should come quickly. That was last night, sir. When we got to the Ladysmith police station last night, we found it closed, so were unable to get our papers in order. We decided to travel from four o'clock this morning to Bloemfontein and report to the nearest police station – which we have done, hoping that the police will understand that we were not trying to break the law, sir.'

'What's your name?'

'Abdel Fattah and this is my wife, Jawaria,' he said, going on to reel off the other names.

'You had better come with me to your car. Corporal!' he shouted, and when the latter appeared, said, 'Take this family through to the European waiting room and let the ladies use the toilet, if they wish. I am taking the driver to the car so that I can inspect it. Hand me his keys, please.'

'But Sir…the European waiting room and toilet.'

'You kept these people in a cell without any facilities, no food and I'm sure that the ladies will want to use the toilet. If you can't bear the idea, just look away… Get one of the kaffirs to wash out the lavatory with Jeyes Fluid after they've gone.'

'Fattah, open the boot and a car door. I want to look inside.' Manie lifted out the suitcases and peered about inside the car with a detective's eye; then satisfied, after inspecting the contents of the cases said, 'All right, you can go. I'll get the corporal to hand back your passes. You must exit the Free State today and report to the Colesburg police station. I'll phone ahead and tell them to expect your car. All you have to do is to go in and get the release paper signed, which we will get from the corporal. They won't delay you. Where are you stopping overnight? If you get as far as Beaufort West, contact a Dominee Barnard who looks after the Coloured folk. He'll find a place for you to stay overnight. Do you need food? Your children must be hungry, even if you grown-ups are not. I'll drive ahead of you to the nearest café and come with you inside, just to make sure they don't kick up a fuss about serving you.'

'Officer, sir, may you be blessed for your kindness. Salamu-'Alaikum.'

Manie stood outside the café and watched the Indian's vehicle disappear into the distance, the children waving. Driving back to breakfast and his sister, his tummy rumbling, his mind continued to dwell on the circumstances surrounding the mysterious death of Theresa O'Brien. Who was Julius Nkoko and why was she carrying a florin so twisted out of shape that it was useless as a coin – and that stone…? Were the latter just keepsakes, or did they have a greater significance, he wondered?

You could see a family resemblance between Manie and his sister, although she was slightly freckled and a few inches shorter. She had been engaged to a dashing South African Air Force officer attached to the meteorological department just before the Second World War until she discovered that he was carrying on an affair with another girl. She broke off the engagement with such disillusionment that she remained a spinster, from that time on devoting herself to teaching at the girls' school. With the effluxion of time, she took up the post of Assistant Principal. She encouraged a love of classical music among her pupils with the dream that no girl would complete an education at the school without being able to read musical notation and to play an instrument. The De Aar School duly gained a reputation for such endeavours and many a girl distinguished herself in the national Eisteddfods.

She was taking the holiday break to visit her brother, and a cousin who owned a sheep farm at Wamakersdrift, near Koffiefontein. When their cousin, Jannie van Niekerk, was not preoccupied by the farm, his wife and their children, he pursued the study of termites whose anthills were a feature of the landscape.

Manie, her brother was content with his lot of rising to detective inspector, hoping that he would have reached Captain, or perhaps even Lieutenant-Colonel by the time of his retirement. Of late, he developed a nervous twitch in his right eye which caused him to be nicknamed 'Winker Marais'. The nervous tic was occasionally misconstrued by prisoners during interviews and a few women. During the war years he had been posted (as a Key Worker and thus excused from joining up) to Jagersfontein, about an hour and a half away, on an untarred and dusty road. Here, his time was taken up with the usual commotions associated with the Italian prisoners-of-war camp and the 500 South African detainees. The latter were considered to be dangerously active in the extreme right-wing organisation called Ossewa Brandwag (Ox wagon-Burning Watch / Sentinal). One of the detainees, a Hendrik Verwoerd, was to rise to prominence after the war by becoming a Senator when the right-wing Nationalist party swept into power in 1948. It was a matter of continuing amusement that Jagersfontein was the source of the enormous Jubilee Diamond, presented to Queen

Victoria on her Jubilee and the prisoner of a Senator bitterly committed to ridding South Africa of British influence. It was now 1949 and Manie was proud that predominantly the Nationalists were now in power, even though his interest in politics did not burn brightly.

It was early closing day, and he humoured his sister by driving her into town to shop at Fichardt's and Sonop. Shopping was his least favourite chore but, because it was his sister, he persevered. The last port of call was Ivan Haarburger's in a high, pressed-steel ceilinged, musical instrument shop where she bought viola strings and tried out the new uprights which, mysteriously, had found their way from Leipzig, behind the Iron Curtain. Tucked away, in a far corner, was a celeste, slumbering in its cobweb heaven, until awoken by Nerene's fingers.

He broke the news that he had to drive to Wurasoord on the Monday before they went across the road to the Bings, who had invited them for dinner that evening. He was relieved when she said, 'Well, perhaps I should come with you after which you can drive me to the van Niekerks – if they agree; I could visit them first and then come back and visit you for second week. Good idea?'

There was a bowl of orange river lilies on the dining table. The Bings liked their food and Cecil always took over from the Coloured maid when it came to the preparation and roasting of the beef and potatoes. He claimed that few knew how to make gravy properly – and that Bing was one of them. This he shouted to his guests from the kitchen during the critical roasting process, meanwhile quaffing a fair portion of the glass of cabernet sauvignon intended for the gravy. Cecil would grumble that it really should have been mature Bordeaux, but beggars could not be choosers.

Their other guest was a Father Jacobus, an extraordinary

Flemish priest who had driven his careworn bakkie from his parish near the border of Lesotho and would stay overnight with the Bings, departing early in the morning to arrive at dawn in time to administer communion to his indigenous flock. The main purpose of his Bloemfontein visit was to collect donated food supplies from Fichardt's and some other stores. He was an enthusiastic painter though some Free State cognoscenti disparaged his fauve de Vlaminck-like pictures of donkeys, farm labourers and sunflowers as 'daubs'. His hosts would switch to Afrikaans to deter him from attempting to speak what the priest imagined to be English. Even to understand his almost incomprehensible guttural Flemish was difficult, despite the fact that both languages – Afrikaans and Flemish – are akin.

Sales from his paintings went towards supporting the poorest of his Tswana flock at his little school near the border.

'So the Russkies now have the bomb too,' said Cecil. 'Now we've got both the Yanks and the Soviets able to blow us all to smithereens – mind you, it could turn out to be a Mexican stand-off…enemies with hands on their six-shooters, wondering who's going to fire first. A pity about the Russians – great music, great literature, great art, but ghastly leaders. I read that their bomb was tested secretly somewhere in the Kazakh region, wherever that is, of middle eastern Europe. It was only discovered by American surveillance aircraft reporting a surge in radioactivity. There's much agitation in the airwaves as well…Bill Thatcher, a sub on the paper is a ham radio enthusiast. He invited us around to his house the other day to listen to the first broadcast of Radio Free Europe, transmitted on shortwave from Munich, and aimed at Soviet-controlled countries. Interesting – but a bit too much brazenly anti-Communist rhetoric.'

'Agree, let's talk about something else. Sussie, that was

an awful return to Bloemfontein you had – Manie, you too, although I suppose you've been hardened to such sights. Who was the girl?'

'I can't tell you more than you've read in the papers today, as you realise that we're still investigating…I believe you have travelled always from Thaba Nchu, Mr – er – Father,' Manie said, changing the subject. 'Now our Nationalist Party is in power, I was told privately of the intention to create a self-governing territory there and in other places where the Twana peoples predominate. There's even talk of developing a casino resort to generate income when independence is established. What do think of the idea, Father?'

'All that is news to me. What is your source?' he asked, as Cecil, the journalist, became all ears.

'This is just talk behind closed doors,' Manie said, 'but it seems reliable…'

Gutturally, Fr Jacobus exploded into Flemish: 'It would be the end of innocence, and attract corruption and prostitution and probably a wave of illicit drug-taking as well. It's the worst idea I have ever heard. Surely, if your new government wants to implement a divide and rule principle, there are far better ways of creating wealth for the new principality. If what you describe does come about, I will pack up and go home to a saner society in Belgium.'

'But surely, the idea of separate development is worth considering? Here we have eleven different tribes of indigenous peoples proudly struggling to retain their identity against a flood of the worst evidence of westernisation which is destroying their culture – sacrificed for rattletrap motorcars, tin cans and alcohol – you name it – to join the other two tribes of South Africa, the Afrikaans and the English, who – even they – are struggling to come to terms with the elements that divide them? Would it not be better to implement separate development, gradually easing the tribes into the twentieth century?'

'This is social engineering in too small a country,' said Cecil, mindful of the Pogroms his parents suffered from in Lithuania where the Jewish quarter was regularly invaded by Gentiles, at Easter, shouting, 'You murdered Christ, so you must die!' His grandparents had lost their lives in one of those episodes. 'Development might work to preserve the tribes in the Amazon, on the other hand, but here they lived in giant and remote regions, barely penetrated by "civilising" elements. That might work, even though ecotourism will ruin them in the end. No, South Africa can do without a vision of *Brave New World*, developed by a Stellenbosch pro-Nazi professor in an ivory tower; and again, it is mad logic to plonk a "sin resort" right in the middle of a tribe you're hoping to keep separate to protect their endangered culture. It's bonkers.'

Spotting the dangerous direction the conversation was heading (Manie was bristling to retort), Bing's wife said, 'I think we artists are an endangered species too. What can we do to protect us struggling artists, I wonder? Manie, would you like another helping? Just hand me your plate,' and this was enough to head off a political argument, with Cecil saying, 'As the zebras on Naval Hill might tell you, there is protection and strength in numbers – so why don't you form a group of enlightened artists and writers here – I can think of a few more – like that writer near Koffiefontein – and see who could be found to help promote your interests? There's much talk about the furtherance of Afrikaanse Kultuur, at the moment, so I'm sure that a person of influence could be found to support the idea. Perhaps you could call yourselves "The Zebra Group", or something.'

'Ag Ja, well, now fine. It's a good idea but it might start with hubris and end in a muddle – you know how independent artists are – we all even squabble among ourselves. Incidentally, Father, have you had the opportunity of visiting Basutoland recently? I hear a Chinese couple have opened a new restaurant in Maseru and their speciality is sweet-and-sour fish sticks!' which made everyone laugh, the capital of the mountain kingdom being so very far from the sea, fish would have seemed to be the most unlikely pièce de résistance on the menu.

'On Maseru visits we used to enjoy lunch at Boccaccio's, owned by an Italian in Half Moon Street. Amazing how Italians can make any restaurant they open a roaring success, no matter how remote it is. Maseru's hardly a metropolis. Delicious food, until it was burnt down.'

By the time the dessert of home-made ice cream was served in a bowl of scooped-out pawpaw, the conversation had moved back to the Cold War in Europe and speculations about the future, blurred in a haze of good wine and cigarette smoke. Beatrix had fallen asleep where she sat – she always nodded off after a glass of wine or two.

'Yuss,' exclaimed Nerene, as they pushed open the garden gate at Manie's house. 'You certainly trod on the priest's toes when you talked about a casino! He is certainly revolted by the idea of forced separate development, too, isn't he?!'

'Well what else does he think we can do with all these Kaffirs? Thank God Bloemfontein has a solution by getting them out of town by nine o'clock at night – less chance of our being murdered in our beds. When I hear a nine o'clock sound I'm comforted that the town is secure. About tomorrow…I'll get up early and phone Bethany Mission station about our visit.'

While, by 1949 it was possible to make direct-dialling telephone calls within city limits, this was not so to rural settlements. For Manie to call the mission station near

Reddersburg, he had to book a trunk call through the Bloemfontein municipal switchboard. Voice quality was poor and callers had to bellow to be heard.

'Is that Pastor Roentsch?' he howled down the line.

'Yes, who's calling?'

'It is the Detective Inspector Marais, of the Bloemfontein police station. I wish to call on you today to make enquiries.'

'Is it about the dead girl? Terrible business. Yes, she stayed here for one night several weeks ago, but I know nothing much more, though you are welcome to visit. We will have a lunch ready for you. Goodbye,' then he heard a rattling click as the receiver was put down.

The phone rang immediately again, and it was the pathologist on the line. 'The girl was alive when she hit the top of the train. No sign of an attack and no sign of recent sexual activity. Thought you'd like to know.'

'We could see you coming from miles away by the cloud of dust set off by your car. Come into the house and meet my wife,' the pastor said, and then shouted, 'Hannah! We have visitors… . It's so hot, let's sit on the stoep. No, second thoughts, let me give you a quick tour first.'

Nanabessie trees sheltered the simple Lutheran chapel, school and other stone buildings at the mission.

It was settled among thatched Griqua huts that dotted the hills that surrounded the mission, among other shelters put together from industrial scraps and rusted corrugated iron. The style of layered thatching of the traditional huts distinguished the tribal dwellings from huts found elsewhere. Children, poultry and dogs abounded.

'You haven't visited before, have you? Well, here we like to think of ourselves as self-sufficient, so my flock is encouraged to learn vegetable gardening…and, over there – the modest results of our animal husbandry – we have six milking cows and a bull; that's him munching away and looking very docile but, in fact, not quite so when he gets in amongst his girls. Here's a workshop where we teach carpentry, carpet and blanket weaving – some of the women have started a tapestry which will illustrate the biblical stories, but adapted to Griqua interpretation, and…the women are naturally creative and delight in making patterns. They're fond of beads and even porcupine quill head attire, when they dress up. This is our little school which instructs the children in early reading and writing, basic arithmetic, a bit of a Griqua history and so on, plus special lessons in the other language, English. I don't have to tell you that our flock speak their version of Afrikaans, and this is the general medium, but we feel it good to stretch their horizon by introducing the other language as well. There's the bell for lunch. Hannah and I will answer any questions you have about that tragic girl – Theresa, she said her name was – all the way from Ireland and attached to the Durban museum as a student archaeologist. Came out to South Africa as soon as she could get a passage after the war – it was very difficult to do so, I believe…some complicated arrangement with her alma mater University in Dublin. Couldn't speak a word of Afrikaans, but we managed to communicate quite well.'

Over a cold lunch of cheese from the dairy, meat slices, avocado pear, lettuce, small, boiled potatoes, radish and waterblommetjies, the discussion dwelt on the girl.

'She had hired one of those surplus jeeps from some place in Bloemfontein and despite our warnings that Africa was not Ireland and it was unsafe for a girl to travel about the Free State alone, she ignored this. When you make enquiries at the station – just down the road, my guess is that you will still find the vehicle parked outside.'

'Did she explain what she was doing?' asked Manie, and winked at Hannah, who was pouring a beer. Nerene spotted Hannah's puzzled look and said, 'Manie has a nervous tic in his right eye and can't help his winking.'

'Yes…vaguely. She explained, as far as I could understand, that she was researching rock paintings by the bushman (some people called them the San) and establishing the differences in imagery and half-human-half-animal representations left on rocks in the Free State, compared with those in Natal's Drakensberg. Apparently it was unusual for the bushman artist to paint animals and humans upside down – as if falling. And that's all we know.'

'Well, not quite,' Hannah said. 'I've seen some of these paintings displayed in the Bloemfontein Museum where the curator said that rock paintings could only be done where there were adequate overhangs to protect the images from the weather. In this vicinity there are no substantial overhangs so the bushman artist had to resort to chiselling images onto the rock. The museum woman explained that the San believe that their ancestors lived inside the rock and that the paintings established a communion with them when a shaman went into a kind of trance-dance.'

'Hang on, we received a postcard from her about a fortnight ago posted in Ladybrand. Would you like to see it?' he asked rising from the table to fetch it. Returning, he handed it to Manie.

It was scuffed and dog-eared. On the front was a montage view of Leather Avenue, Ladybrand and a painted portrait of Lady Brand, wife of a president of the Orange Free State. On the reverse was an undated handwritten message, which read, 'Dear Pastor and Mrs Roentsch, thank you again for your kindness. I have been visiting a wonderful rock art site near Tandjesberg. A treasure-trove! Hundreds of San paintings…

cattle, elephants, bees, birds and half-animal / half humans. I hope to see you soon. love, Theresa.' The handwriting was feminine but firm.

'I would like to hold on to this for a while. May I?'

Nodding assent, Roentsch's wife said, 'By the way, I keep on picking up rumours in the village that your government is planning to uproot my Griqua and shift them away from Bethany. This would be disastrous, not only for them, but for us as my mission was founded here to improve the lot of such people. For us, we would have to close down. Have you heard anything to this effect?'

'No,' Manie said, 'news to me…'

Sure enough, a surplus Jeep, coated in dust, was there outside the station though stripped bare of any human possessions, if there were any. Manie, with Nerene, who was caught up with the fascination of the enquiry, clambered up the railway bridge and discovered that a portion of the railing had been broken and removed – possibly stolen. The station master, when he was found, said that the Friday train from DeAar was 'express' and did not stop, so he hadn't been present when it slowed down to the mandatory crawl as it passed through.

Later, Marais drove into the little dorp which boasted a farmers' co-op, a bottle-store, and precious little else, except the Dutch Reformed Church and the Dominee's home. Here, Manie made a bellowing phone call instructing the police to tow in and impound the vehicle, dust the steering wheel and handles; and to trace and interview its owner.

'Also, bring a native out-of-uniform constable (make sure he's a Tswana) with you to make undercover enquiries among the railway workers. Get him to watch out for anyone offering him something suspicious for sale – like a wallet. Have a

report for me by the time I get back from Koffiefontein.'
(He had said all this while Nerene charmed the Dominee in
his parlour, when Manie had closed the living-room door.)

Chapter Two

It was a bone-shaking ride along the corrugated road from Reddersburg to Koffiefontein, so the Marais siblings elected to pause halfway and picnic overlooking the Orange River, sitting beneath a grand old Namaqua fig tree. Beside them, a spruit rippled its way between sandy banks to join the Orange. It was a favourite spot of Manie's and his dead wife's when the children were very young – way back in 1930. The boys used to chase the dragonflies which hovered over the stream, he remembered. He would intrigue the children by panning for gold in the spruit. Nerene had never seen him do this and was intrigued when he went to the boot of the car and fetched a sieve and pan.

'Shouldn't you be looking for diamonds, rather? Isn't it near where some children found the Hope Diamond?'

'There are certainly diamonds, but there's alluvial gold as well, in many parts of the Free State. You know all that. Just you watch…'

Manie scooped a little shovel full of pebbles and earth, taken a few feet up the bank, and then emptied it into the sieve, designed to retain pebbles bigger than an eighth of an inch. This residue he discarded, after making sure there were no nuggets caught up. He allowed the silt to fall into a shallow brass pan, rather like a miniature wok, but with layered ridges on one side. Then he crouched down at the water's edge and allowed the stream gently to carry away most of the earth, half tilting the pan. He kept on doing this until there was little left and what there was, was caught in the ridges.

'See those specks that gleam? That's gold – being heaviest, it's been caught in the ridges.'

Finally, he sucked up the gold with a little bulb which terminated in a small glass tube, and squirted his findings into a test tube, which he corked.

'There you are, about five pounds worth. Haven't done that for years and years. The boys would spend hours copying my example. Come on, we must get to see our ant-man and family, and we've got another eighty miles to go.'

'What do you feel about the girl?' Nerene asked. 'Was she pushed, or was she desperately trying to escape from someone and jumped on top of the train opportunistically? The train just happened to be there at the right moment?'

'I think she jumped to escape some very nasty people. Keep the knowledge about the stones and everything else to yourself, please Sustertjie. At the moment, the whole thing is a mystery.'

Manie's thoughts dwelt on the gems in the little drawstring bag he had locked away in the small safe in the boot of his car. He was driving into the low western sun and dust accumulating on his windscreen was making vision difficult, so he was very relieved when they passed the old British blockhouses and the ugly giant coffee pot monument at the entrance to the town. 'Strange to think that our present-day leaders were imprisoned here during the war,' Nerene said.

'Their farm's about eight miles further on, remember? near a place called Wamakersdrift, we'll spot it by the old ox-wagon at the entrance and the name, Uitspan, in metal letters on the driveway entrance wall.'

Turning into the drive, they passed fields and fields of purple-flowering lucerne, until they reached a single-storeyed and sprawling, green-roofed house surrounded on two sides by generous verandas embraced by creepers. Driving through to the back, they were greeted by a couple of Great Danes, who barked excitedly and ran beside them. Marielese, Jannie's wife, waved a welcome while encouraging her hens back to their pen by dribbling corn ahead of them. Farm machinery lay about in front of several large sheds, with housing for the Kleuringe lying a good social distance away under pawpaw trees.

'Haloo!' shouted Marielese as she bolted the poultry gate for the night and pointed to where they should park.

'You've arrived just in time for Sundowners. Maandag!' she shouted. When the Griqua manservant appeared, she told him to take the Marais' suitcases to their bedrooms and said, 'You will find the bathroom next to your bedrooms. We are out on the front veranda where Jannie's pouring drinks for neighbours Sandra and Etienne. They arrived just before you – coming in the other way – you remember them? They have that big home on a farm over there. Jannie would have rushed to meet you, but they brought an English guest, some sort of journalist and writer with whom Etienne has been corresponding, for some time. His name's Graham Greene. We're having a braaivleis later on, because there are too many to fit at the table – and besides, it's so hot – Mr and Mrs Hardcastle are coming, just as soon as they've managed to put their children to bed. He's the mine's surface manager.'

Greene half rose from his seat as they entered but Etienne remained seated, or rather slouched on a wickerwork couch and Jannie waved the soda fountain at them, in a form of greeting, as he replenished the other guests' glasses.

After the usual introductions, Manie's cousin asked Manie,

'It's a long way from Reddersburg to here. What were you doing in that godforsaken place…isn't there a mission station nearby? Was it about that murdered girl?'

'Yes, I was making enquiries, but there is no suggestion, for the moment, that she was murdered. I can't say anymore because, you'll understand, our enquiries are ongoing and confidential. How are your white ants doing?' The detective explained to the other visitors Jannie's absorbing interest in the white-ant colony he was observing on the farm, and that he had dug a small arena facing the termite heap and cut away a section of it, replacing it with a large panel of observation glass.

Jannie explained how his interest had been stimulated after reading *The Soul of the White Ant* by Eugene Marais, who shot himself years after discovering that a French scientist had plagiarised swathes of his book and published it as his own, winning a Nobel Prize as a consequence. He said that the plagiarist had 'neither seen an ant nor put a foot on the African continent'. There was absolutely no mention of Eugene's writings and work – neither in the references nor the bibliography. 'May I read you a snatch of what Marais had written?' And without waiting for any response from his guests, he opened a well-worn book from a table, saying, '"The white ant territory is a separate and composite animal, in exactly the same way that man is a separate and composite animal. Only the power of locomotion is absent…it has a brain, a stomach, a liver, and sexual organs for the propagation of the race. It has legs and arms for gathering food, and a mouth: If natural selection continues to operate, the final result may be a termitary which moves slowly over the veld."'

As if to underscore the researcher's sad death there was an explosion of sparks from the braaivleis which a manservant was dousing with splashes of water, thus allowing Jannie's wife to divert the conversation away from ants, by saying, 'You must find it very strange to be so far from home, Mr Greene,' to which the visitor replied, 'I spend most of my time far from home – in fact, so often, that I am not quite sure where "home" is any more. Essentially, I am a foreign correspondent for a newspaper which chooses to send me all over the globe, giving me the perfect opportunity to write novels based on my experiences in such parts. I have very little visual imagination, so it's invaluable to be able to write novels in experienced settings. I can't help thinking that your work, as a detective, and mine and Etienne's are very similar – except that yours is more down to earth and productive. After all, we three observe, make notes, follow clues and make deductions from our experience of human nature with all its mores and flaws.'

Etienne, stirred, said, 'Well, yes and no. That comparison is as good as it is, but it doesn't touch on the signposts in the mind, fantasies and innuendos. I'm tinkering with just such elements set within preparations for a wedding between two rich winery families. Now the Mixed Marriages Act has come into force, I'm going to have a lovely time pulling away the façade of respectability and explicitly reveal what actually goes on behind-the-scenes between these bloody snoots and the kleurlinge in their backyards and the rondneukery within the families. A divided society – what goes on in the dark of night is contradicted by what is said during the daylight hours. It will probably be banned – another sign of growing intolerance of the actual truth.'

'What are you going to call this novel, Etienne?'

'I don't know…But a working title could be something like "The Week Before the Wedding" or "A Week at the Steins". Some members of one family fry their brains with dope, and the other lot are busy staring too deep into the bottle… . Ah good…here are the Hardcastles – just in time for the braai and bring us back to the world of Wamakersdrift. All quiet at the mines, Fred?'

'Like farming, there is always something to do. We've discovered some ancient skeletons buried in shallow graves at the West End of the tailings. Not a happy discovery. The burial position for the native workers is usually in a sitting position, after the body has been carefully wrapped in an ox skin or similar, and graves often contain prized possession; but not so, in this discovery. The skeletons are in disarray and the sites are quite old. Discounting mining accidents, there were many deaths from epidemics in the old days, as well as from tuberculosis and these seem to be some of these bodies. Sorry to mention this but we are preoccupied with burying them again with dignity. Yes, thanks I need that drink.'

The women, who had disappeared into the house during these conversations, now reappeared, bearing large kiaatwood bowls of seasoned salads to accompany the lamb and Boerewors sizzling away on the griddle. Manie had remained silent much of this time, thrown out of his depth by Etienne's utterances but pricked up his ears when he heard Hardcastle talking about the rock engravings on a cluster of boulders on the koppie behind the mine-manager's house.

'I have never seen these things; but I have to leave first thing in the morning. Nevertheless, I wonder if you could show them to me before I leave.'

'Certainly – can you be at our house at seven tomorrow? Our children wake us up well before then, so I'll be ready for you. It's a short trudge to the koppie, so boots or veldskoene. We needn't bother about snakes…too early in the day.'

Chapter Three

He crept past Sandra's whimsical paintings in the hallway and out, past the wisps of smoke drifting from the remains of the braaivleis pit to his car, for the short drive to the Hardcastles' house.

The veld spiders had woven their spells just before dawn, so that a miniature sea of cobwebs was ready to catch the early morning dew. He could hear the children racing and down a passage of the house, as Hardcastle opened the yard door. 'Right,' said the engineer. 'A quick coffee and a rusk, before we go? Joy has a secret recipe for rusks… You can taste the condensed milk in them. Better than those packets of rusks you buy, I often say – to keeps her making them.'

Firebreaks had been burned towards the hill, so that their boots crunched over the blackened stubble. The two engravings at the pronounced foot of the koppie were of a black wildebeest and a warthog – chisselings on a vertical rock face and done with keen observation and artistry.

'And there they have been for the last 250 years or more, I'm told. I've often wondered how they were cut, as the bushman had no metal…couldn't help wondering if the artist had discovered a diamond to use as an engraving tool. And why these two animals? Did they slaughter them – or were they offerings to the artist's ancestors living in the rock, one wonders? There are two more at the top of the hill – care to climb up to see them?'

These were the first rock engravings in situ Manie had ever seen, yet while his overriding motive was to familiarise himself with the interests of the dead girl, in a flash of insight he saw in his mind's eye a small Khoi artist crouching and scraping away the rock while, a thousand miles further south, Dutch settlers were exploring the coast east of the little settlement of Cape Town. Another 250 years…and the Khoisan would have to flee into the Kalahari desert – those that had escaped the bullets of the trek-Boer invaders.

Hardcastle was fit and strode up the hill with Manie panting and sweating after him. When they got the top, the former said, 'What did you think of all that conversation last night? For my part, I could stand so much and no more of all that artistic flubbery to last me for a month.'

'What did you think of that Englishman? He's knocked about the world a bit. Didn't say much but I watched him observing us and soaking it all in…I bet we'll find some of us in his next novel. Ah! Here they are – see, two elands. Seen enough?'

Alone, Marais turned his car towards Kimberley, a hundred miles of doglegging through Jacobsdaal then taking the road across the Modder river. He counted seven wind pumps on the way and a huge ugly silo, out of kilter with rest of the flat landscape.

The entrance to the Diamond Laboratory, an auxiliary to its head office in Pretoria, was in a small cul-de-sac sandwiched between the stables and the grand old lady of Stockdale Street, of Kimberley brick, fronted by a second-floor veranda with white-painted railings of cast iron and wood. The only sign of the laboratory was a brass plaque marked 'DL' beside its front door.

Dr Pieter de Lara's office-cum-laboratory exuded quiet study, reflecting the man himself, a tall sharply boned forty-year-old who wore rimless spectacles. There was a hint of Spanish about him.

'I oscillate between Kimberley and Pretoria – more so the latter, although our home is in Kimberley. Now, what can I do for you?'

Manie pulled out of his pocket a little cotton bag containing the stones, explaining where they were found and that the investigation was ongoing, saying, that they were so large that it seemed impossible for them to be genuine.

'Well, we can soon sort that out,' de Lara said. 'Amazing to think that diamonds were created about four and a half billion years ago, deep down during the world's formation and it's only luck that so many were brought to the surface by volcanic eruption. Plenty more down there we'll never get our hands on. Mind you, gold is even older and brought from outer space during stellar collisions, while the earth was still forming. Only some has been brought to the Earth's mantle during early eruptions.'

'Now, let's take a look at the less interesting sapphire first – if it is a real sapphire.' Upon which he opened his mouth and breathed on it. 'This is just a parlour trick – not a jeweller's! Well, it's such a huge stone that I was very doubtful that it was genuine, but it could be. If it had remained misted over for long, it would have been a fake – possibly glass. Gosh, it really is a whopper. Mmmm…is it synthetic, let's see?' And picking up a jeweller's loupe he squinted at it with screwed-up eyes. 'Yes…I can see little inclusions and characteristics that confirm it's the real McCoy. I would just like to shine a white light through it, for final assurance. The genuine article will project the same colour. A fake would scatter the light. Yup, it passed that test too, with flying colours; seems a very old cut – could be Victorian or substantially older. But where from? Hang on, I just want to go and find a book,' he said, returning with a leather-bound volume and turning over pages and pages, as he walked back to the desk. There was a long pondering silence until he said, 'I think the stone is from the Sutra Placer at Nezametnoya. That's in the old Tsarist Russia. Now how on earth could this land up with that poor girl? This is extraordinary! Such stones seldom reach the West, except through an important auction house like Christies – and then more so in New York where customers have particularly deep pockets. After the Russian Revolution those aristocrats who did manage to escape the slaughter landed up in a parlous state in the West, having to let go of the jewels they brought with them.'

De Lara looked at Manie in puzzlement, causing Manie to say quickly, 'This must remain highly confidential for the moment, you will understand. I am as surprised as you are, but remember you are contributing to the ongoing investigation we are conducting.'

'Oh, of course, of course! Now, I have a funny feeling that these stones aren't fake either. If so, why aren't they in the Kremlin Armoury? Let's see.. We'll do the simple tests first – anyone can do this. Now what happens when I drop them into a tumbler of water…? Yes, they sink like stones. Next…does it scratch glass? May I?' he said, and turned to a small panel of glass cemented to his work desk 'Yup, it scratches. Now for the interesting stuff,' he said tightening a little screw as he put each one into the jaws of a small brass clamp and picking up his jewellers' loupe again to squint closely at each one in turn.

'No real diamond is flawless – in the sense that diamonds

extracted from the earth always have a pattern of very minute inclusions – impossible to see with the naked eye – which is the key mark of a genuine stone. Synthetically manufactured stones do not have inclusions, except for the presence of a "starter speck". The little traces can suggest where the stone was mined. This means that the elements in the volcanic type which brought the diamond to the surface will differ from region to region. I'm going to take the stand into my little darkroom hoekie and project a beam of pure white light through them to see what the spectrum might tell us.'

He emerged, once again from his darkroom carrying a clamped stone, muttering to himself as he set the clamp down on the bench again and wandered off to his book shelf. Returning with a heavy volume of images, he ran his finger down page index, halfway through the volume, and said, 'Yes, here we are! Mysore, India. Inclusions – traces of cobalt, hydrogen, and nitrogen. Major source for Romanov crown and related ornaments. Wurra wurra wurra – it goes on and on. I want to see what happens when I shine a short-wave ultraviolet light through the diamonds. Come with me to the darkroom and we'll see.'

The darkroom was lit by a single incandescent bulb which plunged the room into darkness when he switched it off until he turned on an ultraviolet beam which flooded each stone in turn, making them glow red, a glow lingering even after the UV light was turned off. The glow slowly faded away, once again leaving them in darkness until he turned on the feeble incandescent bulb.

'Now let's weigh them,' he said, moving to a laboratory scale. 'I should have done this earlier, but I was so fascinated, I forgot for a moment. Here we go,' as he polished the stone with a soft cloth, he donned white gloves and delicately placed each one in turn onto a pan on the scale. 'Well, there you have it – the first is 35.02678 carats and the other's a shade over 36. The ancient cut matches that of much of the Romanov jewellery…. My friend, you have a mystery on your hands. Look here, this has taken up most of the afternoon and you mentioned that you were intending to drive back to Bloemfontein today. Why not stay at our house overnight and start off refreshed early tomorrow morning? Yes?'

'That's very kind of you,' Manie said.

'Capital! I'll suggest that we treat you to a little restaurant called *The Star of the West*. Let me phone Hazel immediately. We've a journalist friend staying with us – a girl from the *Diamond Fields Advertiser*, who we can bring along to make up a foursome. She's on loan from *The Friend* newspaper in Bloem.'

The de Aral homestead was a generous Kimberley brick settler house with ubiquitous white timbered verandas. Dogs bounded out to greet the car as it crunched up the gravel driveway. Hazel and her friend were seated in cane chairs and even before de Lara could introduce her, the wife's friend said, 'I'm Joy,' as if announcing her part in the Everyman Miracle Play. She might just as well have said, 'I'm Good Deeds' or 'Knowledge'. Both had already dressed for dinner, Hazel in a grey restaurant frock. A hand was adorned by a splendid diamond engagement ring and a gold wedding band. Joy was dressed in red with gatherings at her shoulders. She was younger than Hazel – pretty, though the bloom of youth was poised to fade in favour of a slight plumpness. Both women looked intelligent.

The American idea of cocktails had not reached Kimberley, if it ever would, and the group was satisfied with sherry and the alternative for men of Opsaal brandy and ginger ale. There were peanuts in a little bowl.

Joy asked, 'I can't resist asking what connection there

might be between the murder or accidental death of that girl, Theresa O'Brien, and your visit?'

'No connection,' Manie lied smoothly. 'I had to drop off my sister at Koffiefontein, where she was visiting our cousin, so I detoured on my way home to Bloem to show Dr de Aral a few "blink-klippe" I picked up near the Orange River some time ago – in the dim hope that they were diamonds – but no such luck.'

'They turned out to be beryls,' de Aral said quickly, 'of no particular worth except as attractive stones to mount in, say, costume jewellery. Sorry about that, Manie,' and chuckled, enjoined by Manie's, 'We live in hope…one day…one day, I'll find something worth a fortune.'

'Of course, you know, as a journalist, that there are a lot of diamonds knocking about the Free State and, inevitably, plenty of illegal diamond dealing – diamond sorters in Lesotho, for example, swallowing an uncut gem or two when the boss isn't looking. It's got so bad that the mines hit on the idea of paying a discounted price for any misappropriated stones handed in, and no names asked…knowing that the thieves never received adequate payment from illicit dealers. Mind you, illicit trading of stolen cut diamonds also comes with the territory. This kind of skivery results from the volume of stones desired by the mink-and-manure set wives and money-launderers.'

The conversation drifted on to politics and Joy said, 'Now the Nats are in government, I suppose there'll be a steady clampdown – judging by the names of the people now in power – it's like voting a Nazi party into power – internees like Hendrik Verwoerd, Oswald Pirow, Balthazar Vorster, Hendrik van den Bergh, Johannes von Moltke, Pieter Willem Botha and the rest…' She reeled them off.

Deftly switching subjects, out of consideration for the

"pro-Nat" sensitivities of heir guest, de Aral said, 'Hazel teaches part time at the Perseverance school and training college for Coloureds – both sexes. She has some interesting stories to tell. Perhaps we can hear about them over dinner – speaking of which, I think we'd better leave for the Star.'

The Star of the West in Tucker Street had been there even when Kimberley was a frantic mining town in the 1880s, populated by hundreds of diggers who had staked their claims to plunder the rich kimberlite pipe on Colesberg Koppie. So frantic and prolonged did their diggings become that the koppie became Kimberly's Big Hole. Their diamond eurekas were most often traded for cash by the canny Henry and Barney Barnato brothers, who had earned a reputation for fair dealing. It was an era of Cecil John Rhodes, who might well have dropped in at the Star to savour the cigar-fugged atmosphere of heavy-drinking miners being entertained by Diamond Delilah and the staccato pianola beat of Scott Joplin.

That atmosphere was still in replication when the de Aral party arrived in 1949 – an atmosphere preserved in aspic. Finding a reasonably quiet corner, after noting that Manie was recently in Koffiefontein, Joy said, conversationally, 'Do you realise that there are over sixty towns, villages and railway halts with names ending in "fontein"? The only other country likewise endowed is Belgium. Just intriguing…I discovered this when had to answer an enquiry from a DFA reader. I did a bit of research and found that when I overlaid the grid tracing the path of the Voortrekkers, they matched – with a few exceptions – like the one east of Pretoria…"Tweebuffe lsmeteenskootmorsdoodgeskietfontein".'

'Manie, please translate that into English for us, will you?'

'It means "two-buffalos-with-one-shot made-dead-stream", recording an actual incident.'

'Omitting those in Belgium, I would like to visit every single place ending in fontein and write up stories for a book.'

'That discovery highlights the importance of finding water in a dry land,' said de Aral. 'Today, I'm told, those treks, wouldn't be possible, if the routes were followed, as swathes of sweet grass regions in the interior have disappeared, with desertification taking hold; no grazing when outspanning the oxen,' at which point the wine waiter appeared. Manie admired the courtesy with which Dr de Aral consulted him about the wines, after determining his guests' meal preferences, as if the waiter was a Master Sommelier, even though there was no evidence of a sommelier's knife. The waiter grew in stature while this consultation went on.

'Are you planning to attend the Voortrekker Monument opening in Pretoria, Manie?' asked Hazel. 'Should be a grand occasion.'

'No, I'm not among the illustrious, but I heard that my cousin's neighbour, Etienne and Sandra, had received an official invitation and they were contemplating going, despite Etienne's disparagement, but the 16th of December is a difficult time for farmers. Let's see.'

'I believe the architect Moerdyk, I think that was his name, travelled to Germany before the war and studied Nazi monumental architecture,' said Joy. 'While there, he was much taken by Pharaonic temple architecture, the study of which was all the rage in Germany at the time, inspired by the discoveries of Carter, with tombs and artefacts emerging from the Egyptian sands. Moerdyk even went to Berlin to contemplate the bust of Nefertiti, the Royal Wife of Pharoah Akhenaten, on display at the Neues Museum, we're told. The Nazis actively implied parallels between the thousand-year reigns of the pharaohs and that intended for the Third Reich.'

De Aral laughed and said, 'I have a picture in my mind of Adolph and Eva Braun's mummified bodies being entombed with thousands of Shakti SS guards to administer to their needs in the Afterlife; but, somehow, I don't think their souls were lighter than a feather, so would never get to see Osiris, god of the underworld.'

'I believe that Moerdyk was so enraptured by the sun-god, Amun-Ra's,' Joy said, 'that he incorporated the mystic sun theme into the Voortrekker monument. The sarcophagus containing the remains of Piet Retief and fellow heroes is to be lit by a shaft of sunlight on the 16th of December, the Day of the Vow…but I don't mean to decry the heroism of the Boers, just the Aryanism inferences…"God's chosen people" and all that.'

De Aral interrupted, saying 'I say, steady on Joy, the Brits have besmirched themselves with their own brand of ideology. Hardly pure as the blown snow. Take Cecil John Rhodes, who held the view that Britain was "God's Gift to the World" and that the concept of empire should be applied to dominate as many of the world's people and economies as possible, regardless of the injustices imposed. Don't forget Kitchener's scorched earth policy during the Anglo Boer War…his concentration camps.'

To avoid a further slide into political debate, Manie asked Hazel about her work at the Perseverance College, to which Hazel was quick to respond.

'What I have to tell you,' she said,' is just to illustrate how much neglected potential there is in the coloured folk, given half a chance. For example, there's Witbooi. He is the son of illiterate, coloured parents who laboured on the farms near Vryburg – and you know what the place is like…. It's the gramadoelas. Through charitable help (the Methodists) he managed to persevere and matriculate in Kimberly and is now teaching…just one example among many; but now our new bloody government wants to suppress advancement like that.'

"But what will he be the fate of all those educated coloureds running about the place? I can tell you it will spell trouble and revolution in the years to come. I have seen this in Bloemfontein's black township where those teenagers who have received some education, are demanding more housing and better roads and so on – threatening to burn their Passbooks and boycotting the sale of potatoes, upon which many Boer farmers depend for their livelihood,' Manie said angrily and winking uncontrollably; at which point the desserts arrived and Hazel contrived to distract by upsetting an almost empty wineglass. A waiter came to mop up, and the rest of the evening dwelt on small talk, during which Manie felt a foot rub against one of his legs. Looking up he saw Joy smiling at him; he winked. nervously.

'I expect to be reposted back to *The Friend*, fairly soon, so may I come and pick your brains if I return to general journalism– and I like to learn a bit more about the goings on with the Native National Congress? It was founded in Bloemfontein in 1912, after all? I'd be interested in learning more of their activities. Any objection?'

'Of course, of course, I might be able to open a few doors for you,' Marnie said, almost with a little too much vigour. There was a stirring in his loins.

Chapter Four

'We have three main lines of enquiry – the first is how the girl lost her life. Was she murdered – pushed off the railway bridge – and who might have done this – or was she rushing to get away from parties unknown?'

Manie and his Superintendent were lunching at the Phoenix, a restaurant off Bloem's Hoffman's Square, renowned for its Spitzbein and draft beer. A serious effort had been made by the downers to capture a Bavarian atmosphere, in the middle of the Free State, nogal, with dark wood-panelled ceiling, mirrors and shelves loaded with bayerische memorabilia. All customers received the bonus of an already-poured thick pea and barley soup, accompanied by slices of hefezoft and butter, as customers sat down, whether they wanted it or not. The soup waiter had an Elastoplast around his thumb, which often found its way into the soup as he served the bowls.

His Super, Lore Herzog, who hinted that he was descendant oof noble Teutonic stock, he would like his friends to know, had inherited a liking for all foodstuffs German. He was portly and his eyes bore a brutal but intelligent look. Manie and Lore liked the restaurant, not only for the food, but the waitresses dressed in dirndls. Their favourite waitress, Elsa, seemed to enjoy the provocation of leaning forward when she served, allowing the men to peek down at her breasts, paying off with a good tip they always left.

'Because the girl was found with Russian gemstones on her person, the second question is, what the hell was she up to?' Manie ruminated aloud, after a good swig from his tankard. 'We're examining her notebook in detail to see if there're any clues there – for example, was she seen meeting someone, or people, at one or two other sites listed in her notebook? She strongly underlined "upside down dead animal". I'm going to follow a hunch I have about them. Rare sites. Why underlined with the word "Sibelungs after them? That's Norse or Wagnerian! Here and there she has entered "Therianthropes". What's that? Is it a codeword? Are her rock painting interests merely a cover for something more sinister? It seems so. There's a name in there of some native called Nkoko. That's a Xhosa name and we'll have to find out who he is although there are thousands of 'em. How on earth could such valuable gemstones come into her possession – and why Russian? That's another thing. Did she bring them with her from Ireland? And why, therefore? I don't think she was into Illicit Diamond Selling – the pattern is all wrong. For the moment, I won't call in the IDB Branch – I think they'll just make a mess and not contribute.

'Therefore, the third line of enquiry is to find out who the hell she really was, if she was merely using her archaeological enquiries as a cover (and I think this is likely to be the case). If that is so it means we we'll have to dig out her background – the South African Police Commissioner to the Irish equivalent Commissioner – by telex – and you know how long-winded and troublesome that could be, bearing in mind Ireland's current shitty attitude towards us.

'Meantime, fingerprints on the vehicle left at the Bethany railway station are good for a beginning. We checked them against the girl's in the morgue – but there are lots of others so tracing those is also on our bucket list.

'We've allowed the garage owner to take back his jeep and keep the deposit the girl paid. It adequately covers the half-empty petrol tank. By the way, her full name is Theresa Aoife Ciara Roisin O'Brien – what a mouthful. We found that out by phoning her workplace in Durban – the archaeological section of the museum. I spoke to a woman by the name of Sofia Klizinska, who said she – not O'Brien – was Polish and that Theresa was Irish, with an excellent and ambitious enquiring mind. The girl's name was entered into various documents concerning her work at the museum and her relationship with the Dublin university where she started her postgrad degree. There is no sign of her passport, apparently, so I'll have to search her lodgings at the boarding house off Broad Street in Durban…owned by a grumpy-sounding Mrs Bell. When I made a trunk call to her she got shirty when I instructed her to double-lock the girl's room and not to enter it until I got there. Apparently, her rent is due.'

'Yuss, this could be politically interesting…could turn out be an intelligence operation,' said Lore. 'Personally, I would like to keep this investigation under our hat for the moment – we don't want some fool setting off alarm bells ringing in Pretoria. This is what we're going to do,' he said. 'I'm going to take you off all other duties so as to allow you to concentrate on it – we'll get in that Mompara in Welkom to cover for you…I'll let the Commissioner know only in very general terms and say that it might – repeat might – be necessary for you to travel to Ireland to investigate the girl's identity – and that's all – explaining that telex communication with the Irish Garda, long-distance, is slow, up to shit and cumbersome…far better to be there at the coalface…do your own knocking on doors. He'll understand that. Okay? Let me know when you wish to travel if necessary, and I'll make arrangements, and ask our Commissioner to clear the decks for you in Ireland. There'll have to be an inquest once you have investigated as much as you can. Keep me posted…okay?'

Manie had travelled only once beyond the borders – and that was only to Rhodesia; his other memorable holidays being with his family in Durban. For a moment his mind's eye drifted back to splashing in the paddling ponds with his young children and wife at the North Beach. The sight of his young wife sliding down the water chute with the boys remained as fresh as yesterday. The prospect of travelling abroad on police business, filled him with a mixture of apprehension and excitement.

Manie's way back to the police station took him through Market Square and the entrance to *The Friend* newspaper offices, so it was no surprise to bump into Cecil Bing mounting the shallow steps.

'Oh, hello,' Cecil said. 'Time for a chat? I might have a snippet of information for you concerning that dead girl.' The beer at lunchtime had mellowed Manie's inclination to apply himself to the mountainous in-tray awaiting him back at the office, so he gave way to Bing's invitation, and accompanied him upstairs to his office, past a façade made up of worn wooden type pieces, backdropping a Heidelberg printing press which dominated the entrance hall.

'That,' said Bing, pointing at the machine, 'was the press used during the second Boer War when Rudyard Kipling was the editor.' A framed picture of a walrus-moustached man stood beside the machine. 'That's him.'

It was Manie's first visit to a newspaper newsroom, and he was fascinated by the sight of a cigarette-smoky roomful of journalists and subs clattering away on typewriters, making phone calls between-times. In a corner, a bank of telexes chugged away adding to the din. To an outsider, the noise was bedlam.

'Yuss! What a noise – how can they concentrate?'

'Oh, you get used to it. Nowadays I find it difficult to sub without all the background clatter. Come into the interviewing room where we can find some peace.'

His eye caught sight of a *World Mechanics* magazine open on a coffee table, proclaiming that computers would be shrunk, in the future, to weigh a mere one-and-a-half tons and he wondered what a computer was. He had heard of them vaguely.

Bing, closing the door, said, 'That girl found on top of the train…you can understand that her death and the whole incident is hot news for us, so one of our journalists has been digging about Reddersburg. No doubt your men have been doing the same thing, so what I have to tell you may not be news for you at all, but it appears that the railway platform gardener saw a girl answering to the reported description, screech her jeep to a halt at the Bethany station, which was otherwise deserted, and race to the platform. Another car arrived shortly after and two men got out, one white and one native. Immediately she spotted them, she raced up the bridge steps, just as a passenger train was approaching at the mandatory five miles per hour, when passing through the station. The men were clearly after her, so on the spur of the moment, she raced up the footbridge and jumped through a missing part of the railing onto the top of the moving train to escape. The train picked up speed as it left the station. The men then got back into their car and raced off, in a cloud of dust. My guess is that they intended to intercept her before she arrived at Bloemfontein station. Look, we're competing with *Die Volksblad* on this story so please don't pass this on to them.

'Describing the two men in the car, the gardener said that the black man was not from these parts. He was a Xhosa and dressed in city clothes. As for the white man – but you know most whites look the same to natives – he said that he looked about forty-five, dressed in khaki – shorts, not longs – and had a crooked knee, so that below the knee stuck out at a funny angle, making it difficult for him to walk quickly. He wore an old wide-brimmed farmer's hat and veldskoene, and had a bokbaard. Almost forgot, the Xhosa wore reflecting sunglasses – you know the type favoured by Totsies. The gardener said their car was "very strong" and was brown, like the sand. I suppose that means beige. There it is…you realise, I'm sure, that we cannot appear to be in the league with the police, but in this case, we are as eager as you to follow the story. If we hear anything more, we'll let you know. You could get a call from Eggy Mollet, the journalist who picked up the trail. His initials are E.G., so that explains his nickname. Let me show you out,' and back they went through the newsroom. 'Eggy sleeps at that desk over there, but he's out at the moment, otherwise I would've asked him to join us.'

Back at the station, Manie instructed a uniformed junior to spend the rest of the day and the next day telephoning all petrol stations within a 500-mile radius of Reddersburg, enquiring whether anyone answering the description of the man with a bokbaard and a crooked left leg had gone to the counter to pay for petrol…and there were not so very many garages in those days.

'How do we get the phone numbers?' asked one of them.

'Use your bloody loaf – call the oil companies and get the address list of their garage customers. Here's a map and a pair of compasses. Typing in the numbers onto the telex would take far too long so get them to read them to you and note them down.'

A couple of sightings, Manie reasoned, would indicate the direction of travel and narrow a later dragnet. He spent the rest of the afternoon visiting the archaeologist at the Bloemfontein Museum in Charles Street, boning up on rock art and its significance. The engravings at Koffiefontein opened a new world to him and he became fascinated by the history. On the way home he stopped by his usual garage and was amused to see the sign, 'Spaar water. Ons is in die greep van 'n droog!'…'In the grip of a drought'. 'Bang goes this year's Free State's wheat harvest,' he thought. Swirling dust devils began to buffet the car on his way home and reduced visibility forcing him to reduce speed to a crawl. It was as if all the daemonic sands of the karoo had come to gather about the cocoon of the car.

On turning into the drive, he found the gardener sitting on the kitchen door step.

'Baas, I am waiting.'

His pay was five pounds a week plus two meals a day – the first of putu and tea and a lunch break of bread and meat. He was a faithful retainer and they got on well, in a master-servant way that had stretched back for years. Questioning matters of inequality had not occurred to either of them. It was a prospect impossible to imagine, although the maid did allow him into the kitchen when Manie was at work.

'We're going to have a storm, so I'll drive you to your bus stop. Come, get in the car.'

Automatically, Baboki climbed into the back seat and wondered at the comfort of the leather. After paying him his wages, Manie drove him to his 'Non-European' stop, which was a long way down Andries Pretorius Street. The first pellets of hail began to strike the windscreen. By the time they reached the stop, the full roar of the hailstorm pounding the car made it impossible to converse. When the bus arrived the hail was beginning to change to a furious downpour, with lightning flashes striking the shunting yard rail lines, which ran alongside the street at that point. Baboki's bus to the Location (a curious term for the slum that it was) would take another hour before disgorging him into the muddy and ill-lit lanes of the shack town. There was no shelter at the bus stop, so they sat silently in the car until it arrived. Manie told him to take an umbrella out of the boot, then took the car back homewards.

Many of the oldest houses in Bloemfontein, even in the most respectable suburbs, were roofed in corrugated iron, which clattered and roared during heavy rainfalls. Thus it was while Manie ate his solitary evening meal. When the pudding arrived – one of Mavis' specialities – the hailstorm returned and his Great Danes, terrified by thunder, found comfort by lying as close to him as possible, stretching themselves across his feet. That night, Manie dreamt a brandy-fuelled dream of a girl, a comfortingly mixture of his dead wife and Joy.

The overnight storm had brought out the frogs before dawn the next day. With the petrichor of quenched grass wafting through the house, he booked a call to his sister, on a line full of crackles. 'Sussie!' he shouted. 'I have to go to Natal, within the next few days. Would you like to come with me? Could be an interesting trip. We will have to go trekking near Dihlabeng.'

'Where the hell is that?'

'It's near Bethlehem and Clarens, in the Eastern Free State.'

'Are there snakes?'

'Could be, but the scenery is beautiful. An opportunity to see a part of the world we haven't visited.'

'Why do you want to go there?'
"Police business.'
'Is it about that dead girl?'
'Yes.'
'Manie, I come all the way from De Aar and you have to go away. Let me think about it. I'll call tonight.' He could feel her irritation coming down the line. 'I'm quite happy here with Jannie and his wife…I see his neighbours Etienne and Sandra, quite often too – great fun but a bit mad. Call you later.' He heard the rattle of the receiver being replaced.

The phone rang later with the news that his sister had decided to stay put until he returned to Bloemfontein.

Police stations smell of old tobacco smoke, paper files, disinfectant, faeces, urine, and human misery. Manie's station was no different but his office was well away from the cells, and considered a *sanctum santorum*, adjacent to that of the Superintendent's. Since his wife's death he had buried himself in police work, gaining the reputation for thoroughness – leading to intolerance of sloppy work in others. The Theresa O'Brien file was beginning to swell, though the main questions remained unanswered. He poked his head around the superintendent's door to mention that he was off to Bethlehem and Clarens, tracing up sundry leads. 'Give my regards to Sgt Roussouw and his wife Heloise,' Lore said. 'He still owes me a beer, tell him. If you're going into the native bundu keep a rifle in the boot as well as your Webley; and take Corporal "Izambane" too. You never know. Remind him, plain clothes if he's got any. I presume you'll fix up his accommodation in the hotel's servant quarters wherever you stay. He must be incognito, like you, and snoop. It's some hours; drive, so take padkos,' the superintendent grunted, and waved casually while still looking at the paperwork in front of him. ('Izambane' was a Zulu and the nickname referred to his huge appetite for mashed potato, the Zulu word for this vegetable.)

The men broke their journey to eat padkos beside a large dam. Neither said much, the silence broken only by Manie remarking, 'Ja, over 350 Boer children died in a British concentration camp over here. They died of starvation and disease.'

Izambane grunted, but said nothing, though thought of his own children, over the mountains in Mtubatuba who often went without food – even though he sent much of his pay home.

They reached the Dihlabeng rock overhang on foot, after several misdirections, many of which, Manie suspected were deliberate, for while Izambane spoke fluent Southern Sotho as well as his Zulu, the locals disliked Zulus – particularly those who worked on the railways 'because they steal our women'. It had rained overnight so the winding veld paths were muddy and overgrown with long grass. 'Pasop for rinkals, Baas,' said Izambane (his real Zulu name was Lungelo). 'The rain makes frogs come out. Snakes like them – they spit in the frogs' eyes and they die. They can try to spit in our eyes too. After that the snake pretend they dead. You stand on one then they bamba you. If they bite, you can die. What you looking for, Baas?'

'A picture on the rocks of any falling down inyamazane. That's number one. Then we look ground near it.'

'Bheka! Kukhona eyodwa.' (Look! There's one.) They stared at a faded fawn and white rendering of an antelope depicted on a rock face, upside down with long spindly legs and thin, tapered ears.

'Was the impala killed to bring rain?' Manie pondered;

'Or perhaps, by merely painting the picture on the stone, the artist could communicate with the ancestors who dwelt within the rocks?' Then out loud he said, 'Painted long time ago by the bantu basehlathini, the little people who lived here before you Zulus and we whites chased them away.'

'Behka!' Izambane said again, pointing to strange figures seemingly in flight, towards the left of the overhang, half human, half animal, some with long kangaroo-like extended legs and long antelope ears. Manie suddenly thought of the entry 'Nibelungen' in the girl's notebook – the half-human creatures with mythical powers in Wagner's *Siegfried* and the treasures of gold and jewellery they had stolen. Elsewhere, there were representations on the rocks of bees and running human figures. 'Now where are our little dwarfs' treasure buried?' he muttered.

'If anyone comes to ask what we are doing you can say we are scientists "from the museum"…Now we must look where someone has been digging and then covering' (he gestured with his hands) 'so that no one can find it.'

It was once again, Izambane who was the first to spot a slight, tell-tale sign…of pebbles out of place, as if brought up by digging and, carelessly discarded on the surface of the soil against a rock which appeared to have been dislodged. Manie had brought along a short camper's digging tool which he handed to his companion, after they had moved the stone out of the way. His spade soon hit a metallic-sounding object, not a stone, about a foot and a half below the surface, which he levered loose and lifted out. It was the size of a large workman's lunchbox of thick aluminium alloy and sealed in sturdy waterproof wrapping. It was locked.

'Izambane, you have the eyes of a fish eagle!' Manie exclaimed with great satisfaction. 'Wait! Just leave it on the shovel and slide it into this bag. We have to fingerprint the wrapping and the box – that'll give us a lot of clues. Excellent!'

Night falls quickly in Africa. Mist was gathering in the valleys and the sun had already set, when Manie said, 'Misa usubenza! Stop work for the day. We must go to the hotel in Bethlehem and pretend you're my driver. Tomorrow we go to Clarens. Perhaps the spooks in a big cave there can tell us some more.'

Driving to Clarens next day, Manie said, 'I know we call you Izambane because you like mashed potatoes but what do you call me?'

'iWashi'

'iWashi?' That means "watch" doesn't it? Why that?'

'It's a joke about you: "Iwashi lakhe liyamtshela uma elambile" – he who looks at his watch to tell if he's hungry. At home we eat when we are hungry, when we have food to eat, but people like you look at your watch and at one o'clock you say you are hungry. Then you go and eat.'

The approach road to Clarens winds between two basalt-striated, sandstone cliffs, inherited from a period 200 million years ago in the days of Gondwanaland, the mega-continent, when the swampy region dried up and became a sandy desert, overlaid and then upheaved with volcanic basalt ten million years later. Compression of the sand into exceptionally rugged sandstone followed. Water erosion did the rest, to create today's landscape. The cliffs glow sandy-golden in the sun, hence the entry to the area being dubbed 'Golden Gate'.

Lungelo (and that was what Manie now called him) was instructed to park the car around the corner from the police station, where Manie left him in the car, and sauntered to the station. He was able to drop the persona of 'a wealthy Free State farmer' once he was ushered into Sgt Petrus Rossouw's office and the door closed. He said, 'My Super says you owe him a beer.'

'Wragtig!" said Rousseau. 'That story is wearing a bit thin! Although, mind you, he did manage to get me out of a hole, but it's a long story which we won't bother to revisit now. How are you, anyway – and why all this hush-hush business?'

'Maybe crazy that I am here covertly, but we don't want to reveal that exceptional police enquiries are ongoing – so, for the record, I'm here as a Free State farmer paying his respects to the memory of a close burger relative who died in Paul Kruger's Kommando at the Battle of Naauwpoortnek on the 29th September – tomorrow. His name's on the Battle monument – you know the one in the main square. I'll go and stand there for a bit…leave a bunch of flowers…before I leave town.'

"So that's your fairy tale. What's the real reason for your being here?'

'No, this monument bit is true. My sister asked me to commemorate when she heard I would be in Clarens on that day – but the truth is we have to dig up the entrance to a cave full of rock paintings near the town without anyone noticing.'

'Stop right there. I know the place you mean, and it was fenced and gated a fortnight ago, because tourists were spraying the paintings with water to enhance images for photography. They were also chiselling bits away. The only person who has authority to enter the site is Rentia Myburgh, our local archaeologist-cum-palaeontologist (fancy title, huh!), who runs our little museum just a short walk away. It's Wednesday, so she'll be there. I'll ring her to forewarn her and request her cooperation. Okay? She lost her husband about seven months ago, when his tractor overturned on their farm near here. He was driving up a steep incline on the diagonal. Bloody careless.'

'I'll go there right away, but could you send one of your native cops to go round to the car and invite Lungelo back to his section and give him some grub? Tell him to be discreet. Say I'll collect him later. It's the brownish Studebaker with a normal OB numberplate ending in 9564.'

'Where are you staying overnight?'

'At the Ou Waenhuis. May I invite you and your wife to supper?'

'Sounds good. I'll phone Heloise right away. Perhaps she can persuade Rentia to join us – she needs bucking up…living alone now in that farmhouse – they didn't have any children.'

She was sitting at a wide desk, surrounded by open reference books and a collection of what seemed to be rock samples. The museum was small with racks and glass cases of objects relevant to the town's history – dinosaur teeth, a large bone fragment, voortrekker era household objects and clothing. On the walls were framed sepia daguerreotypes of glassy-eyed Grant-Woodian couples, and groups of bearded men holding broomstick rifles, surrounding a portrait of Paul Kruger. Seemingly incongruously, a photograph of the *Titanic* steaming out of Cobh, hung beside a painting of a cliff resembling the prow of a ship. An unusually small Pierneef was on the wall behind her desk.

She was in her mid-thirties, attractive, in an earnest care-worn way, wore round spectacles and her hair was up in a chignon. He wondered how she would look with her hair down.

Without looking up, she said, 'I'm told you've come to dig up my precious San sites and that I must cooperate. What's it all about?…In our little rural backwater, this is exciting!'

'Thank you, but before we talk about that, can you recall encountering a young foreign archaeologist girl student

making enquiries about visiting the rock art cave near here…
answered to the name of Theresa O'Brien?'

'Yes, very well. She told me she was Irish and signed the
visitors' book. Look…here it is, but no address,' she said,
after turning back the pages. 'I can't understand what she
added as a comment. Can you?' Manie saw, carefully penned
beside her name and date in almost copybook handwriting
'Músaem beag suimiúil!'

'No; but foreign it is, for sure. Looks Swedish. Probably
Irish. May I take a photograph of it please?' which he did,
of the whole page.

'She stood out since we very seldom get Irish visitors – if
at all – and because she was knowledgeable and spoke English
with an accent that could have been Canadian. She was alone
and drove a dust-covered jeep. Parked it right outside the
museum. Why all this interest?'

'She lost her life by falling from a railway bridge near
Reddersburg, recently.'

'Oh God! How awful. So, she's the one…the papers have
been full of it. Oh, I am so sorry…look, she gave me this
strange little ring, said it was a 'Claddagh', and showed me
how to wear it on the hand opposite my wedding ring hand.
I told her that I had lost my husband recently and she said I
should wear it with the crown pointing inwards and it would
bring me good luck. See, it's of silver, with a heart clasped by
hands, topped by a crown. We got talking "shop", about my
old hobbyhorse of the therianthropes – the half-human half-
antelope images often painted by the San in a trance-state.
She remarked that similar mythical creatures were common
in ancient Irish folklore – mentioning the blue-eyed golden
hare, reputed to transform into human form to steal milk
from the cows – and so on. But I think these folk beliefs are
common to many countries. How did the accident happen?'

'I can't really tell you much – it would only be speculation, but I'll let you know before more becomes public – if it ever does. Did you take her to the Bushman cave?'

'No, I indicated where to go, then I was distracted by the arrival of some noisy American tourists asking stupid questions and the last I saw of her was her driving off in the general direction of the cave.'

'We will have to keep the purpose of my visit quiet, please, so, for the public ear, I'm not a policeman but just a Free State farmer, but I would like to investigate the cave in the early morning, before anyone else is about.'

'Well, I'll have to be present and any digging you do must always be under my supervision. Is that understood? Any fragments you dig up must be recorded by me, including the level down at which the bits are found and all non-police interest relics will have to be left with me and the soil returned, the disturbance marked. That means an early start. You'll have to collect me from my farm at six o'clock sharp. Okay?'

Beside the Ou Waenhuis entrance, sheltered by a Doringboom tree, were a cluster of rocks, deeply scored by wagon wheels. They had been rescued from the route of Hendrik Potgieter's trek party near Vegkop. The restaurant, attached to the small hotel, was within the original timber-beamed wagon shed, decorated with Potgieter memorabilia.

Manie rose from his chair when the Rossouw party arrived; Petrus clutching his meerschaum and walking ahead of Heloise and Rentia. The latter, he saw, had released her hair from its chignon prison and wore a simple sleeveless blue frock which set off her figure to its best. She was wearing the Claddagh with the crown pointing towards to the palm of her hand.

'Heloise is an unusual name for this neck of the woods,' Manie said, as an icebreaker.

'My mother studied French in the process of tracing her Huguenot ancestors and was absorbed in the novel by Jean-Jacques Rossouw, *Julie, or the New Heloise,* which she read when she was pregnant with me; so you can understand her delight when I married this old smelly pipe-smoker and settled in Clarens – seeing that the novel is set in that other Clarens – the little village at the foot of the Alps where Oom Paul Kruger is buried. I'd like our children to be *drietalig,* when they grow up – Afrikaans, French and English. French for a window on the world, Afrikaans because it's our tongue and English because we have to.'

'And you, Rentia?'

'Afrikaans, Latin and English. Die Taal because it's ours, Latin because it's the lingua franca of science so I can understand names like "Massospondylus carinatus" – you can blame Carolus Linnaeus for that – and English because most of the best studies are printed in English – often exclusively.'

'The what!?'

'Latin for "long-spined vegetation-eating biped". If we were sitting here during the early Jurassic period, the place would be swarming with 'em. The females laid their eggs (tiny! size of hens' eggs) high in the banks of a river that flowed quite near here. I've discovered some – they laid clutches of more than thirty eggs at a time – and now some are sitting on my desk, leaving me wondering how the hell to look inside them. I really need a magical X-ray.'

'She's off,' said Petrus. 'Before she frightens away the natives shall we decide what we're going to eat?'

After the main course was cleared away and the women were dithering over the choice of dessert, muttering something about their figures, Heloise asked Manie what he thought about the government refusing entry to Seretse Khama and his British wife Ruth Williams, and Manie saying, 'Well, what could they have expected? Mixed marriages were banned earlier this year. The elders of the Bamangwato tribe in Bechuanaland didn't like the Khama marriage either. In their minds Khama should have married a high-born virgin from the tribe.' All this was being discussed in the presence of a sadly servile Tswana, waiting for their dessert orders.

'So you're coming to see my Nibelungs in the cave tomorrow,' Rentia said, 'or at least that's what I call them. The part-human, half-animal images the San painted on the cave walls.'

'Nibelungs? Aren't they Wagner's dwarf creatures that protect the gold stolen by Alberich from the Rhine daughters out of which he makes a magic ring?' Manie asked, winking involuntarily. 'My wife and I had all the purple patches on scratchy records. It reminds me of her when I play some.'

Rentia said, 'One of my greatest wishes would be to watch the whole Ring at Bayreuth – though that'll be impossible, now Wagner's musical reputation has been sent down among the dead men, all because of Hitler.'

Heloise nudged her husband and murmured; 'I think Rentia has acquired a sterretjie [little star]. It's about time, né?'

'But why Bushman rock art "Nibelungs"?'

'Because in rock art therianthropes are equally fantastical as the Nibelungs of ancient Norse beliefs, though the little bushmen's jewellery were finger-rings and bracelets made of ostrich egg pieces rather than gold.'

'What's that ring you've got on your right hand?' I haven't noticed it on you before,' asked Heloise. 'May I take a look?'

'Oh, I just wore it again on the spur of the moment. It's

a Claddagh…long story, but if you wear it with the crown towards the knuckles, I'm told, it means you are available. Otherwise, not.'

Heloise discretely nudged her husband again.

When Manie arrived at Rentia's farmhouse next day, the bantam cock was crowing. 'He's called Chanticleer Rentia said on opening the door to reveal a bush-whacking figure in khakis, with her hair imprisoned again in a chignon. Mist still haunted the valleys as Lungelo drove them – formally sitting as whites together on the back seat, as far as they could go, to park the car at a farmstead called Schaaplaats. Then they had to trudge the rest of the way on foot along a dew-wet and overgrown path, winding around the hillsides before descending to trace a small river.

'Pasop vir slange,' Lungelo said.

'You're right, Lungelo, but maybe too early. They need the sun to warm them up, like the lizards – maybe later in the day they get dangerous – but we must pasop for baboons. Some like to sleep in the cave and we don't want to meet a mother with her babies coming out of the cave. They climb over the fence with ease. See if you can spot those little brown bats – the Rusty Pipistrelle, they call them, rushing back home to sleep in the back of the cave in the daytime. I tell you; it's all happening in this little nook of the woods! Important things, bats…we must look after them…without bats, no bananas. Bats pollinate them.'

'There you are! Petrified footprints of my Massospondylus carinatus, my long-tailed biped…two hundred million years old. See, Lungelo.'

Once they got used to the light inside the cave, Rentia led them to two sets of half-animal creatures, then pointed out a hunt scene where men were preparing to kill a rhebok. 'Strange that they should do that, as the rhebok is distinctly nasty to eat. Perhaps it's a warding off, in deference to their love of their eland. And look…there's a khwa-ka xoro, the rain animal which looks like a mixture between a hippopotamus and an ox. These are very difficult to catch because they control very heavy rain and thunder, but once caught the creature is led to a place of slaughter where the blood is allowed to flow. The female of the "species" was thought to bring a gentle drizzle…and there is a shaman doubled up with pain in his stomach, so strong is the medicine. It has made him go into a trance state. In this state he can leave his body and wander. We must remember that the images are reflections of life within the rocks itself. These are the portals. Seen enough – I never have!? Where's Lungelo gone to?'

'He's looking for what we set out to find, representations of an upside down, dying antelope…Here he is again – perhaps he went off to pee, but by the look on his face, I think he's found something.'

Beckoning, Lungelo said, 'Woza. Iseduze [Come. It's outside],' and turned, leading the way, slashing at the grass with his stick. A little distance up a steep rise led to a short extension of the overhang, where he stopped and pointed at a flat surface of rock, recessed from the weather. There, concealed by the substantial foliage of a shrub, was a small, faded painting of an upside down antelope, with slender legs in the air and long thin ears. 'Lapa,' he said and unfolded his small shovel.

'Well, I'm damned. He really has the eyes of an eagle,' she said, and unslinging her Zeiss, saying, 'Wait! I must take photographs of the site before it's disturbed. Lungelo, please hold this matchbox beside the painting – so'; then she took several more of the scene – one with Lungelo, as the hero

60

of the hour. Then she allowed him to commence digging. Manie noticed her clutching a pocket tape measure and little notebook in readiness. After dislodging and shifting a rock, digging did not take long before there was a now familiar thud and the spading up of an aluminium box, wrapped in waterproofing.

'Yuss! There's always something new out of Africa! I suppose you won't open it – no, I suppose not. Fascinating! What on earth was that girl up to, one wonders? Up here, one realises that the San always chose a good view for their dwelling places. One can imagine their sitting here on the lookout. Now what?'

'It's back to Bloem with booty.' Running her back to her farm, Marnie said, 'I have to investigate the same sort of thing on the Natal side of the Drakensberg in the Cathedral Peak area. Care to come along in a few days' time – your archaeological insights might be very helpful indeed? This is a strictly professional invitation.' – Which of course it wasn't, as he was immensely drawn to her and suspected, hoped she felt the same.

'It's an interesting thought but I couldn't possibly get away,' she said, gabbling out several reasons…pressure of work…the farm and so on, while thinking the opposite: might this be the one?

At the farm she turned and waved at the departing car crunching down the gravel drive. It turned a bend and disappeared. Suddenly, she felt very alone.

Chapter Five

The dogs recognised the sound of his car, and he could hear them barking in the closed-off back garden where they were confined until his return. Mavis appeared, putting on a kitchen apron, in the expectation of cooking dinner, and said, 'Missus Sussie said you must phone her. She sounds far, far away. The telephone was all crackly, and her voice was very soft.'

He booked the call and then settled down with the *Volksblad* and a generous splash of Opsaal brandy, his mind drifting between the paper and thoughts of Rentia until, restlessly, he turned on the wireless for the seven o'clock news, in time to hear Prime Minister Francois Malan expressing determination that the system of apartheid would be pursued, no matter what the cost and disagreement that might arise from time to time.

The call came through just as Mavis brought in a jelly, with a, 'It's nice and wobbly raspberry this time. Here's some cream for it.'

'Ja, Sussie. How are you? Mavis told me that you had phoned. I've just got back. How are you? Enjoying yourself?'

'Very happy. I've got to know the mine manager and his wife quite well with the children. Then Etienne and Sandra come across every evening, for sundowners.... He is very eccentric. Quite mad, and Sandra is a little bit up the wall, but they're entertaining. When are you coming to fetch me?'

'I have to go to the Drakensberg for a couple of days, on the same mission Will you come with me? I must go and look at another cave.'

'Is it in the bundu? You know how I dislike even the thought of snakes. No, I think I had better stay on at the farm until you get back. Then you can fetch me.'

Next day at the police station, fingerprints on the packing bags and boxes confirmed they were those of the dead girl.

'During your absence, we located the men who chased the girl onto the railway bridge.' His Super said that they must have been tipped off, because they belted for the Swaziland border and managed to get through – the black Totsi had a genuine Swazi passport and the white with a crooked leg carried a forged one. Scorched bits of it were found in the car. They were traced heading for Mhlabanyati on a very bad road to the Foresters Arms hotel when their car overturned on a notoriously bad bend. It tumbled down into a ravine, where it burst into flames. The black man must have survived and has now faded back into the wallpaper, but the white man must have been trapped and was roasted alive in the burning car.

'His body was still in the wreck. The local agent got there ahead and managed to extract the man's lower jaw with a pair of pliers. He also rescued a very charred pocketbook from what was left of the glovebox. That revealed his parents' home address in Mooinoi…

'It's a small dorp not far from Britz in the Magalies mountains. It turns out he ran away from school and became a big cheese in diamond smuggling, by the name of Frikkie du Buisson. His leg had been badly set after falling onto rocks… came from poor but respectable family…nine children. Gott!

How some of us breed…as bad as the bloody natives. Our man found a mixture of uncut and cut stones too, which were handed over to the IDB cops. So that's the end of them, as far as we are concerned, except the need remains to establish the how and why and where the dead girl contacted them. I will pursue.'

Manie and his Super were sharing koeksisters and coffee in the Super's office when Lore pulled a large bunch of keys out of a drawer, between mouthfuls, and eventually found one that fitted both locks. It was the last one on the chain. 'Typical Sod's Law that it should be the last one. I've been collecting these keys for years and they've come in useful, time without number.'

'Now we can establish the supplier of the locking device and perhaps the manufacturer of the boxes, and eventually where these were sold. A long shot, but worth following up. Over to you.'

The key, surprisingly, fitted both locks. Inside each box were wads of hundred-pound notes, twisted put-out-of-shape florins, and several foolscap pages each or so of typewriter printed numbers in groups of four.

'Either she was some kind of illicit diamond dealer, which I doubt, or this is some kind of plot. Crooked or political? Probably both. Only a cryptographer could construct or decipher that lot. If we sent them to Police Intelligence in Pretoria, there they would sit until some momparas conclude that they couldn't break the code. No, we'll try to crack it here in Bloemfontein.'

'Uhuh, don't touch the pages with your sticky fingers. Go and wash them! You say Mozambican spotted them beneath areas of disturbed ground? Well, they're not exactly the Dead Sea Scrolls and he's no goatherd, but, between you, you seem to have uncovered something pretty startling.' (The newspapers were filled, at the time, with the sensational discovery of the Scrolls by a goatherd wandering into a cave after a stray goat, at Qumran near Ein Feshkha on the northern shore of the Dead Sea in Palestine. Their deciphering cast new light on the emergence of Christianity and Judaic learning.) 'Perhaps we should buttonhole that military intelligence fundi at Tempe near here.'

'I would prefer to keep it out of public view – in other words military – for the moment and would prefer to go and consult the professor of mathematics and statistics at the Bloem University. Okay?'

It was left to Manie to see the professor whom he found down a long corridor eating a hamburger at his desk. A breeze and the open windows contrived to clatter the professor's certificates and a few family photographs on the walls. Folders of paperwork on his desk were weighed down with kitchen-scale weights engraved as 5lb, 2lb and 6oz.

'They never put enough onions in these things nowadays,' he said, while half rising to pull the windows to. The clattering suddenly stopped, and he said, 'It's so bloody hot with the windows closed. Now what can I do for you – you were sufficiently mysterious on the phone that my curiosity has been aroused.'

'I've kept the two lots of papers separate, which we discovered somewhere – I can't go into any more details than that, but I wonder if you could look over them and possibly decipher them?'

'You say these are from two separate sources? Well at first glance I think they are in an unbreakable code – firstly because they seem to have been encrypted using what's commonly called a one-time key. The encryption changes with every message, meaning that even if you managed to decode one set, you would have to start all over again for the second set of papers. Secondly, you won't be able to break the message, basing your task on recognising number or letter repetitions, because the number is unlikely to represent the same letter twice.

'The top of the first page probably carries a unique set of numbers which differs from the next set. That's a clue that it's the key, but, if you don't know to what the key refers to, you're flummoxed Quite clearly the producers of these manuscripts have no intention of your finding out. My guess is that the original message is encoded and then encrypted with a key set of numbers known only to the originator and the person intended to decrypt them. Only these two parties will know the significance of the magic numbers and, likewise, know the key reference to the code. Without that information these messages are uncrackable.'

'The only people who would go to such lengths are a secretive state or a very sophisticated criminal network. Also, they could be in a foreign language, for all we know. I would tend to favour the first idea. Perhaps you should try to locate the typewriter's owner.'

'That's good thinking, but I believe the owner is dead. Nevertheless, we're pursuing that thought at the moment.'

'Look, you can leave them with me, and I'll see what I can make of them overnight. Come back and see me tomorrow lunchtime. All right?'

The next day was overcast, still and muggy, and by the time Manie had parked his car and reached the professor's office, he was sweating. The latter was perspiring too and was overweight. On this day there was no zephyr and the frames on the walls were still, despite both windows in his office being pushed out to the full extent.

'I ordered a cheeseburger for you too, with extra lashings of onions. Help yourself to a coke in the fridge, the glasses are over there. Well, as I said, these documents are unbreakable. Sorry, I tried every trick in the book, only as I forecast, to come up against a brick wall. Sorry! Enjoy your cheeseburger.'

That night, after booking a long-distance call to Rentia in Clarens, he sat on the veranda anxiously waiting for the call to come through. His heart was in his mouth when it did, and he realised he was behaving like an uncertain teenager. 'Helloo. It's Manie here – you remember taking us to the rock art cave?'

'Oh helloo – yes of course, what a surprise! How's life in the Big Nartjie? Any progress – oh I forgot; you still can't talk about it.'

'Yes, it's about that enquiry. I need your expertise to pursue the same investigation in the Drakensberg's Ndedema Gorge. Can you join us for a short expedition there? I know I suggested this before, but your knowledge would contribute greatly.'

Manie realised, only to well, that this was a semi-fabrication used to persuade Rentia to join him. 'I know I mentioned this before, but I'm raising it again, in the hope that you can break away for a couple of days. Strictly professional. We would have to stop over at the Cathedral Peak Hotel for first and third nights, camping at Leopard Rock Cave on the second. My black corporal policeman, you remember him, will be with us.'

There was a long pause before he heard, 'I'll think about it. Phone me early tomorrow,' and there the conversation ended, with the click of a receiver being replaced.

Next day she said that she had managed to arrange several

days' leave due to her and yes, with the understanding that this would be a strictly professional journey.

Chapter Six

It had been a long day. The journey from Bloemfontein to Clarens took about five hours, compounded by delays on arrival at the farm, while Rentia busied herself with orders to the staff; then it was another four hours of slithering down a windy Van Reenen's Pass. The road, a cleft through the mountains, was untarred and a rainstorm had turned the surface into mud, making steering downhill, without wheel-chains, very difficult indeed.

Manie pitied the floundering ox spans struggling up past them, heading for Pretoria. The waggoners were reenacting the original Great Trek, made a century earlier. The volk huddling under the wagon canvasses looked doggedly miserable; even more so, the sodden voorloper, leading the oxen.

After Bergville was reached on the Natal edge of the mountains, they had to branch right past Winterton before the faint lights of the remote Cathedral Peak Hotel were spotted, nestling beneath its mountain.

Early next day, they left the hotel, parked the mud-splattered Studebaker at the Indian store down the road, climbed through the barbed wire fence behind the shop, and set off for the Ndedema Gorge. Lungelo was carrying an extra-large empty pack for the collection of kindling along the track, in case, while the other two's rucksacks contained sleeping bags and food. All the rucksacks were aluminium framed…the latest thing.

The grassy path led down to a marshy area near a shallow mountain stream, more pebbles than water. In the distance, a tall stick beside the stream suddenly transformed into a heron when it spread swings and flew away. It had been standing stock still, waiting for tiny fish and crabs to come within snatching distance. Its departure coincided with rumbles of thunder. Moments later lightning began to strike the marshy ground.

'Quick!' shouted Manie, remembering his training. 'Our rucksacks have metal frames, turning us into lightning conductors. Take them off quick-quick, leave them away from you and hasten up that bank, but spread away from each other. Crouch, like this, so only your shoes touch the ground, and keep your heads down!'

For what seemed like a very long time indeed, the clouds grumbled the lightning away until Lungelo walked towards the other two and said, 'God always angry in mountains.'

The rudimentary path was overgrown and the black man said, 'Pasop vir slange [Lookout for snakes].' By the time they reached Sebaayeni cave – more of a deep overhang than a cavern – it was dusk, with only the mountain tips still in sunlight. Manie assembled some stones, sooty from an earlier fire, for Lungelo to set the kindling beneath heavier logs. Soon there was a merry little blaze. 'What's for supper?' he asked, to which Rentia replied, 'Steak and kidney pie from Uruguay,' brandishing two round flat cans, 'and mushy peas. Lungelo, I know you've brought some putu, so perhaps we can have a little too, to soak up the gravy? And for dessert, we each have a banana.'

The corporal wandered off at this point to arrange his bedding for the night at the little Zeni overhang nearby.

Later, when Lungelo had left them after supper, and Rentia and Manie had curled up in their separate sleeping bags, Rentia murmured, 'Strange to think that, thousands of years ago, someone had stared up at that same carpet of stars and wondered. In the Clarens caves there are plenty of depictions of comets, but not on this side of the mountains.'

He leaned over and kissed her. She said softly, 'Not tonight, but soon. Perhaps.'

Manie awoke in the middle of the moonless night to hear a small herd of antelope grazing, down in the valley. Closer, a nightjar sounded warning of a predator. Manie recalled what Lingelo had said: 'Lots, lots eyes looking,' pointing at the bearded vultures circling high above on a thermal, on the watch for carrion, and a family of baboons tracking their progress. He had read somewhere that the region was home to nearly three hundred bird species, and thought back to the sight of the hummingbirds, hovering around a wild honeysuckle bush they passed. Just before, they had startled a Kudu, which scrawled up a steep ascent, then turned to watch them.

It rained again before dawn, the raindrops thudding on the ground outside the cave dripline, with the sound of a thousand impi assegais beating Zulu shields.

The primus was hissing away when he woke again, to find Rentia up and looking at the overhang. 'Before you go looking for little boxes,' Rentia said, 'I want to show you what we were sleeping beneath. Come. See…those are female dancers painted on the rocks, perhaps in a trance, and an eland. Look at their strange hats. And there are bees…and more people, perhaps crossing a stream.'

'Bheka,' said Lungelo, beckoning them and pointing to a spot at the small Zeni rockface. He was about to move a stone when Rentia said, 'Wait! I want to take a photograph.

You two, both of you for scale, stand beside that little giraffe painting. Manie, hold a matchbox flat beside the giraffe for scale. Okay, you can move the stone now.'

Lungelo unfolded the camping trowel and started digging carefully, until there was the familiar thud of metal being struck. Like the others, the sturdy aluminium box was wrapped in waterproof. Carefully, he levered it out and slid it into the linen bag Manie was holding ready.

The return hike was uneventful until they reached what was a shallow stream but now presented as a swollen torrent – on reflection, no surprise, considering the rains. Early French missionaries visiting the area had dubbed it *Mont-aux-Sources*, being the headwaters of the Tugela, Orange, Elands and Wilge rivers. They had a choice: either to sit it out for the next five hours until the water level had dropped, thus having to stumble back to their car in the dark, or to take their chances and wade across. They chose the latter, so Manie went off to find the widest part on a curve.

Returning, he said, 'I've found the place. We're lucky to have put everything in dry bags, so we can float the rucksacks across, tied to us. We must link arms. Lungelo, you're the strongest, you first, me next and Rentia, hang on to me tight. See that point on the other side of the river, at the wide flat bend…with some stones and grass? Keep your eyes fixed on it, all the time, as we cross. Take small steps and tiny shuffle along – like this. Always keep your stick upstream. Important…lean against the current all the time, like that.'

The water was clear and cold. The deeper they got, the greater the tug of the current. Manie's blood froze when he stepped on a slippery rock and nearly toppled the three of them. Never was the feeling more comforting than when they managed to scramble onto the far bank, startling a little duiker. All three lay flat on their backs with relief.

'River enamandla [powerful],' said Lungelo.

'Two tight squeaks are enough,' sighed Rentia. 'You do realise we could've been washed away. They'd find three dead bodies, later, floating down the Umzimdusi. Aisch!'

The only clothes the Indian storekeeper could offer were highly patterned Hawaiian shirts and army surplus trousers. After buying some strangely large towels, he allowed them to change one by one in his back parlour, pervaded by the scent of incense and curry.

With Lungelo safely lodged and fed in the servants' quarters, Manie and Rentia joined some of the other guests for stiff sundowners on the hotel patio. Rentia still wore her marriage ring, so the others assumed they were married; an assumption neither of them made any effort to correct. There were two couples sitting nearby and one of them asked, 'I hope you don't think I am being intrusive, but are you from Hawaii?'

Both laughed, and Manie explained that they had been obliged to ford a swollen river after an overnight thunderstorm in the mountains – and that they had been there to examine rock art paintings in the vicinity.

'We had to buy some clothes from the Indian store down the road, as we were wet through. The hotel is kindly drying out our clothes in the laundry,' Rentia said.

'Oh! Did you know that we've some fine rock paintings high up in the Kamberg escarpment, quite near Dundee? I'm Peter MacPhail and this is my wife, Wendy. We're from thereabouts…just taking a break away from the coal mine I manage; and my friends, here, are down from Kenya – may I introduce them? Colonel Bill and Dulcie Greenwood.'

'Colonel?'

'Retired to Kenya. British Army India. Now we live on that "little hill" called Nyeri, within sight of Mount Kenya…

farm coffee – and cattle between crops. Coffee is easier, but it's four years before the first beans. One has to do something in the meantime, other than drinking at the Outspan Hotel or Treetops. We flew down to Durban by flying boat last Thursday – to meet up again with these rascals, just to make sure my cousin hasn't set his coal mine alight yet. Interesting trip. Took off from Lake Naivasha…preferred by the pilots as we settlers are more adept at clearing the waterway for them. Bit of a bundu-bash to get there though – must detour through Nyahururu. From these parts?'

'Certainly far closer than Nyeri. We're from around the other side of the mountains – the Orange Free State.'

'Oh yes. My coal-man cousin tells me that things are quiet down here…got things under control. Would you agree? We have rumblings in Kenya, the Kikuyu want us to vamoose and just to focus our minds, they've invented a secret society called the Mau Mau or something that sounds like that, about which we know very little, except that there have been some nasty murders of white settlers in the Highlands recently. Lots of bloodcurdling secret oaths and mumbo-jumbo. Don't know who to trust any more, not like the old days. A couple of weeks ago, we found our two Rhodesian Ridgebacks writhing in pain with all their leg tendons sliced – and our best house boy has disappeared. We had to put the dogs down. We've seen the earth go around the sun for more than sixty years now and I don't think we'll be able to put up with this fearsome turn of events – so we're exploring South Africa. Know anything about a place called Knysna?'

'Not very much. It's on the Cape coast – your cousin will know more about it. Land is expensive there I believe.'

Peter MacPhail tipped in and said, 'There was a lot of unrest in Durban at the beginning of the year – not against whites but Zulus against the Indians – the excuse being that the Indian shopkeepers were charging black market prices for essential foods like mealie meal, bread, sugar and tea. The fact is that post-war prices have risen steeply and I suspect that the real reason was the imposed division between Indians, who are treated rather like "third class whites". They are allowed to buy liquor, whereas the blacks are forced live in compounds separated from their rural families, cannot buy liquor, except so-called "kaffir-beer" in municipal beerhalls, and are prevented from bettering themselves or their families, at every turn. In the countryside, even near Dundee, the rural Zulu is still living in a beehive grass hut with no move from the authorities to improve access to clean water, hygiene, schooling and so on. We do what we can at the mine, but it's a drop in the ocean; it's an uncomfortable truth that if we don't introduce effective changes for the better, rebellious change will come about, and all will be swept away. It's the country's Achilles Heel, ripe for exploitation by the Communists – and that means the bloody Russians for their own ends…end of the Empire, and all that.'

Manie and Rentia remained silent as they were taken aback to hear such remarks. Nevertheless, they did accept the invitation to join the cousins for dinner, with Manie remaining circumspect about his occupation, merely saying that he worked for the administration in Bloemfontein. Rentia, on the other hand, fascinated them with the talk of rock art paintings, therianthropes, San trance dancing, her prehistoric temnospondyl and other strange beasties. By dessert the cousins were all for joining the archaeological society.

It was customary for the hotel to show a film on Saturday nights. That night it was *The Third Man.* It all seemed so very far away.

That night Rentia shivered and moaned in a prolonged

duration of ecstasy and Manie proposed. He wondered how his sister would react. His sons would approve, he thought and slipped into dreams of zebras and his dead wife.

Chapter Seven

'Soe! Roep die wandelaar uit, en laat sy bondeltjie goed sak, [Phew! sighed the wanderer and let drop his bundle of goods],' said Nerene, recalling the opening lines of *Somer* by C M van den Heever, a shared memory from their preparatory school days. A tired Manie had just dropped his rucksack onto the Kruis Street veranda on his return, then sighed and sank into a deck chair beside his sister. She was listening to *The Trout* Quintet and got up to turn down the volume.

'And so? How was it? I got tired of Koffiefontein…a small ingrown society clustering against the diamond mine. Grotty little lookalike miners' bungalows, one after the other. All that talk on the farm of lucerne, groundnuts and potatoes, and his interminable termites got me down after a while. They took me up a koppie to see an overgrown monument to the First World War dead – and then to see the relics of Italian murals at the POW camp. Erasmus and Vorster were detained there too, they told me.'

'Yes I know, you forget I was one of the police supervisors there, towards the end. They had an easy life with a shop, a college and playing fields. Before that Vorster had been locked up in a cell…he was always complaining about the food in the camp.'

'All those bloody makalani palms everywhere…makes you

feel as if you're in a Sahara oasis, so hot and dry. I'm glad to be back in Bloem.'

'We found what we were looking for, but the plot darkens. The Drakensberg is beautiful. Pour me a drink and I'll tell you about it – not least the rooineks I came across there.' Rentia, he decided not to mention. It just felt inappropriate, for the moment. Naval Hill seemed to have shrunk in height and prominence after his experiences in the mountains, and Bloemfontein had returned to what it always was – dry, flat, dusty and provincial; but it was home. 'It's back to the smelly police station tomorrow, but tonight I'm putting everything related to police work out of my mind. Somehow, Sussie, I feel most at peace when you are here. I see you've bought a lot of papers.' Reaching for the *Volksblad*, he said, 'What the hell are these? English papers…?'

'I picked them up at the CNA and was just curious to read what the other side was thinking about. One's a major magazine called *Drum* and the other thingy is a paper I've never seen before – *New Age/The Guardian*. An article in there might make your hair stand on end – some journalist called Ruth First wrote about black kids who disobeyed the Pass Laws and were sent to pick potatoes on Bethal farms. Maybe it's just propaganda from the English pinks, but if there were a shade of truth, it makes uncomfortable reading. It claims that the kids had their clothes removed and replaced with hessian sacks to wear. They had to dig out potatoes with their bare hands because there were no implements, and were sjamboked often by the overseer. First claims that deaths went unreported. Bodies were secretly buried, and relatives were never informed.

'When the matter was raised in parliament, Verwoerd dismissed the report and described it as "a most unjust attack by unwarranted generalisations".'

'Manie, if this is true it's not right. Look, there's another article in *Drum,* the native magazine – with pictures. Now the blacks have all refused to harvest the entire potato crop in protest and that explains why you'll have no potatoes tonight. Mavis says there are none in the shops. Any shop attempting to sell potatoes is boycotted.'

'It's probably just kaffir-boeties stirring up trouble. You know what they're like. It could suggest trouble ahead, nevertheless, but rest assured, we'll be able to sleep safely in our beds for a long time to come.'

After dinner, Nerene dragged him off to attend a recital at the university School of Music preceded by a short talk on the role of the cor anglaise among the woodwinds. The recital that followed was an agonising quartet, at least to Manie's ears, performing a work by a Dutch postwar modernist, Madalena Huistenbosch, which comprised an unrelenting series of syncopated squeals from the cor anglaise competing with a discordant jazz piano, a double bass and an occasional shriek from the flute. The bass player was Chinese, whose whitened face and scarlet lips mesmerised him as she rocked to and fro with staring eyes, while plucking and slapping the wood. He learnt her name was May Ho Why. Looking about, he studied the eager faces of students and wondered if they were really enjoying it, or trying to convince themselves that they were, and then caught Nerene's gaze, which she raised slowly heavenwards.

'What did you think of it?' Nerene asked on the way home.

'War's gruesomeness destroys Arts' equilibrium. Take Dadaism after the First World War. The last war did the same thing to that Dutch woman composer. She was in a concentration camp, according to the programme notes. That "music" is the result.'

'Ah well, when we get home, we'll put on some Schubert brain-cleaner.'

★★★

Mornings start early at police stations and Manie's was no different, but, on this occasion, he insulated himself from the routine, the collecting of prisoners to be taken to the magistrates' courts by uniformed men and the arrival of new charges for the usual fingerprinting, paperwork and general temporary confinement. That was not a detective's business. In the Super's office, he sat down with a sigh and said, with a compulsive wink, 'There's nothing for it but to go to Durban and search the girl's room myself – bearing in mind that her caretaker's moaning like hell that she's losing out on valuable rent; and I don't want anybody down there messing with the evidence.'

That night he broke the news to his sister, over dinner, and received the expected reaction, by her saying, 'I'm not seeing much of you, am I? It's almost time for me to get back before preparation for the next term, so would you please book the next train for De Aar, leaving in the morning? It takes about five hours.'

There's something about train departures…the incomprehensible squawk of platform speakers, the misspelt names on passenger lists, the solitary wheeltapper testing the integrity of wheels…the random mustering of strangers. While Manie was no Odysseus, he began to feel that he was in search of some sort of personal Teiresias, still very far from Ithaca, as he clambered aboard the train at Bloem station, pointed in the opposite direction to the one which had carried his sister away to De Aar – the day before. No one had been at the station to see him off, he thought, as he and his fellow 'Menschen im Eisenbahnabteil' greeted each other and settled down in their cocoon, to books and periodicals, and the comforting rhythm of the next twelve hours. The world he knew was temporarily withdrawn.

He learnt that his three companions were a Swiss horologist, new to the country, who had boarded the train in Cape Town, an Anglican minister returning from a ministerial gathering in Bloemfontein, and a dried fruit broker from Breede in the Western Cape. Manie said he worked in the Bloemfontein administration. When the dinner gong sounded in the corridors, they all agreed to share a table in the dining car.

The bilingual Spyskaart / Menu decorated with proteas and other wildflowers was the focus of attention. 'Bilingual', in South African terms, meant printed options in Afrikaans and English. It was inconceivable that any indigenous language might be included, although some French chef-ese had managed to sneak through. He saw, with satisfaction, that Afrikaans preceded menu descriptions, thus 'Dik haricotboontjie-en-tamatieop bretonne' preceded 'Thick haricot-bean and tomato soup bretonne' although he wondered what 'bretonne' meant. 'Krummelhoender met groen ertjies' preceded 'Crumbed chicken with green peas'.

Over the wine, the Swiss clockmaker challenged their credulity by saying that pendulum clocks were affected by the gravitational pull of the moon and the dried fruit man claiming that his products contained more than three times the fibre, vitamins and minerals than fresh fruit, which led to a banter about the quality of the food they were eating. Manie noticed that before the minister commenced eating, he closed his eyes momentarily, and broke off a small piece of bread followed by a sip of red wine.

There was much debate about the founding of the 'German Democratic Republic' with the Swiss saying, 'At

Yalta, the American President Roosevelt gave away half of Europe to that butcher Stalin and the world will be very sorry in the years to come that he did such a damn stupid thing. All those countries, Poland, Lithuania, Estonia, half of Germany and the rest are now in the grip of the Russian bear!' to which they all nodded their heads, by which time Manie was beginning to feel very tired after much wine. He wanted to lie down, so excused himself and stumbled off to the compartment, which, he discovered, had been magicked into four bunks, complete with fluffy railway sheeting, pillows and blankets. Gratefully, he managed to clamber onto one of the top bunks and fell asleep, waking only later when the train ground to a halt, for no apparent reason, in the middle of the dark African veld, and realised that he was still dressed. He lay there listening to the others snoring, took off his shoes and tie, then got into bed fully clothed. A goods train passed on a parallel track and then the train began to creak forward as he fell asleep again.

At breakfast, as telegraph wires swooped and Pietermaritzburg slid by, conversation was desultory, with each to their own thoughts as they munched railway bacon and eggs. The Anglican minister, who had drunk little wine the night before, was the only one to chatter. It turned out that he was an enthusiastic member of the Durban Historical Society and launched into a defence of Durban's British Empire buildings, which progressive architects were calling for replacement with 'glass and aluminium contraptions'.

'Take the Durban railway station we'll soon see… . Detractors described it as a badly iced cake, ignoring the fact that it is a rare example of late Queen Anne Revival style of the late Victorian era. It's an imported treasure. When you leave the station, spare a few moments to study the outside of the building and the architecture of the General Post

Office, the gigantic City Hall and the Cenotaph. At least they won't be able to knock *the latter* down. The Post Office is a magnificent example of the Corinthian style designed by an Irishman, Philip Dudgeon', at which point the Swiss clockmaker said,

'As a matter of fact, my job here is to rescue the post office clock! Apparently, it's been gaining time ever more quickly, caused by cog wear. It's going to take many months to repair.'

'Well, well I never! We must stay in touch.'

'By all means. I'll be staying at the Marine Hotel until I find something more permanent,' at which point Manie pricked up his ears, and said, 'I'll be staying there too for a short while, until I've finished my business down here. No doubt, we'll bump into each other.'

Returning to his hobbyhorse while waiting for the coffee to arrive, the Minister said, 'Then dwell for a moment when you pass the City Hall…how can those Philistines wish to destroy part of Durban's history! Ah, here's our coffee. It's an extraordinary example of Edwardian neo-baroque style squatting here at the sharp end of Africa…part of the hubris of the British Empire, fast disintegrating, alas. Destroying it would be rather like pulling down the Brandenburg Gate just because von Pfuel, the Nazis, and Napolean had strutted through it. Oh, Good Lord, there's Kloof Station! We'd better get back and pack.'

All this had passed over Manie's head, but he bristled at the idea of preserving relics of the British Empire. He wondered who von Pfuel was.

Disembarking, Manie took a rickshaw to the Marine. He had booked for a third-floor view of the bay. Although the rate far exceeded a policeman's hotel allowance, he had elected to pay the balance himself, in order to return to the Marine of his happy marriage. It was still the same…the splendidly turbaned Indian porter administering his minions and taking charge of his luggage – past the odiferous Vogue hair salon in the foyer and the Ladies Bar boasting the only woman bartender in Africa; then being whisked to his floor by the same, now very old, lift man. His balcony overlooked tall palms lining the Esplanade and the bay.

Chapter Eight

He had arranged to meet Detective Simpson at the Three Monkeys. To that end he had cut through Union Castle Arcade, so that he might catch sight again of the huge model of a Union Castle liner. His young sons were fascinated, as was he, by the accuracy and its twinkling lights. Yes, it was still there, the large plaster cast of Mizaru, Kikazaru and Iwazaru, still squatting in the window of the coffee shop, in front of the three big bean-grinding wheels. He was led there by the coffee smell which wafted down West Street. Simpson was to be identified by his reading a copy of the *Natal Mercury* and an orange on his table.

'Hello,' he said, folding his paper, half rising and shaking hands. 'Good trip down? Takes a while to get used to the humidity. The owner, over there, assures me that the best coffee in the world comes from the Yirgacheffe region in Ethiopia, gets it straight off the boat, so I ordered some to go with our croissants…you like croissants, I hope? Now, pleasantries aside, how can I help? The girl's room remains barred by us, following your request – much to the fury of the owner, Mrs Bell. As you know, fingerprinting has been done, and nothing much has come to light. Just her prints, the cleaners and smudged prints of previous tenants – those least fresh.'

'Thank you. I'm looking for any correspondence with

Ireland, or any other paperwork, concealed or not, perhaps books. I understand that a scientist working in the museum has her passport and so on, but any extra correspondence might help. I've arranged to visit the museum after lunch.'

'Right. Let's catch a trolley up Smith Street. The town retired the trams last March and the drivers haven't got the hang of these new vehicles yet. The overhead poles keep on coming off.'

Theresa O'Brien's room was up a flight of careworn stairs and overlooked a small, tired garden with an emaciated tree sulking in the corner. The bathroom was down the passage and shared with three other residents. The men disentangled themselves, with difficulty, from Mrs Bell, the owner, who wanted to accompany them to O'Brien's room and stood at the bottom of the stairs complaining.

There wasn't much to investigate. Manie caught sight of himself in the girl's wardrobe mirror and wondered what she was thinking of when she stood before it for the very last time before departing by train, ultimately to her death. There was a shelf of books, mainly of a reference nature, with few paperbacks. Beside the bed a bedside light stood on a small set of drawers, along with two novels and nothing else besides. He was struck that these favoured leisure time books were left behind.

'We'll have to work through every single book back at the station but make a note that I've borrowed these two books beside her bed. I have a hunch. They're *1984* by George Orwell and *Brave New World* by Aldous Huxley.'

They spent the rest of the morning dismantling, examining and then reassembling the few sticks of furniture, then bundling her clothes into a suitcase that remained under the bed, containing some treasured items, including several twisted florins, items of modest jewellery, a metal cloisonné box of beads and a sewing kit. Oddly, there was no correspondence, but there were two faded brown photographs of a man and a woman in an unfamiliar domestic setting. Tightly wedged in a pocket of the suitcase and stuffed beneath a crumpled newspaper sheet and a pair of stockings, Manie found a minute folding triptych depicting the Mother of God surrounded by New Testament figures. He studied it with puzzlement. It was hand-painted on hinged wood and partly gilded and was the first he had ever seen. He felt, in his bones, that it was particularly significant.

'I would like to take this along to the museum this afternoon and perhaps establish its origins. Okay? Include them on the list.'

They spent the rest of their time listing everything culminating with Simpson saying, 'It's past lunchtime and you'll have to hurry off to the museum, so I'll arrange for the suitcase to be taken to the station…see you tomorrow morning, at about eight. The easiest way to get to our Aliwal Street police station from your hotel will be by rickshaw… you will have noticed the rank around the corner from the Marine.'

Natural History museums tend to whiff of pickles, given off, ever so slightly, by the residual formaldehyde used as a preservative, and Durban's was no different. The door to Sophia Vitali-Kluczynska's office lay behind a diorama of a lioness' lair sheltering her cubs, after passing by the skeleton of a Dodo. In a glass case. Manie had written down her complicated name on a slip of paper and had this in his hand when he knocked and pushed open the door, starting to ask a woman behind a vast desk, when she looked up and said, 'Yes, yes, that's me, with the difficult name. Come in, come in. Just call me Zosha. You've come about poor Theresa, haven't you? Ach! Such a sweet girl – and such a good student…what a loss. But before we talk further let's have some tea. If you do not mind filling the kettle at the gents down the passage?'

On his return he found her emptying some gingernuts onto a plate and drawing up a bentwood chair to her desk, which was littered with photographs of swallowtail butterflies, samples of pupae, chrysalises, caterpillars and a butterfly field guide.

'We cannot talk about Theresa, please, until the kettle whistles…I'm the museum's entomologist and am writing an article for the *African Butterfly News* on the camouflage of the Citrus Swallowtail during its four stages of metamorphosis. Durban people who own lemon trees know all about it when it's a caterpillar. Wonderful creatures. Sugar and milk? Do you know that butterflies lose all memory of their previous life as caterpillars? That's the latest research.

'The young caterpillars of the one I am studying resemble bird droppings and the full-grown ones' green colour with grey bands makes them well camouflaged. The chrysalis resembles a broken-off twig.

'Now,' she said, 'brass tacks,' pushing her work aside, and unlocking and rabbiting around in a cupboard. 'Here's her passport (she didn't trust her landlady) and all the correspondence I have between her, the university in Dublin and me concerning her extended African studies. She and I became friendly, through our mutual professional interests, our daily contact, and because neither of us knew many people.'

Zosha said that post-war turmoil had brought her to Durban after she managed to extricate herself from Poland. Her officer-father had been shot by the Russians at Katyn, and her mother and sisters lost their lives during the Nazi Polish blitzkrieg.

'Theresa and I got into the habit of going for a swim at North Beach early in the morning after meeting up outside the Coooee tearoom. The beach is beautiful at that time of the morning when there is no one else about. You should consider trying it while you are down here.

'After she got to know me better, Theresa told me her life story. She came from abject beginnings. Her grandparents were illiterate farm workers and were so poor that they ended their days in what was called a workhouse in an Irish town called Wexford. They were buried in an unmarked graves. Her mother and Theresa went to Dublin in search of work and dwelt in a place called Swift's Alley in an area called The Liberties. I remember this because she showed me a newspaper cutting reporting its demolition. See, it's in her paperwork…I recall her expression of joy while she showed me. It almost seemed excessive. Her mother died of tuberculosis in a squalid room there, she said, which now is no more. Miraculously, she was rescued from a life of drudgery, and a similar fate by being adopted by a childless couple – a Mr and Mrs Fitzsimons who lived in a snooty part of Dublin called Merrion Square. She was rather proud of that and showed me a picture of the square that she seemed to treasure. There was a marvellous library in the house, while being tutored at home – kept separate from hoi polloi children, culminating in her being sent to Château Mont-Choisi Finishing School in Lausanne for a year. This explained her excellent command of French. Her English pronunciation had a marked French "twirl" – though her command of English was also very good… . During this period she developed a hunger for learning…but this paradise was destroyed when, soon before her return, the Dublin house caught fire and her adoptive parents died from smoke inhalation. Fortunately, she was now old enough to survive on her savings, while seeking work. Good fortune was with her when she landed a post as a filing clerk in the Trinity College library in Dublin. A professor, hearing of her background, took her under his wing and arranged for her to study and complete an archaeological degree, the subject which fascinated her. Unfortunately, he died before her graduation, but it was this qualification which brought her to Durban.

'So, there it is, and here we are at closing time; there's the bell, but before we part, let's have a drink. I have discovered a beautiful sundowner. Come…hand me those glasses over there,' she said, while taking ice, gin and a bianco style of vermouth from a little fridge. 'It's my Great Durban Discovery. Theresa and I used to drink them, sitting on these very chairs…dobre zdrowie!'

'Look,' said Manie, 'solitary dining in the Marine is a sad experience. I booked in there because my dead wife and I spent our honeymoon there…and went back again with the young children. Way above a policeman's travel allowance. I wonder if you'd care to join me for dinner in the hotel's West Room this evening?'

She thought for a while, then said, 'Yes, thank you, why not – but I must be home well before eleven at the latest. I have a Little Topolino, but I prefer not to drive at night. You'll have to arrange taxis.'

'Just before I go, can you identify this?' he asked, unwrapping a tissue he had taken from his pocket.

'Why yes – it's an Eastern European triptych perhaps Russian – a travelling icon. That's why it's quite small. It's customary for Eastern Orthodox believers to carry one. Where did you get it?'

'A friend found it.'

'This is a hand-painted one. Ach it is beautiful and quite valuable.'

'Is it not Irish, perhaps?'

'No, no – definitely not.'

★★★

After walking back to the Marine to book a good table he decided to take a turn past Dick King's Statue and the yachts parked on their chocked cradles, the riggings slapping gently, to sit on an old barnacled bench at the end of the Mole. He and his wife had sat there in the gloaming, so long ago, listening to the sounds of the harbour. The water had been so still that they had heard a fish plop.

Turbaned Indian waiters were not the only feature of the West Room. It was truly an emporium of plaster decoration excelled only by the ultra-rococo interior balcony, just big enough to accommodate an accordionist and two string players who struck up with a discreet nuevo tango music, just as the head waiter ushered them to their table. Zosha had arrived dressed in a red cotton dinner dress.

As they were being seated, she said, 'This is the first grand hotel I have entered since my father took my mother and me to dinner at the Hotel Grand Polonia in Warszawa… Warsaw before the war. It was my mother's birthday, and she too wore a red dress that night. As she looked about, her eyes glittered with tears, while candles were lit.'

They were encouraged to choose a first course of prawn cradled in an avocado with Marie Rose sauce and Manie was relieved that the ordering of wine would be simplified by their both ordering citrus-braised lamb shank accompanied by buttered mashed potatoes, green beans, roasted cauliflower and a young tomato salad. He ordered a Western Cape claret and asked the wine steward what Eton Mess was, which he spied among the list of desserts, to which he replied, with his nose distinctly elevated, that he believed it was served at the annual cricket match between Harrow and Eton.

'Never heard of either,' he muttered as the waiter withdrew.

During the meal, she spoke about the brutal occupation under Nazi-then-Soviet rule, the random arrests and executions of Polish intelligentsia by the combined efforts of the Gestapo-NKVD until Germany's declaration of war against Russia, which later triggered an uprising to be once again crushed by Russia.

During Nazi rule, posters throughout the city emblazoned the latest executions. Warsaw was reduced to a provincial backwater, to be replaced in time by neo-Nazi architecture, for which two German architects were imported to mastermind the project, though fortunately never commenced. The purpose was to humiliate and crush the Polish spirit for ever, she said. Zosha managed to vanish by joining the underground, about which she said little except to mention her participation in the blowing up of railway lines.

During the turmoil at the end of the war, she managed to smuggle herself out to the West with her pre-war graduation certificates and, through a series of happenstances, wound up in her present position at the museum.

'By comparison, my life has been humdrum,' said Manie, and he described his early life, growing up in DeAar with his sister; the boredom of attending Dutch Reformed Church with his strict parents every Sunday and the instilling by teachers that South Africa belonged to the Afrikaner nation 'It was our God-given right…drilled into us – in a sense, that we were the master race. The Coloureds – half-caste servants and labourers – only spoke "Kaaps" (that jumble of Afrikaans and other languages, some indigenous) and we just ignored the occasional black unless we had to interact – and even they spoke a simplified "kitchen-Afrikaans" with us, as their language Xhosa remained incomprehensible. These people just jabbered away at it in the kraals It never occurred to anyone to learn it.

'We seldom heard English spoken until, one July, we came down here to Durban on holiday in Pa's shiny new car – juss! It was a long way – where everyone spoke English and I was tongue-tied – even going into a shop to buy sweets was a stumbling embarrassment. Later, I took English as a second language in high school but was taught by an Afrikaans teacher who had barely mastered the rudiments of English himself. Yet from that time on I was resolved to speak it as well as I could.

'Both parents loved music and encouraged us to learn to play their piano. Nerene showed much talent. Money was short, so my parents favoured my sister in studying further, leaving me with three options…to work in a shop or the railways at De Aar, or join the police – this was well before the war, remember, when opportunities for a young Afrikaans boy "from the middle of nowhere" were few and far between. De Aar was pretty isolated too, and there was much resentment of anything English. My parents retained ugly early memories of the Boer War British concentration camps of women and children. There was great suffering.

'When war was imminent, policemen tended to join a new anti-British movement called the Ossewabrandwag, but, ironically, I spent the war years guarding Afrikaans pro-Nazis detained in Koffiefontein.

'I was a good student and passed many police exams until I became a detective. One day, as a senior policeman and OB member. I stumbled across a copy of a secret German document which described the OB as "based on the Führer-principle, fighting against the British Empire, the capitalists, the Communists, the Jews, and the system of parliamentarianism…on the base of national-socialism". This was a bridge too far, so I lost interest in the OB movement until it was absorbed into the Nationalist Party after the war.'

What he didn't reveal was the discovery of the rock art site boxes and their contents, O'Brien's encounter with the IDB crooks and the recovery of the Tzarist jewellery; and although he did talk about his dead wife and his children, his sister's shared love of music, he felt it inappropriate to mention Rentia.

'Look, your eyes are beginning to droop, and I don't blame you – listening to this old mompara rambling on. I'm going to call you a taxi.'

'Not at all, but I'm no longer used to the Grande Standing lifestyle and it's well past my bedtime. I won't invite you in, but please see me home. I don't like climbing three dark flights of steps at this time of night. You can guard me to the top of the stairs. My block of flats has a funny stairway lighting system. You must push in a timer on the wall, then scramble to the next floor before the lights go out again.'

Back in his hotel room, he stared out at the midnight harbour and traced the pinpoint of a police launch as it worked towards C-Dock, then turned in, after flipping through some pages of O'Brien's *Brave New World*, wondering why she had underlined 'an angel in bottle-green viscose' in a passage which read 'The flush suddenly deepened; he was thinking of Lenina, of an angel in bottle-green viscose, lustrous with youth and skin food, plump, benevolently smiling.' He assumed that the girl was one of those habitual underliner-readers, who marked passages that resonated with them, and turned out the light.

A few moments later he sat bolt upright and turned on the bedside lamp again, took the book, and counted the number of letters in the underlined section. They were exactly twenty-

94

six. In fact, she had not marked the last letter in 'viscose', which would have made the letters twenty-seven.

Paging through the rest of the book he soon found another passage with twenty-six letters underlined. It read, 'Most human beings have an almost infinite capacity for taking things for granted. There's only one corner of the universe you can be certain of improving, and that's your own self.'

Opening Theresa's paperback of *1984* he almost yelped as he read the first few lines of the first chapter, 'It was a bright cold day in April, and the clocks were striking thirteen. Winston Smith, his chin nuzzled into his breast, in an effort to escape the vile wind.'

'It wasn't the books she was keeping, it was the keys to the codes, hiding in plain sight!' he said out loud, then turned out the light again. The pillows he snuggled into smelt of hotel laundry. The night was so still he could hear the faint bells of the town hall clock striking all four quarters, then One. 'Out of tune,' he thought as his mind drifted into sleep.

Dressing, the next day, a Wednesday, he paused to watch the lavender-hulled *Warwick Castle* liner being pushed sideways by tugs towards its B-dock berth.

The rickshaw man outside the Marine was not one of those fancy beachfront beings, but a simple human taxi, waiting for hire. 'Where to, boss?'

'Aliwal Street police station, but you needn't stop at the entrance; stop just a little bit before we get there.'

The swaying, squeaking progress took him back to riding in one with his young wife, perhaps explaining why he gave him a generous bonsela at the end of the trip. As he walked towards the police station, a nondescript brown car screeched around a corner, and headed directly at him, forcing him to dive for cover into a shop alcove, as the vehicle mounted the pavement, missing the rickshaw which had been pulled away, but scraping several parked cars with an almighty din before careering back to the correct side of the road and disappearing around the next bend, from which blaring horns emanated, marking its onward path.

People ran out to see what had happened but, perhaps because of the bonsela he had received, it was the rickshaw man who ran to his assistance and helped him into the station, then disappeared.

'My God, what happened? Did the lady at the museum beat you up?'

After having his arm iodined and bandaged, and a stiff brandy, Simpson said, 'We'll find the car and driver, but it's too late now to chase after him. It was a "him" was it? Was he a white?'

'A white with round spectacles…I'll swear that it was deliberate. I can't recall seeing a number plate…no, there wasn't one – I remember that the place for the plate was bare – you know how you spot things. It was a prewar Chevrolet sedan. Brown – and battered. I remembered that streamlined figure above the radiator grill.

'Well, when you're ready, come next door to the case room where there's a big layout table. There isn't much.'

The girl's few possessions, the picture frame, the books, her cosmetics had been opened – split open in many cases. and the linings of her clothes had been unthreaded.

'The silver picture frame is hallmarked SG (for Séamus Gill), the second is the symbol of the Irish Assay office, followed by the number 925, guaranteeing 92.5% silver… we called in someone from Randles to explain this. Nothing wrong there. It's impossible to identify the middle-aged couple in the sepia photograph, but the cardboard mount is embossed 'Edgar Adolphe, Dublin'…only correspondence with Dublin could check that. Odd…there are no letters, invoices or receipts.

'I can explain that – the museum woman had the letters – O'Brien didn't trust the landlady. But I think I've found the keys to that coded stuff. Not the full answer by a long chalk, but it might be the beginning – way past me. I'm keeping a copy of everything and I'll be sending off the originals to the Pretoria momparas.'

'And these twisted florins?'

'Dunno. Maybe a quirky way of identity reassurance when encountering someone else in the net – to establish they're kosher. I seem to remember they were used as a means of identification when RAF airmen, downed in France, were smuggled over the mountains to Portugal – like a baton in a relay race.'

'What about her effects?'

'In normal circumstances, we'd hold on to them until case closed, then send them to her Irish relatives, but there don't seem to be any; so we'll hold them locked up until it's over… That's two people without known relatives, I've come across recently, one alive – Zosha at the museum – and the O'Brien girl. So we're done then, for the moment, and thank you for your help. I'll keep you posted – let me know if you locate that crazy driver. I'll leave for Bloem first thing tomorrow morning. Time for lunch before we finish off?'

'Well, why not? Let me introduce you to the best bunny chow in town. Officially it's an Indian restaurant so whites are barred, but I know the owner and we all look the other way. It's at the end of the line, literally – the Umgeni end of the now disused tramline. Samosas, bunny chow and a lager – you won't get those in Bloem – except the beer.'

'Bunny chow?'

'Mouthwatering – and eye-watering too, for some,' said Simpson, as he pulled into the start of Umgeni Road and staring, for a moment in the rear view mirror. 'Well, "chow" is just the local slang for food, and "bunny", it is said, came from "Banias" – the caste of the Indian family who owned an Indian café in town, way back. Bit of a long shot…lots of stories…one of them is that natives were not allowed to enter Indian eateries, so, never to lose the chance of an extra bob or two, the owners hit on the idea of selling curries in scooped out halves of bread through a back hatch. Funny, I must be imaging things. A car seems to be trailing us, two cars back…Probably imagining things – I'll just park for a moment. Nope…it's just gone past…must be going cuckoo.'

Back at the hotel, he watched the flying boat from Victoria Falls croon overhead before describing a foaming path as it landed at the head of the bay. The phone tinkled. It was a call from Simpson, saying they had located the car that nearly ran him over, burnt out, in the bushes beside the Kwa Mashu road to the native location. 'No number plates, but we identified it by the numbers stamped into the engine block and so back to the dealers. It was stolen outside the post office in King Williams Town over a year ago. Kings – that's a long way away, about nine hours from here…probably used as a getaway. Of course no one knows anything about it… the usual, but we'll keep trying.'

'I'll be interested to hear how you've put the puzzle together. Sinister?'

'Yes, very sinister, I think. I can see myself having to travel to Ireland to unravel that end; so you're likely to see me back here to catch that flying boat up Africa.'

★★★

He packed, went for a stroll again and, returning, bumped into the clockmaker, agreeing to dine together, in the hotel's supper room – far less grandiose than the West Room.

Although Ernst Carli was Swiss, he explained that he came out to Durban contracted by one of the few tower clock manufacturers left in the world, in England. In between mouthfuls (he ate with his mouth open) he discussed the perils of tower clock repair, and said he was not looking forward to clambering up the ladders to reach the clock chamber. Bird nests and bat droppings were his least liked encounters – secondarily the draught inside the clock chamber, along with the cobwebs and large spiders.

'This clock was made in 1883 and she's beginning to show her age. It probably needs a cog-by-cog cleaning. The untimely acceleration is probably due to just one piece that I'll have to replace, making a new one. This means I'll have to dismantle the mechanism and bring it down to my new workshop. Each cog has a synchronism mark, which will help me put everything together again. A big blessing is the detailed instruction manual I expect to find left beside the clock.. That's standard procedure…heaven help me if it's been blown away.'

Carli was a short bespectacled man, past thirty-five, with receding fair hair who spoke a Teutonic-tinged English. After his parents' fatal off-piste skiing accident, he was brought up in an orphanage, he told Manie, and apprenticed in a Swiss horological college. To widen his experience in the final year, he spent some months at a famous firm of Leipzig tower clock makers, where he was recruited to apply his craft in one of the few tower clock maker and carillon foundries in Croydon, England.

Manie encouraged him to ramble on and reflected upon

the number of people he had encountered recently, who had lost their parents or their past through accident, poverty or war. Was this not too much of a coincidence, he wondered? As is often the case among those who talk much about themselves, the clockmaker showed little interest in Manie's Free State wanderings, except when his mouth was full – Manie glossing over the true reason for his Durban visit.

He did ask him about living conditions in Britain and he replied that Croydon was badly hit during the Blitz in '41/'42 and was still recovering when he left for Durban. 'Lots of propped-up ruins. Being Swiss, my wife and I were technically neutral, so I was not recruited, but spent most spare time fire-fighting as an air raid warden. She joined the WVS, feeding the blitz victims…night after night; then the doodlebugs, the most awful, except for the V2s…we all used to dive for cover when we heard the flying bomb engines cut out…then boom! Meaning some poor buggers had copped it, and their houses. I lost my wife and child. It made me loathe the Nazis, as I still do.'

'Copped it?'

'Blown to pieces. Our factory had switched to munitions, and my specialism was designing delayed action fuses. I can tell you more about that kind of clockwork than you can shake a stick at.'

'Shake a stick?'

'Sorry, it's an expression.'

Escaping upstairs, Manie parted the curtains to look out on the night harbour. The palm tree fronds were thrashing about before the electrical storm that followed and the lights across the bay were suddenly obscured behind the sheets of rain. He stayed at the window, exulting in nature's tantrum. Before turning in, he booked a trunk call to Rentia for six the next morning; farmers woke early, he remembered. He had kept the two underlined paperbacks and turned to *1984* again, this time merely for the pleasure of finding out what happened next, and read "…*How often, or on what system, the Thought Police plugged in on any individual wire was guesswork…*"

The bedside phone rang in the dark. 'Clarens exchange here. I have your caller on the line. I'll interrupt when your time is up. The lines are very busy today. Go ahead, caller.'

'Is that you, Rentia? – I can hear other voices and clatters in the background? Lots of crackles on the line.'

'Yes, it's me. Marvellous to hear from you… . Hang on, I'll close the door to the kitchen. It's the maids jabbering away. I thought you had gone to ground. Where are you – still in Durbs?'

'Yes, I'm high up overlooking the ships in the harbour. I'm catching the train back to Bloem this morning. Have you thought over my proposal?'

'What do you think? Of course. Much, and the answer is maybe. As I said, I love my job and the farm, but I would like to marry again to the right man, and you seem to be he. But we live poles apart at the moment and I can't see a way of resolving that. Let's sit down and talk – perhaps we can meet up this coming weekend?'

'Yes, but I might have to go to Ireland very soon.'

'To Ireland! Gott Almagtig!' At this point, the operator interrupted and said, 'Time's up. Sorry caller, we must terminate your call.' Then the line went dead, only to ring again immediately, with the hotel switchboard operator saying 'A call for you from Pretoria, sir. Will you take it?'

'Who is it?'

'It's police headquarters, sir.'

'Brigadier – General van den Bergh here. Is that Detective Inspector Marais?'

'Yes sir.'

'We've been quietly following developments in this O'Brien lastige raaisel. Have you made progress? Don't give details over the line.'

'I have learnt much useful information, but the mystery deepens. It's a plot, of some kind and we don't yet know who or what is behind it. I don't think it's IDB.'

There was a grunt from Pretoria before the voice said, 'I've arranged for you to go directly to Ireland as quickly as possible. We've squared it already with Scotland Yard and the Irish Garda. As you are in Durban, catch the flying boat to Southampton, then by rail down to Fishguard for the Irish ferry to Rosslare. Cook's will sort you out – issue tickets, overnight stays en route and so on, so we have transferred adequate funds to Thomas Cook in West Street, Durban – they'll issue you with travellers' cheques, plus adequate local British and Irish cash. You must keep receipts for everything, even bus, tram and train tickets. The police have an account at Greenacres and Cuthbert's, so you can buy adequate clothes and luggage. It's cold over there so you'll need a winter coat. Get your requisitions from Aliwal Street headquarters. Report to me when you get back. You have one month. Goodbye.'

Chapter Nine

He found himself sitting beside the British Consul, who, with his wife and children, was taking up his new post in Bulawayo, Southern Rhodesia. Manie had had to phone Rentia about the plan change and likewise his housekeeper, Mavis in Bloem, after arranging with his bank and Bing to pay Mavis and the gardener.

'Where are you off to, then?' the Consul asked.

'Ireland – the republic.'

'Good Lord, a long stretch. We were all very sorry to see Ireland leave the Commonwealth. It's a fearsome task for such a new country…to go it alone. Mind you, there's still that special connection between Ireland and Britain, joined at the hip. I suppose it's just as well…the Irish didn't like us very much. Alas, Britain's so broke now after the war that the Empire's disintegrating – can't afford it any more…the end of the Raj in '47 and look at what that has led to – all that bloodshed between the Hindus and the Muslims. And then there's all the turmoil in Europe still… Iron Curtain and all that. Do you know Southern Rhodesia well? I don't know it at all…read up a lot about it if course, but the children are already getting excited at the prospect of seeing the Victoria Falls from the air for the very first time, as Pamela and I are. The Zimbabwe Ruins as well. We got off at Durban, instead of going on to Beira, as we wanted to see a bit of your country first. Are you going to Ireland for pleasure?'

'No, on government business.'

'You're a fellow diplomat, are you?'

'No. I'm a detective.'

'I see. Can you tell me what it's about?'

''Fraid not'

'No, of course you can't. It must be fascinating work… intrigue, murders, clues and all that. But your journey must be very important, otherwise you wouldn't be travelling on this flying boat – reserved for the posh, the very rich, and diplomats like us. International diamond smuggling perhaps? I know a lot goes on through Beira. Ah…there's the lunch announcement…my word, we could be dining at the Savoy… bone china, silver service, napkins, BOAC napkin rings – all this after wartime rationing is a bit of a culture shock. Mind you, travelling to Durban aboard the *Union Castle* softened the blow somewhat. Just look at my girls over there, eyes like saucers. Thank heavens Pamela's taught them some table manners. They're looking forward to landing on the Zambezi. Quite a splash. They must clear the strip of crocodiles and hippos, hours ahead of our arrival, I'm told.'

They flew well below twelve thousand feet, sometimes obligingly much lower, to view the huge herds of antelope and elephants. As they approached the Zambezi, the pilot dipped lower and circled over the Falls' gorges with their rainbow tiaras, before voicing preparations to passengers for their river landing. 'Jove…angels in their flight,' murmured the Consul. He was of course referring to a remark written by David Livingstone, the first European to come upon the Falls ('scenes so lovely must have been gazed upon by angels in their flight!')– a remark which went over Manie's head.

'Well, here we are. Bumpy landing, what? Into the launch

and onto the jetty…Customs now. Have we got everything Pamela….children and all their things? See that notice over there, girls – "Beware Of Crocodiles"? We're staying at the Vic Falls Hotel,' he said to Manie, *Jungle Junction* they call it, don't they…and entraining for Bulawayo in the morning. A pity we've missed the All-Blacks match. They were thrashed by Rhodesia, I believe. We'll see you up there later.'

Padlocked sacks of post were unloaded first, then luggage. Motoring through the veld on the way to the hotel, they passed a row of broken trees. 'Why are all those branches broken?' asked one of the children, to which the shuttle driver replied, 'Elephants.' A mural dominated one wall of the foyer, depicting tropically dressed tourists in twenties clothing, staring at the falls with binoculars, the bridge in the background. On the patio, ready for sundowners, passengers were greeted by a smiling Odwell, the head waiter, in his red coat covered with buttons, and an African xylophone group playing 'I want to be Happy' with Matabele and Makalolo variations.

'They're catching up,' said the Consul. His wife, Pamela, was away, upstairs, seeing to the children. The consul and Manie were staring at 'the smoke that thunders', from the lawn's viewing site, sundowners in hand. 'My parents took us to *No, No, Nanette* at the Palace in 1925, a world away. The war's like a mountain range, isn't it? Everything happened either "Before the War" or "After the War"… . They'll be playing "Tea for Two" next! There you are! Listen. I think I prefer this African version.'

'By the way, I'm Richard Bayley, originally from Broadstairs in Kent. There's a South African connection through the novelist John Buchan. He wrote *The Thirty-Nine Steps* there. He was brought out to South Africa and fell in love with your beautiful country. I believe there's an engraved stone in his memory overlooking a stretch of water in Magoesbaskloof – pardon my pronunciation. Peter Pienaar, a retired Boer scout features strongly as a "Mr Standfast" in many of Buchan's Hannay novels, you will recall.'

'And I'm Hermanus, or Manie, for short, Marais, from a hot, dry railway junction in the veld called De Aar, in the Northern Cape. I'm amazed about your knowing about Magoesbaskloof!'

'A mind like blotting paper, I'm afraid. Had to…the only thing that allowed me to stagger through a degree. It's a pleasure to meet you,' he said, shaking Manie's hand, who responded with 'Aangename kennis!'

'Marais…that's a French name.'

'Yes, I think it means "marsh". Afrikanerdom is peppered with French names, like our rugby team. There's a saying that if you look between the blankets, you'll find a Huguenot.'

'Ah yes, of course, they settled in the Cape and elsewhere after the Edict of St Germaine in 1685. Look here, would you care to join Pamela and me for supper? The children will be tucked away by that time. It'll be an opportunity to soak up more inside knowledge about South Africa. I've been cautioned that saying "Kitchener" to an Afrikaner is like saying "Cromwell" to an Irishman…. I believe that the à la Carte range is very good. Eight o'clock in the Livingstone Room then?…We can meet up in the anteroom, at about 7.50 or so? I believe they've done away with dinner jackets since the war and "smoking" or blazers will do. Dinner's our treat…. We must all remember to take our quinine before supper.'

Pausing at little hotel shop, Manie spotted a paperback of *1984* and bought it along with a copy of the *Bulawayo Chronicle*. Upstairs, he flung himself down on the bed beneath the mosquito-netting and read 'Front halts African housing?', then lay the paper aside and listened to the night sounds. Away on the bridge, a train rumbled slowly and whistled.

Over dinner, he excused the nervous tic of his right eye and Pamela related the often funny moments she had negotiating the minefields of communication in Katmandu. It turned out that Bayley had worked in the DFID and before that for a German engineering company in Bangladesh. Before that he had read Anthropology at Cambridge. Pamela had a way of listening to a guest intensely, and Manie soon found himself talking about happy boyhood times on his father's De Aar sheep farm, and the perceived simplicity of the Coloured Volk.

'What does 'De Aar' mean?' she asked, and he explained that it meant 'the artery', referring to the town's bountiful aquifer.

'Well, there we are,' Richard said at last. 'Time for us to join the children. Early start for all of us tomorrow…you to wing up north on your secret mission and for us to catch the Bulawayo train…I believe the town has the longest railway platform in the world! Will we ever learn what your mission is all about?'

'Perhaps. Goodnight!'

'Well, we're off to White Mischief land,' said his new travelling neighbour as the pilot announced that the bar was open. 'Hello, I'm St John Morris (he pronounced it as 'Singin') and that's my wife Phoebe and son, Littlejohn. It's going to be quite a leg, so we might as well introduce ourselves.'

Manie shook his hand, asking, 'White Mischief?'

'So-called about the goings on of the set in the Kenyan Highlands. Famous unsolved murder and trial. My wife, Phoebe, over there with my son, and I are both British lawyers doing the round trip via Mombasa, so we're ever interested in the story. Right in the middle of the war it was too – the UK made a meal of it. Better than talking about the blitz.'

'You're South African are you? Perchance a lawyer?'

'No, I'm a detective.'

'Good lord – well…this is right up your street – a classic unsolved mystery. Flying on business or pleasure?'

'Business'

'I was referring to that unsolved murder in 1941 of Josslyn Hay, a high-ranking British ex-pat. Everyone suspected it was Jock Broughton, as Hay was carrying on blatantly with Broughton's much younger wife, let alone other men's wives, leading to one enraged husband horsewhipping Hay on the Nairobi railway station; but Broughton's guilt was never proven. Suspicion fell for a while on someone called Cholmondeley, pronounced "Chumley" and a lot of others, as Jock wasn't popular. Broughton got off scot-free, defended by a Harry Morris, a brilliant South African lawyer. Ran rings around the prosecution. The Mischief gang…lots from the British and Anglo-Irish aristocracy…were leading a hedonistic lifestyle…worse than King Farouk…much drunkenness, wife-swopping, morphine and cocaine – they were all at it. Gatherings focussed on the so-called Djinn Palace, a Moorish monstrosity of domes, turrets, and cupolas built in 1927 by Hollywood actor Cyril Ramsay-Hill. The quip also referred to the enormous glasses of gin they all downed. We might even fly over it when we come into land.

'To complicate things, Hay was in British Army Intelligence, monitoring German trickery in Tanganyika. So, there was also some speculation that a German spy had somehow managed to bump him off…. Well, I'm duty bound to take my son upstairs to the observation lounge to see all the wildlife herds down below. Big place, Africa. Tarah.

Looking forward to lunch,' he said, easing himself out of the huge airline seat, and gesturing to his son.

'The British like talking a lot,' concluded Manie, opening his *1984* with relief. *"I allowed the word 'God' to remain at the end of a line. I could not help it!…The rhyme was 'rod.' Do you realize there are only twelve rhymes to 'rod' in the entire language?"* he read.

They landed on Naivasha lake that afternoon, after the pilot had made a pass to ensure that the pelicans and hippos had been chased off. As they landed, the view through the windows was obliterated by spray.

'Most passengers overnighting at the Outspan, I gather, but we're off to spot the wildlife at Treetops before being whisked off to Nairobi and finally Mombasa,' said Morris, shaking hands. 'So cheerio and happy hunting in Ireland!'

That evening, Manie was invited to dine at the airline master's table – a much coveted invitation, as Master Airline Pilot Dudley Travers, DFC's social status was next but one to God, in those heady days. There had been sundowners on the terrace, beside Paxtu cottage, the erstwhile home of Baron Baden and Olave Powell.

'I rather like the circle surrounding a dot on Baden Powell's grave nearby…that's the trail symbol for "Going Home",' the Master Pilot remarked. 'Of course, you understand the meaning of "outspan", being South African, in the name of the hotel, but I doubt that the other passengers do. Good name, that. I think it refers to the temporary relieving oxen of their yokes when they are watered and given a rest…after grazing for a while. Is that right? I noticed your profession on the plane's manifest. After anything interesting?'

'Yes, but can't talk about it for the moment,' Manie would

say, involuntarily winking, beginning to secretly enjoy this newfound 'Mystery Man' status. And so the pattern was set for the rest of the journey with five more stops in Khartoum, Luxor, Cairo, Augusta, from suffocating equatorial heat to the arrival on a freezing and foggy day at Southampton, where, suddenly, the flying boat assumed the appearance of a small dragonfly floating among towering ships. At each overnight stop he had airmailed cards to Rentia and others back home, including Mavis. He chose the most exotic photographs, liking the Souk ones the best. A picture of a Cairo belly dancer he reserved for his station commander, hoping it would shock the verkramp post-mistress. While flying towards Khartoum, he had received a telegram from the steward which read, YES + RENTIA. He scribbled a reply, which read +JA EK OOK+EK SAL LATER BEL+MANIE+ ['Yes, Me too. I shall later phone'].

Preparing to step from the Southampton jetty to dry land, he felt a huge push in his back, which catapulted him fully clothed in his overcoat into the stinking freezing harbour water. His floundering shouts brought a swift reaction, with a cabin steward throwing him a jetty lifebuoy attached to a line then clambering down the steel jetty ladder to help him. Harbour water flotsam builds up beside a dock and that at Portsmouth differed little from harbours elsewhere. He was conscious, during his floundering, of his face encountering a sodden loaf of bread, oily discharge muck and a dead mackerel. Passing through his mind was that all his travellers' cheques and passport papers were being turned into pulp or perhaps floating away. There was a burning sensation as water began to enter his lungs, which stayed with him even as strong arms began to hoist him to safety, then laying him on the wooden dockside with hands pumping his chest until he was turned on his side to vomit the water and part of his last meal.

'He's breathing again. Quick, some blankets,' he heard a voice shout, though it was muffled by his water-clogged ears. Another voice took over and said, 'Okay, I'll take over now, if you'll help me get him into the car. I'm the police officer that was here to welcome him. My wife's a nurse so I'll get him home and before a good fire; she knows what to do.' The voice turned to someone else and said, 'I'll need his luggage please.'

There were fumbled delays, until, fully conscious again, and shivering uncontrollably, he was wrapped in blankets, placed in a wheelchair and trundled through several corridors to the waiting Police Wolseley his Samaritan had summoned to the entrance by radio.

'I should be catching the train to the Irish ferry,' Manie said weakly, to which his rescuer replied, 'You're not going anywhere for the next forty-eight hours, sir, except to the police married quarters. Just opened. The last one was flattened during the Blitz. We have a guest bedroom. My wife's got a warm fire going and you'll have to put up with my ration clothes until we dry you out. Besides, we can't miss Terry Thomas, can we? He's on the telly tonight. I'm Detective Sergeant George Baker, sir. They call me "Biscuit". We were alerted by our Commissioner to render all possible assistance on your arrival. I'm sorry you got such a watery welcome from Pompey, sir. Our driver is Corporal Taylor…passed his Advanced Police Driver as top of the class.'

'Pompey?'

'That's what we call Portsmouth, sir, due to all our naval pomp.'Fraid you're not getting a flying boat supper tonight. Just pea soup, followed by toad in the hole, cabbage and mashed potatoes, Judy tells me – and a whisky, of course. Booze is off ration now, like sweets.'

'Thanks greatly for your rescue,' Manie said. 'Oh, my luggage!'

'We have it all stored safely in the boot of the car. You let go of the hand luggage, fortunately, before you decided to inspect the quality of our seawater.'

'I was pushed. Did no one try to grab him?'

"Bear in mind it's dark. I'm told that a figure wearing a hooded raincoat rushed out of the night and disappeared before he could be caught. Someone tried to chase him but fell over a bollard and lost him. Everyone was distracted by your falling, sir, keeping in mind that passengers and crew were concentrating on stepping ashore, in freezing night weather. Believe me, the docks are being scoured as we speak. I'll keep you informed.'

Judy Baker was one of those young women others would describe as 'sensible', but her kindness was unrestrained. Baker helped him strip bare before the fire while she was clattering away in the kitchen behind a closed door, then dried and clothed him in regulation clothing. Baker set to laying out Manie's passport, correspondence and travellers' cheques to dry on a towelled side table, after joining him in a whisky by the fire.

'You're in luck. Our Pompey police complex has a laundry! Otherwise, we'd have had to send off your coat and so on to the Chinese laundry. Judy'll sort all that out. Now, it seems an unfair question to ask after your dowsing, but what was the seaplane journey like? It sounds like a trip beyond our wildest dreams.'

Judy had joined them in easy chairs at the fire. He found himself talking about Africa, its vastness, the normalcy of faraway places, his dusty Free State home, rock art and plant-eating dinosaurs, vast herds of elephants viewed from the air and landing on the Zambezi at Jungle Junction, so that his listeners forgot all about watching Terry Thomas. He discovered that he was holding them entranced, the spell interrupted only once while Judy served the toad in the hole.

'My goodness,' Judy said, 'the wildest dreams of Kew are fact in Timbuktu!' deliberately misquoting Kipling. 'Africa seems like a romantic film set, unlike us in stodgy toad-in-the-hole Pompey. Mind you, we've had enough excitement during the Blitz to last a lifetime – for those of us who survived.'

'You're being forced to convalesce tomorrow, so Judy'll show you around the interesting bits. I'll be on duty and will join you later. We'll pop you onto the train, the day after that… . It's all right, we've notified everyone about the delay.'

Lingering by the fire after Judy had retired, Baker said, 'Clearly, someone, or something, seems rather keen to bump you off,' after Manie described the Durban car incident, 'so we've instructions to shadow you on the train, all the way to the Fishguard ferry. You won't notice him or them or her, but they'll be there. We know you're travelling to Rosslare in Ireland, to unravel the mystery of that O'Brien girl, so this might contribute to getting to the bottom of the puzzle, before it's too late. We'll see if anyone's following you and will keep in touch by police telex with our Irish counterparts.'

That night he dreamt that he was in Bloem, as the faint naval dockyard noises changed into the distant clangs and hoots drifting up Kruis Road from the railway shunting yard. It was a deep sleep of relief. He awoke late with Judy knocking on the door and announcing that porridge was on the table and that there was a dressing gown hanging on the door hook.

'Your clothes are back from the laundry,' she said, gesturing at neatly folded clothes. 'My word, you slept the sleep of the dead…it's almost lunchtime. Biscuit's at work and I have the day off, so, if you're up to it, I'll take you on a Cook's Tour of the town – plenty to see, then we're booked for an early supper at the Royal Albert Naval Club – cosier than it sounds. Your train for the ferry at Fishguard departs at nine-fifty tomorrow, and takes hours to get there, just in time for the ferry to Rosslare. You'll get to Ireland close to nine that night, and then your train on the ferry jetty will get you to Wexford close to midnight so Biscuit has booked you in at White's Hotel in Wexford. He made quite a lot of phone calls, so your opposite number, or the duty officer, will meet you at the Wexford train station and take you up to the hotel. From then on, it's over to you.

'Bacon's rationed and still mingily rare, and none in the fridge this morning. Have some energen rolls!…I'm afraid bread's still hard to come by, and the rolls taste like crisp blotting paper but delicious with lashings of marge, when we can't get butter, and honey. We have a secret suppler of it, from a farmer up country.'

The doorbell rang and a wifely neighbour arrived. 'May I introduce you to my next-door neighbour, Mrs Cartwright? Maisie, this is Detective Inspector Marais from South Africa. He had an unplanned swim in the Solent yesterday.'

'Hello. So, you're the one who sends us all that snoek and whale meat,' she said, shaking his hand. 'Not popular. I tried both once. Ugh!…went back to Spam and chips after that.'

'Maisie belongs to the local historical society and knows absolutely everything about Pompey, so I've asked her to join us for our tour just now, although I rather want to have a peek at Dingle's. Perhaps it's open for tea. Maisie's husband's also a detective, chasing, for the moment, spivs using dead people's ration books. Lots of them.'

'Tonight's meal at the Royal Naval Club and Royal Albert Yacht Club: quite a mouthful even before you get to eat. Very navy-yachty as you gather. On a clear day you can see the Solent from the balcony and the Isle of Wight…far less stuffy than it sounds. You can return the honours if we ever get to visit.'

Chapter Ten

The train was freezing as it had been standing in the shunting yard overnight and only in the past few minutes had the engine driver allowed the steam heating to trickle through. Biscuit had managed to book him a coupe seat in first class – one of the only bookings available in a crowded train. It was approaching departure time and Manie, huddled in an overcoat, thought he would have the carriage to himself, when there was a rapping on the window and a woman's voice shouted,' Hello, this is my cabin. I wonder if you would take in these parcels through the window for me. The porter's lugging my suitcase around to our door when he stops grumbling. Could you throw it up on the rack?' She wore bright vermillion lipstick. Several carefully labelled brown paper parcels followed up from the platform.

'Brrrrr!' she said, holding her gloved hands to the heater. 'You'd think they'd warm up the train – but no, it's British Rail. Probably some union regulations. This entire country's controlled by "the wukkers" now, ever since Atlee got in. Travelling far?'

'Yes,' said Manie, compulsively winking, 'all the way to Ireland…I was lucky to get a seat. Last minute.'

'Like me, almost had to bribe the ticket office. Do I detect a South African accent? I'm an ornithologist and went to the western Cape to study tern colonies, so my ear got used to Cape voices.'

'Right first time, almost, but my hunting ground is further north in the Free State. I admit I've found it difficult to understand some of the English accents.'

'You're not alone! Some are so guttural…pity about the English…some of them seem to be hell bent on mangling the language so oddly they'd frighten a Scotsman. I'm travelling back to Ireland too, so we're stuck with each other for the duration.'

'Look. If you'd be more comfortable riding with another lady, perhaps I could swap with one from next door.'

'Certainly not. You look respectable. What is your occupation?'

'I'm a detective.'

'Good Lord! Well, that's respectable enough. I wondered, at first, why you winked at me but was quick to realise that your eye has, if you don't mind my saying, a nervous tic. Rather a long way from home for you, isn't it, at the moment? Do all South African detectives read books like *1984*? [She had spied the book he had beside him.] If so, it must be a somewhat literate police force.'

'Oh,' he said. 'No, I bought it in Khartoum as the only book at the hotel stationers I could find, in a language I could at least struggle through. It was either that or week-old English newspapers. My home language is Afrikaans, and I'd never heard of Orwell.'

'Khartoum! Curiouser and curiouser…why on earth?'

Manie rather liked this romantic persona he had acquired. He imagined starting a comment by saying, 'Last time I was in Khartoum.' It would seem as far away as Kathmandu, to the average Free Stater, and said, 'I had just arrived from Kenya by flying boat, and was overnighting at the Acropole Hotel there…swarming with archaeologists, journalists and Greeks,' then said, 'Tell me about your terns. Are you Irish?' as a diversion from further questioning.

'Gosh, how very romantic…I'm Anglo-Irish. The true Irish harbour a long-term resentment of us and given half a chance they would drum us out of town…nearly did when the Shinners were burning down the Big Houses. Many of us are descendants of landowners, and even some are still landed gentry – but nowadays "land rich yet cash poor". A few have inherited titles which are not used there, and some have become "more Irish than the Irish"…but you'll avoid all that begrudgery when you get there, because the Irish brigade fought on the Boer side in the last Anglo-Boer war, didn't they?

'I'm returning from a conference on terns. Plymouth Beach is an important breeding ground for four varieties of tern – hence the conference venue – and Lady's Island in County Wexford is another, where we are heading. The terns like sandy pebbly places, where they can scratch away a hollow between the pebbles, lay their eggs, then camouflage them with markings resembling the little stones, unique to each female, so she can identify them as hers. It's a mystery, even now. I'm researching the unique identifying patters on the eggs and how a bird can spot her eggs on a crowded beach. Terns start to arrive, for breeding, in late April and depart for the Arctic regions in August.

'Unfortunately, their breeding grounds are also attractive to people and increasingly, by night-prowling foxes, So there is talk of providing anchored rafts covered with shingles. At Lady's Island lake they're not so bothered…more deserted. How are you finding *1984*? Dying to read it. What's it about?'

'I'm only at the beginning of Chapter Three. I think it's a warning about how fear, in a technologically advanced dictatorship, is used to manipulate the population's behaviour and crush dissent. Perceptions are manipulated by announcements riddled with factoids. It's reminiscent of

Stalinism and Nazism. There's lots of talk about rationing, so Orwell must have written it during the war.'

Conversation lapsed and Manie took to watching the landscape swoop by as she picked up a women's journal, spread a rug around her legs and began to flick through the pages, before settling in to read an article that caught her eye.

She forewent lunch but Manie elected to investigate the railway's post-war menu so set off for the dining car, to find himself sharing a table with two Irish construction workers and a journalist from Slough, where Manie was exposed to British-instilled insularity. He assumed that sharing a table implied that conversation was likewise shared and was taken aback when this was disproved. The Irish workers turned out to be brothers, who ate their food in the manner of bulldozers, shoving huge mouthfuls past arrays of broken teeth, and communicating with each other in an incomprehensible language. The journalist, on the other hand was only too glad to ask him about Africa – after learning as such, even though he lacked geographical grasp, muddling Kenya with Rhodesia and Rhodesia with the Union, but was interrupted by one of the brothers who said suddenly, 'D'ya know what they call Jamaicans imported to rebuild Britain after the war? Black Irish. That's why we can't wait to get out of here. Sick 'n tired of seeing notices, 'No Blacks. No Irish.' You do the same in your fekkin country, don't you – in the name of appetite [that's how he pronounced 'Apartheid']? "No Blacks, No Coloureds, Whites only." You're a toerag bunch of bastards.' The author of these words had downed a brandy and was well into his second beer. 'You're just as bad as the fekkin British. Worse! – a least John Bull doesn't make appetite laws.' His words were beginning to slur.

Manie indicated to the journalist it was time to exit, to avoid a fracas, and they departed from the table with 'Fekkin

Boers' ringing in their ears, saying to the journalist, 'That fellow could start an argument in an empty room.'

By the time the train had reached the Fishguard ferry, the compartment was a cocoon of warmth, but stepping onto the sleety windswept railway platform was another matter, the porters saying again and again, 'Careful, ice underfoot,' as passengers alighted.

Manie helped the tern girl to alight, with her parcels and both of their luggage, thinking, 'My God, what a miserable place this is,' the ferry crossing confirming these thoughts, as the Irish Sea had been whipped into a white horse frenzy of crests and troughs, causing the *St Andrew*, for that was her name, to sway and yaw, waves splattering the glass windows, as the ship creaked with under strain. A thump and shudder, as if the ship had hit the seabed during departure from the harbour, made passengers contemplate the worst.

'You're travelling on to Wexford, aren't you? Would you mind our sticking together, as I'll need help when we disembark?'

Manie liked the girl who was in stark contrast to those emitting robust derisions in the dining car. He noticed that the journalist had turned a pale yellow with seasickness, slumped like the other passengers in easy chairs. Coming from a land where lower class was applied uniformly to people of colour, the separation of classes was less well defined for Manie – yet nevertheless there.

A newspaper on the coffee table caught Manie's eye with the headline, 'The Lady of the Lake dies'; after which he gave up trying to read and slumped in his easy chair, like most of the other passengers, including two habited young nuns, who, despite the clutching of crucifixes and thumbing of rosaries, had no effect in calming the waters. One of their faces looked strangely like Rentia, and she caught him looking at her. Some erstwhile rowdy American students had given up defying gravity and lay curled up on the carpet. During one particularly steep pitch, a plate, with a slice of cake on it, slithered away on a carpet trajectory of its own.

At Rosslare, railway porters helped ferry passengers with their luggage directly from the ferry to the train, stationed parallel on the dock, while, in the distance, the steam engine was being revolved on the turntable, to reverse back to the carriages Once again, Manie found himself helping the tern woman onto the train, with her packages.

'So here we are again,' she said. 'What a crossing! Gosh it gets so dark! Nearly there – it's only a shortish journey to Wexford. You've missed Wexford's opera season…well over…but from mid-December everything, such as it is, goes slightly frenetic. Perhaps you didn't exactly choose the right time of the year to make contact with officialdom We're a poor country, for the main part, and most people will be struggling to make ends meet; but even the humblest of us go a little shopping crazy. Of course, the thin upper crust, the professionals and the few landed gentry, will have closed for the winter… . My brother and I have an "extra slice of bread" or two, so you could say that we're in the middle of the sandwich, which is a roundabout way of saying we're landowners and sort-of poor gentry.'

'I'm sure it'll be less dull than Khartoum. At least you speak English here, even though we have always spoken Afrikaans at home, I can understand half the people I speak to, and I expect to be busy. Anyway, I have my two books to keep me company.'

'You're staying at White's, you said? Look here…I'm Anne Butler. My brother Michael and I share our parents' old house on Forth Mountain, above the town…bit wild, draughty and slightly cut off, but my brother's got a car…

hopefully you'll meet him at Wexford station. If you find you have to stay over Christmas and have nothing to do over the festive weekend, you're welcome to spend the days with us ss our house guest. Do you ride?'

'Ride?'

'Horse-ride'

'I haven't ridden since a Jagersfontein ride-out five years ago. Now, I might find it difficult to decide which is the front of the horse.'

'I asked because we have a brace of hunters and a spare and may ride out on St Stephen's Day (I think you call it Boxing Day), the day after Christmas, at a place called Ballinaboola. It's out in the sticks, but fun. Think about it. You could at least enjoy the stirrup cup. And perhaps ride with the hill-toppers – more leisurely, no jumping. My brother Michael must stand in as a Field Master, so we're obliged to go…well, there you are – and you're welcome to share Christmas roast with us and sundry others. Our housekeeper makes a mouth-watering stuffed turkey. I'll phone you at the hotel much closer to the day.'

The detective did his best to exude urbanity, but inwardly, he was assailed by a series of cultural shocks, overlaid, not only by a sense of imposture, but instinctive curiosity, and an alertness to unforeseen clues and personal dangers. The Portsmouth dowsing had shaken him more than he would care to admit.

Detective Inspector Brennan was less than pleased, hunched, crow-like, late in the evening, in the driving rain on the Wexford train station. The waiting room had been locked by this time, and the overhang provided little protection. The only other figure on the platform was sheltering in a nook and Brennan joined him, not caring if he was a tramp. When the train did squeal to a halt, only three passengers alighted, one with a walking stick who hurried away, and another man and a woman with many parcels being helped by the former.

'Michael! Hello,' said the woman, as the man from the nook came forward with a large, unfurled umbrella, 'This is Mr Marais from South Africa. We'll be seeing him again, perhaps, for Christmas,' whereupon Detective Inspector Brennan joined the group and claimed him.

In the car, Brennan said, 'How do you do,' shaking his hand. All I know is that you're investigating the death of a Wexford girl in South Africa and that I was to meet you off the train. It must be a pretty important investigation for you to travel all this way. You're booked in at White's, I understand, so I'll drop you there and then scurry away. We'll meet up tomorrow at the Garda station in Roche's Road. Say, tennish?'

Manie found he was registered in as Mr Monni Maray, and it took a little time to convince the receptionist that he was indeed he. 'You're in the Speranza Suite, sir. It's the only room left, because the hotel is packed tonight; I see you'll be staying here for at least a week, so we can move you tomorrow, if you so wish. The bell boy'll show you to the lift and take your luggage.'

'Thank you, is the bar open?'

'It is, sir, although you might find it a spot busy, sir. It's the night of the annual Vintners' Ball,' which explained the sounds of chatter and band music coming from behind swing doors at the end of the foyer. Waiters would burst out of the ballroom bearing piles of plates and then plunge into the kitchen, providing glimpses of vintner merriment. All at once, a sense of isolation gripped him, and of his foreignness descended upon him. On an impulse, he, asked the receptionist to book two trunk calls for the early morning– one to Rentia and the other to his sister in De Aar. Never since Neville Chamberlain's stay, just before the War, had the elderly receptionist received such a request, to call someone in this instance, in Africa…with all those heathens; his knowledge of the Dark Continent being limited to the collection for 'The Black Babies', during Sunday Mass.

'I'll try sir, but I can't guarantee any luck.'

'I'm going to the bar and I'll call by, on my way to bed,' Manie said.

'That's the Library Bar, then, through there, sir.'

Leather-lined easy chairs and shelves of ancient volumes, row upon row of them, most never to be read, lined the walls, giving the impression, more of a gentlemen's club, than a bar; so much so, that the barman and the shiny-mirrored bar itself seemed incongruous. Save for a group of bow-tied vintners that had escaped from their wives for a while, he and a melancholy American were the only two to keep the barman occupied.

'You from these parts? This sure is a godforsaken place to do business just before Christmas! When does the town open up again, if ever? I'm from Raleigh, North Carolina, by the way, name's John Scantlebury Blankenheimer…represent Packard…I'm here to evaluate interest. The automobiles'll be imported in wooden crates, ready to go, but it seems, in this town, that the wood's in greater demand than the cars.'

'I'm a stranger too. From Africa. Hello, the name's Marais,' and he winked uncontrollably.

'Africa? Now Isn't that something? Which end?'

'End? Oh, South, the sharp end.'

'South Africa? Yours is the place trying to keep the races apart…watzit called "appetite"? Isn't it a bit late for that – Ku Klux Klan, black hangings and all that shit?'

Marais felt obliged to defend his government and said, 'It's different in Africa. We live among the primitive illiterate and with different cultures…mostly, primitive people, unhygienic.'

'And whose fault is that, my friend? It won't work…it will for a time, but it'll build a reservoir of resentment and hate and in the end you'll get a bloody uprising…in my humble opinion. We're in danger of it in the States – and so what do you do when that happens? Shoot them?'

The debate rambled on until Manie excused himself.

In passing, the ancient receptionist said, 'I'm afraid it can't be done, sir. I don't quite understand the details, but the exchange said the shortwave link is down at Khartoum and besides they can't book a call to a party line, where anyone can just pick up the phone and listen.'

The upshot was that he resorted to sending a telegram to Rentia which read IRELAND FREEZING + RETURNING POSSIBLY FORTNIGHT ADVISE SISTER + MISSING YOU MUCHLY MANIE +

Eschewing the lift, the winding stairs to his room smelt faintly with an inheritance of ancient cigar smoke, whisky, cabbage and Eau de Cologne. He got into bed with relief. On one wall was a large framed Victorian daguerreotype of a Lady Jane 'Smerelda' Wilde, so labelled, with an explanation that she lived in the room after her surgeon husband and folklorist, Sir William Wilde died. It said that she wrote poetry under the nom de plume of 'Smerelda'. She bore a hauntingly Spanish look, although Manie had no idea of her relevance. To lull himself to sleep, he opened his dog-eared *1984* and began to read, '*Winston thought for a moment, then pulled the speakwrite towards him and began dictating…*'

Chapter Eleven

Next morning, he made his way, buffeted by the wind, to the Garda station alongside what the hotelier called *The Faythe*, 'a Green space with trees, sir', by cutting down to the quay boardwalk, past the little steamers and men unloading lumber and coal by means of small hand-winched cranes, and supervised by a man who remarked, 'Not so smelly this morning because the tide's in,' clapping his mittened hands across his chest to keep warm; then up Distillery Road and turning left into Mill Road between the flour mill and Pierce's foundry already thumping away. Roche's Road was icy, and a man passed him said, 'Getting darker…big storm brewing again,' as the telephone wires howled and whistled. At the police station steps he was almost thrown against the entrance by the force of the wind. The building, he thought, looked a bit like a decayed layer cake, with pale bands of horizontal brickwork. Waiting to be admitted, a large potted bush writhed in the wind as if shaken by a madman.

Ushered into Brennan's cramped little office, he was surprised to see Blankenheimer there, sipping a glass of milk and nibbling a Marie biscuit. He was a big-boned man with pale blue eyes and filled the leather chair.

'We meet again,' he said. 'Sorry I didn't reveal my main occupation – the Packard agency is just to a front to explain away the unusual presence of an American in Wexford, at this time of the year. I'm an old-fashioned spook,. still deniably employed by my government. Detective-Sergeant Brennan here is on loan from McKee Road in Dublin. He works for G2 – a similarly deniable counter-intelligence outfit loosely tied to J2 and knows what you're after – clarity on Theresa O'Brien – that girl you found dead on top of a Free State train. Agh! Sorry, I have a peptic ulcer and I'm suffering from that Irish whiskey I stupidly touched last night.'

It was difficult to squeeze into the tiny office. 'So, you're being in the bar was by design.'

'Yup, but a bar's not the place to spill the beans.'

'Well, you fooled me.'

Blankenheimer said that he had travelled all the way from North Carolina to meet up, after Brennan had alerted him to the substance of his coming to Wexford. The detective's message had rung alarm bells in America.

'As you realise very well, investigating O'Brien's death is a lot more than bog-standard police work. There could be greater forces at play, and thank you for sending us particulars about, what seem to be, Russian jewellery…and much other info.

'For the record, neither of our governments, the American and Irish, condone what your new administration is planning to do to your blacks, Indians and mulattos, in the name of so-called "apartheid", but we have to be pragmatic and are instructed to cooperate. I'll say this…the old regimes are collapsing in Africa, and we can see that the Portuguese empire is next, leaving Rhodesia and South Africa politically exposed. Apartheid is your Achilles' Heel, and, in time, your new government could rue the day; but your country's too strategically important to go the way of the Congo – the Cape Sea Route, your gold and uranium deposits and so on – so, like it or not, we're here to assist.'

'I think you will agree that the three of us are detectives, not politicians and that politics is a topic for another day,' Manie replied, 'but thank you for your frankness. By the way, does the sun ever shine here?'

'It's winter. Expect dark over-clouded days, sundown at four-thirty and getting earlier, as we plunge towards Christmas, the cold, strong winds, driving rain and if we're lucky, sleet and a sprinkling of snow. If the sun does come out, expect to be dazzled by it, because the air is so rain-washed clean. Now to business…this telex arrived for you by Lobster.'

'Lobster?'

'That's the nickname for G4's secure messaging service. It's been known to be called less complimentary names when it gets corrupted.'

Manie read, MORE BOXES FOUND OBRIEN CODES UNBROKEN. CONSULT IRELAND and folded away the pleat of paper. At this point, Brennan said he gathered that some Tzarist jewellery was found on the girl's body. 'That is interesting to both the Americans and us. I gather you recall all about the assassination of the Tsar and his family in 1918?'

'Yes, but no details.'

'OK. It's a convoluted story, but here goes: on the night of 16-17th July 1918, the Russian Tsar, Nicholas II of Russia, his wife Alexandra Feodorovna, and their five children: Olga, Tatiana, Maria, Anastasia, and Alexei were shot and bayoneted to death by a group of Bolsheviks under Yakov Yurovsky – allegedly on the orders of the Ural Regional Soviet in Yekaterinburg; but we think the orders really came from Lenin. Also murdered were their physician Eugene Botkin and the three other senior servants they had with them. All the bodies were taken to the Koptyaki forest, where they were stripped, mutilated with grenades to prevent identification, and buried in a lime pit. Jewellery hidden in the hems of the Princess Tatiana's clothes were torn out before her body was removed.

'The jewels next turned up with a Bolshevist fund-raising party visiting New York in April 1920. This so happened to coincide with the arrival of an Irish fund-raising party, headed up by Eamon de Valera and staying at the swank Waldorf Astoria, followed by standing ovation visits to San Francico and Boston. Well, the Irish were spectacularly successful… raising millions from Irish-Americans, contrasting with the Bolshevists led by someone called Martens, who wound up dismally broke. What happened next is barely believable, but the Bolshevists borrowed $20,000 from the Irish (supposedly implacable enemies of the Communists) offering the jewels as security.'

He paused when there was a rap on the door before an orderly appeared bearing a tray of doorstep-thick ham sandwiches, bottles of beer and a glass of milk.

Brennan took over, saying, 'You may ask why the hell we're giving you a history lesson, but you'll see… . When Dev's party returned to Ireland, the jewels were carried back by someone called Bogan and offered to Michael Collins – the soldier and politician who featured strongly in Ireland's struggle for independence. Collins flung them across the table, shouting that they had blood on them – metaphorically; so Bogan entrusted them to his sister Kathleen, to keep them safe during the civil war raids. She hid them behind the fireplace at 15 Merino Crescent in Dublin. And there they stayed, until last year, when questions were raised in the Dail (that's our Irish parliament) – see, I have the transcript here – and promptly started to read from the record: "Question No 31:

'"Captain Cowan asked the Minister for Finance if he will

state the present market value, if any, of the Russian jewels reported by the then Taoiseach, during the recent General Election campaign, to be in possession of the Government and what it is proposed to do with them.

'"Question No 32

'"Captain Giles asked the Minister for Finance if he will state whether the Russian jewels mentioned during the recent General Election campaign are now in the custody of the present Government; and, if so, is it his intention to investigate their origin and the amount paid for them.

'"Minister Patrick McGilligan [Minister for Finance]:

'"I propose, with the permission of the Ceann Comhairle, to take questions Nos 31 and 32 together. The jewels referred to are in the possession of my department. There is nothing to indicate their origin beyond the fact that they were handed over as security for a loan of $20,000 made in April 1920, to a representative of the Russian Soviet Republic in the United States. The jewels are described in the receipt given for them as being worth $25,500. I propose to have the jewels valued and, after valuation, to consider whether and in what manner they should be disposed of for the benefit of the Exchequer.

'"Dublin, 6 March 1949

'"Memorandum to Government by the Department of External Affairs: 'Sale of Russian Jewels', Dublin, 6 March 1949

'"The question has arisen of the disposal of the Russian jewels given to Mr de Valera by the Soviet Envoy in New York in 1920 as security for a loan of $20,000..." And so on,' Brennan said. 'Here's a copy for your records...there's quite a lot more. The upshot is that a representative of the Soviets in London eventually and very grudgingly forked out $20,000 and the jewels were returned. There the trail stops. There's no record of the jewellery finding its way back to Russia, but there have been many intercepts of Eastern Bloc couriers smuggling lots more Tsarist jewellery out of the Iron Curtain and evidence of a lot turning up in New York and some in southern Africa.'

Manie chipped in saying that it was all part of the vigorous, often illegal, trade in big stones already awash with local gems, to fund big crime syndicates, down his way. Diamonds were the gems of choice, but other high value stones had their place.

'But of course!' exclaimed Frankenheimer. 'You know far more of that trade than we do; but you did mention, in this context, that your diamond expert in Kimberley claimed to have identified jewels you showed him, irrefutably, as Russian Tzarist in origin, and perhaps of one of the Tzarevna's. Weird, huh?'

'By the way, after the attempt on your life in Portsmouth, we had you shadowed all the way down,' said Blankenheimer. 'Not by the girl in your coupe, but from the next-door compartment. You might have noticed someone hanging about in the corridor, from time to time? That was one of ours. We have established that someone or a nasty organisation, doesn't want you to find out more about Theresa O'Brien – and like you, we very much want to.'

'Well, if she was a "bad un" she was a very good bad 'un', Manie said. 'Her academic record was good, and she impressed a Durban scientist and others with her knowledge and enquiring mind. She knew a lot about South African rock art.'

'Sorry, I don't understand. Rock art?'

'Rock art stretches back thousands of years in South Africa, to when an indigenous tribe, the Khoi-San, were masters of painting and engraving images of tribesmen, fantastical creatures and herbivores on rock overhangs, as part of their belief system.'

'Well I never. That's a good example of the type of people we are studying– most of our current suspects…spies…we're monitoring – four of them, and possibly Theresa as a migrant fifth – are very bright and good at their cover jobs. Sometimes at the top of their profession or trade. And there they've sat for years, right through the European conflict, Ireland calls "The Emergency". But you know this can happen anywhere… one only must look in your own backyard – that senior naval officer in Simon's Town, Dieter Felix Gerhrdt – and his second wife…both Russian spies and caught only thanks to our FBI tipping off your people. Fancy that, a man at the top of your naval dockyard for the last three years during the current Cold War! Incidentally his divorced first wife and three children live here in Ireland…no, not implicated.

'Of the people we're looking at (and I'm sure there are at least thirty more in Ireland) who operate independently of the Russian Embassy, one of those we are watching is a manicurist in a snooty hairdresser's on Merrion Road in Dublin, near the British Embassy, another studied political science at Trinity College, Dublin under an assumed Irish name. Another uses the name of a woman who died at the Wexford poorhouse in 1923 and we suspect that your Theresa O'Brien falls into that category. Although the local records are kept at Registry for Births, Marriages & Deaths in Grogan's Road, the trick, for an imposter, is merely to ask Registry for a duplicate birth certificate, after furnishing the full names and past residence of the parents (easy to obtain from local contemporary newspaper archives) and pay one good Irish Punt.

'The Russians have been at this game for a long time, in fact they are obsessed by it…well before 1939, in keeping with its long-term intentions, making it the happy hunting ground for the excessively inquisitive. Three-quarters of all northern underwater cables pass through Irish waters, for example…a tempting window for unfriendly prying; and it's also a breeding ground for Russian agents to emigrate, falsely, elsewhere – to countries of southern Africa and South America.'

'Do you agree that that's enough for one day?' asked Brennan, as he was keen to get to an antique shop before closing time. His wife, he said, collected ink wells – the fancy ones with hinged silver lids.

'We'd better leave separately,' said Blankenheimer, peering out of the rain-lashed windows. 'It's still peeing with rain, but it would still be unwise to leave the Garda station together. I'm still driving my "demo" Packard, but I'll give you five minutes start then pick you up at the entrance to the Pearse Building. As we're both staying at White's we could explain away why we entered the hotel together. We can be seen having a drink at the bar, later. Next step tomorrow is to dig out details at the Registry Office – and I betcha it'll be closed for the season!'

White's was a haven in the storm, which had grown in intensity by the time they reached the hotel and parked Blankenheimer's "flivver", as he called it. Large logs crackled and popped in the Library Bar grate, encouraging people to cluster around it, including a group of bell ringers celebrating a year of ringing the changes with a bar supper and beer.

'It's all a matter of pulling our sallies and tail ends,' said one, with a twinkle in his eye, when asked how bell ringing worked, knowing full well that the answer would baffle the listener. 'The sally is a short fluffy colourful piece attached to the long rope reaching up to the belfry, around a wheel to which the bell is fixed. The tail is the other end of the same rope. When the bells are at rest, their mouths are left facing down; so, you must pull on the sally, repeatedly, to get the mouths resting upwards, before change ringing can begin. When you ring the changes, each bell revolves a full 360 degrees – done by alternately pulling the sally and the tail end – in sequence with the other ringers.

'Our belfry has a framework of eight bells, on two levels, each one a step up in size and weight.'

A man with a thick foreign accent said, gazing at him steadily, 'You like come see?'

'That's Aleksander Turetsky, a refugee from Poland; just arrived…knew nobody, don't know how he got here, so we welcomed him aboard when he showed an interest at the church last Sunday. Thomas, here, arranged a job for him at the forge across town… . At practice last Tuesday, Alex took to the bells like a duck to water. There's another practice on this Thursday before Christmas Day on Sunday, so Aleksander can take you up the tower to have a look. We left the bells resting upwards at last practice. Don't touch them, as they dislodge easily. Okay? Then be here at four.'

'The bell frame's a bit rickety and very old, like me and the staircase…all ancient wood. We'll have to get it restored in the New Year,' said Thomas.

'Heights and I don't like each other, so I'll stay on ground zero, and cheer you as you go,' said Blankenheimer.

As predicted the Registry Office in Grogan's Road was closed for the days leading up to Christmas, but Brennan had instructed the Assistant Registrar to open up for their visit. After much palaver, grumbling and jangling of keys, they were let in and led to chairs while the man rummaged through the 1923 drawers in some remote room, until he returned holding a single page to say, 'Sorry. I forgot. All files up to 1925 were sent to Head Office in Pearse Street Dublin a month ago. All I have here is a list, under the heading, "O'Brien", merely recording the person's surname and Christian names – but no birth and death details. Lots of O'Briens – that's the surname you're interested in, isn't it? – most notably not the Mary O'Brien who was the first person to enter the poorhouse in 1845. The place ceased to function, as such, in the twenties, when it became what is now known as the "Old Hospital" – although no doubt the Pauper's Graveyard is still there with individual graves remaining unmarked. But now, even the Old Hospital is no more and all that's left is an abandoned, boarded-up hulk. You're faced with the difficult task of tracing that daughter and granddaughter – especially as you say they moved away to Swift's Alley in The Liberties. That was the very poorest alley in Dublin…unrecognisable nowadays. Well, there you are, gentlemen. I'll give you Dublin contact details, but I won't be able to help you any further and I want to close up now, so I'll wish you a Merry Christmas.'

'Funny thing,' said Manie as they walked back to the flivver, 'funny peculiar, I mean; all Theresa's records seem to run into the sand. Let's see what Brennan has been able to find out about her. Drop me at the Forge so I can saunter in after you, though isn't your Packard attracting attention? Better not park outside the Garda.'

Inside the Garda offices, Brennan, almost with a triumphal glint in his eye, chucked a Lobster telex across the desk. It read: FROM D BRANCH DEATHS OBRIEN GRANDPARENTS WEXFORD POORHOUSE CONFIRMED + LIKEWISE OFFSPRING DAUGHTER DIED SWIFT ALLEY THE LIBERTIES 1928 + HER INFANT THERESA AOIFE CIARA ROISIN

OBRIEN DIED STARVATION 3 WEEKS OLD 1928
+ BAPTISED FR OREARDON ST NICHOLASDE
MYRA CHURCH + MOTHER AND CHILD BURIED
UNMARKED BULLYS ACRE LIBERTIES NEAR ST
JOHNS WELL.

'So, proved…our Theresa was an imposter,' said Brennan. 'And here's the cherry on the top. The Swiss say that no one answering to that detailed name ever studied at Château Mont-Choisi in 1938 or at any other time. Switzerland did confirm, however, her entry on a tourist visa from Lichtenstein in early July 1938, where she had been staying in a youth hostel in Valduz, and later departure, unaccompanied, in the same month, from Switzerland by train for France, after a stay in lodgings above a café called "Der übliche Ort" on Berne's Brunnadernstrasse. It's quite close to the railway station and, incidentally, the Russian Embassy. The Swiss also gleaned that she made use of a locker at the station, during her stay above the café.

'Lichtenstein records became muddled after the failed coup, probably explaining why there is no trace of her entering Lichtenstein but, strangely, a girl matching her description, but with name of Vera Yelizaveta Tarasova, was recorded as entering the country with a group of Yugoslav youth tourists at that time. It was observed she formed an attachment with a Lichtenstein man and, when it was time to leave, she announced that she was engaged to him and had decided to stay. The returning group lost track of her from that time on. No trace of her companion.

'French passport control recorded a Theresa O'Brien catching the ferry to Dover from Calais, as did the British. The next record is of her taking the ferry from Fishguard in Wales to our Rosslare – all on the same passport.

'Before the war, Lichtenstein was called, in some circles,

"A sunny country for shady people" and we must conclude, until we know otherwise, that that was where she got her forged passport. There are also the usual stamps covering her notional journey to Switzerland from Dublin to attend the finishing school.

'Well, I have her passport with me…brought it here from Durban – here you are…and the stamps corroborate your review: issued in Dublin 26th February 1938 and the photograph matches. The book sure is covered with border crossing stamps, including her arrival in South Africa by Union Castle Line.

'The Dublin issue is phoney,' said Brennan, 'as are all the travel border stamps from prewar Dublin to Lichtenstein, but from then on, the entries are genuine and the passport is as well. It was originally forged using paper and binding that could only have been stolen from an Irish passport office somewhere. Bear in mind that such travel documents were still similar to those issued by South Africa, Canada and so on. See, it says here, "Issued in the name of King George VI", but, unusually, "issued by the Minister for External Affairs"; as for Britain, stating "The Bearer is a citizen of the Irish Free State", Ireland was still part of the Commonwealth in 1936. We only left that club this year… . The passport's a masterpiece of fakery – the only concealment blunder is her claim to have been to that Swiss finishing school, but she only made that claim to your Zosha in Durban…and who would bother to investigate that? She must have learned English as an option in pre-war Yugoslavia, sufficiently well to gain acceptance at Trinity, first as a filing clerk, then a student. After four years she would have absorbed an "educated Irish" accent, with a bit of an unplaceable lilt. The giveaway could have been a lingering difficulty in the use of the article "the", absent in Russian and other Slavic languages like Yugoslavian

Serbian. You don't say "look at the house"…it's just "look at house"…worth checking her correspondence…'

'Brennan, I am truly impressed at what you managed to winkle out – not least, the Swiss,' said Manie – even though it doesn't throw any light on what she was up to in South Africa…and with whom.'

Blankenheimer chimed in, saying,' Vera Yelizaveta Tarasova is a Russian name, not from that multi-ethnic jumble of Yugoslavia, I'll bet my bottom dollar – from the Oblast region…if my training serves me right; worth checking. I guess we can at least assume that she was working for the Russians and her Irish "narrative" truly started when she entered the country and started working at Trinity.'

'Unless we come across anything else, I guess she just laid low and concentrated on her studies,' Brennan ventured. 'Even though we've just cut apron strings with London, we still look to London for any Intelligence dealings with Russia – and, God knows, their relationship with the Russkies is icy…so the Brits will be monitoring every little twitch of the lace curtains and visitor to the Russkie's embassy at Kensington Palace Gardens…even its country dacha at Seacox Heath in East Sussex…not the ideal time for Theresa to make contact.'

'Where's a good bookshop in Wexford?'

'There's a good one in South Main Street. Grandiose looking, used to be the Bishop's Palace. Why do you ask?'

'I want to buy copies of *1984* and *Brave New World* so that I can go on reading them, after handing these copies to Blankenheimer here. These are Theresa O'Brien's books I found in her Durban room, which I must hand over to you, as part of the de-encryption effort. I like her book preferences! Various sentences are underlined in both books. I'm convinced that they're part of the coding process before encryption…unless it's just a hoot…just a way some people underline sentences, they like, while reading and with no further significance – it's a habit of my sister's, for example. I'm instructed by Pretoria, likewise, to provide you with enlarged photographic duplicates of all the encrypted stuff we found in remote parts of South Africa, which have so far baffled us…so here they are…too sensitive and cumbersome to send by mail, and far too long to copy and send by five-step telex. I'll have to ask you for a receipt which I've written out for your signature – just the bare details. What shall we call this bundle in future?'

'How about "the Tatiana files"? suggested Blankenheimer. 'After the murdered Tsarevna. Agreed?'

'Good one,' said Manie, writing the name at the top of the receipt and the duplicate. 'How fast can you speed things along?'

'I'll have to courier it myself to Foynes to catch the PanAm seaplane to Botwood, in Newfoundland then on to Adimn, Block 8, (near Bethesda) after landing on East River, New York, which means you have a Packard to swank around in while I'm away, and that I'll be able to get to my Raleigh family in time for Christmas turkey. I guess it'll be a good opportunity to test your driving skills on Irish boreens all the way to Foynes then you can take it from there. Suits you? As a "trade representative" I have a petrol rationing exemption, which you can use while I'm away, if Brennan condones it?' Blankenheimer said, looking at Brennan, and raising eyebrows twice.

'How do we contact you while you're away?'

'Just signal me, care of this telex number. I know you'll be circumspect. It'll find its way to me.' He handed Manie and Brennan cards imprinted with a number and nothing else. 'I guess you'll continue your stay at White's until I get back?'

Chapter Twelve

Viewed from the ground, the ancient church tower conveyed a centuries-old stability that belied the rough-hewn interior tower embracing the series of steep ladders clamped to the walls. Standing in the ringing chamber, hung about with sallies and tail ends, Turetsky had said, 'You go first to bells. Mind birds.' Ascent to the bell chamber itself was almost vertical and made more hazardous by gaps in the single metal handrail. When, out of breath, both men had reached the walkway of the cobwebbed bell chamber .Manie saw that each bell was attached to a wheel, and was staring up at nesting pigeons, when he felt himself being violently shoved in the middle of his back by one of Turetsky's boots. Manie managed to clutch the handrail and swung about, just in time to see Turetsky felled by one of the bells that had been dislodged by his attacker clutching its wheel. The Pole was propelled back down the ladders. The last sight of his assailant was a flailing figure plummeting, then crumpling to rest with a thump, far below, at the last turn of the ladders. Blood began to seep out of Turetsky's mouth and ears.

'Oh Christ!' Manie screamed, more in horror than in an appeal for divine intervention. Not only was he appalled at the turn of events but well aware of the investigation which would have to follow, at the very worst time of the year, and the disruption of the Theresa O'Brien enquiries. It was clear that Turetsky had plotted to kill him, but he decided to keep this speculation to himself until he had spoken to Brennan.

Clambering down the ladders with great difficulty, he broke the news to fellow bell ringers now gathering in the ringing chamber; asking one of them to find a phone and call an ambulance, then Brennan at the Faythe Garda Station. An old blanket was found in the jumble to keep Turetsky warm while Manie climbed up again, with a few others, to stand guard.

'No, don't touch him!' he shouted. 'Wait for the ambulance men. We could do more damage to his body.' After what seemed an interminable wait, the medics, Brennan and a uniformed garda, arrived at the same time.

'He's not the first,' said the St Johns man. 'There's been a long line of 'em. Last one was a young boy. They should keep the fekkin' place locked. We must get him to hospital double-quick,' and then muttered to Brennan, 'I don't think there's much hope. I'll leave it to your policeman to chalk mark how he lay.'

When Brennan recognised Manie, he said, 'Didn't know you were into bell ringing,' before turning to the onlookers, saying, 'We'll have to seal off the immediate area…no bell ringing tonight, so please go home.'

'I'm not, I merely expressed an interest, while talking to a group of bell ringers in the bar at Whites, so this poor fellow offered to take me up to the belfry and show me how the bells worked. It's a steep climb up the stairwell to get there. The bells are at rest in the upright position, delicately poised, attached to their wheels, so when the man clutched one of the wheels, it tipped and swung down, the edge of the biggest bell hitting him so violently that it propelled him down the stairwell to the landing.' The garda scribbled away in a little notebook.

'What's his name?' Brennan asked while watching the ambulance men stretchering away the body.

The bell ringer Thommas said, 'Aleksander Turetsky,' spelling it out for the garda. 'Polish. I fixed him up with a job at the foundry and they found him a lodging just off Clonard Street. Not married, no girlfriend that we know of, and no relatives here.'

'Right, it's getting too dark to do anything more today, but I'll have to send a photographer up with a fingerprint analyst at first light. Manie, would you come back to the station with me so we can take a written statement? You know the drill, only too well.'

When they reached the Garda station, Brennan apologised and called in a garda to take his fingerprints and asked the South African detective to sign a written statement, but before that happened, he pulled out a half jack of Jameson's and tumblers from desk drawer. They sat in silence for a while, with the wind moaning in the wires outside, then, when his glass was emptied, Manie said, 'Before I sign, you must know something else. The Pole tried to kill me,' and went on to talk through the event in the belfry, explaining that before he could retaliate, the bell the Pole dislodged had done the job for him. 'I didn't touch him, and this is the third attempt on my life – once in Durban, once in Portsmouth and now here.'

'I'm glad you told me. I suspected there was more to it.'

'Before you write in that piece, may I suggest we pull his lodgings apart tomorrow? There's something very fishy. It might affect possible inquest procedures – which, you will find, may have to be held *in chambers,* rather than in public.

Mrs O'Reardon led them and the fingerprint man upstairs, past a bathroom on the landing, to his room. Before they started their search, the technician took several wide-angle photographs. There was very little there, Manie thought, as they pulled on cotton gloves…just an unmade bed beside a curtained window overlooking the cul de sac. A book by Stefana Żeromskiego in inscribed "Do kochanego Aleksiego", and some dog-eared Wizard comics stamped PROP. GWR lay on the bedside table. A squeaky bentwood chair stood beside a mirrored cupboard with two bottom drawers. Tucked beneath the larger lino-topped table lay a large rucksack. Part of the floor was covered by the relic of a threadbare Persian rug. A pair of hiking boots, well worn, lay under his bed, along with a leather-strapped suitcase, marked *Produkt Polski.*

'The GWR boats ply between Fishguard and Rosslare,' Brennan said, 'suggesting that if he nicked them, he could have come from anywhere in Britain, the same route you took…just a possibility…and how the hell did he get there? Something to start with, perhaps.'

What clothes he had, workman's clothes in the main, hung in the cupboard, with a jumble of belongings in the cupboard drawers below. There were many woollen socks. Shaving tackle was left on the window ledge.

'Best chance for fingerprints will be the glass tumbler,' said the assistant, and went about dusting the glass with powder from a thick camel-hair brush, gently blowing away the excess, then saying with satisfaction, 'Yup, good ones, of a solitary person. But I'll check for verification with that metal-handled hairbrush over there;' then again, after another pause, he said, 'Yup, pretty certain it's the same person. I'll lift them both with tape, then do a proper micro-examination back at the station.'

Manie said, 'I gather you want the fingerprints for two purposes – to verify my story and also find out who the hell this guy was?' Brennan nodded. 'Then you'll need some hair samples as well – that hairbrush and comb should do the trick, to match with hair samples left on the bell that killed him.'

Manie pulled out both drawers, ad felt along their backs. Sure enough, he found two envelopes taped to the back of one of one them, containing passports. 'Better fingerprint these too, back at the station,' said Brennan.

One of them was a Bulgarian 'internal passport' stamped Propiska: Bŭgarski vŭtreshen pasport, Sofiya, in the name of Bizer Stoyanov. The photograph was of Turetsky and dated 25th March 1937. The other, the pentagon-starred passport of the Brazil Republic, revealed the same face, but with a bushy beard, in the name of Viktor Muller Ferreira, and dated for the same year but with a different birth date.

'Look like him?' asked Brennan. 'Difficult…typical lousy passport pics – and one with a beard. Yes, probably.'

'So, where's the Turetsky one? We'll have to take his belongings back to the station and knocking on doors will be added to our bucket list – including the door of the foundry foreman. Better check the room again for any other little surprises, before we go and talk to Mrs O'Reardon. I'll need help to move out the cupboard for a last look-see – and the underside of the rest. Let's flip the carpet and disturb the moths.'

Wedged in the bed frame was as a leather wallet containing the picture of a girl and a few Irish Punt.

'I would say that all this will let you off the hook, if enquiries in the belfry support your story…and I'm sure they will.'

An Irish silver florin, twisted out of usable shape, fell out of the Pole's clothing, while gathering up. 'Funny thing to carry around,' said Brennan. 'They stopped minting them in 1943. Maybe a talisman? Probably he spotted it lying about while walking and pocketed it. You'd be surprised how much money people drop in the streets. That's what a geologist friend told me. He was always picking up coins.'

'Maybe,' said Manie. 'This coin has been twisted out of shape with a pair of pliers…look, you can see the grip marks. I've seen one of these before…in South Africa.'

Brennan grunted noncommittally.

Downstairs, Mrs O'Leary expressed her shock and sorrow over the news of the 'Pole's' death: 'Such a quiet man over breakfast, although he held his knife and fork oddly…but I just put that down to him being foreign…spoke only rudimentary English and very anxious to be at the foundry well ahead of his time to start work in the morning. I made him a few sandwiches each night for work the next day. He liked cheese and ham. His bell ringer friend found him an old squeaky delivery bicycle for him – see there it is under the stairs. Used to belong to Ferns' Pharmacy – explaining the delivery basket attached to the handlebar.'

'Did the bell ringer come often?'

'Only once. A kind man, but I could see that they were not close. The man was just doing his best to help him settle in.'

'Have you got his passport?'

'No, I haven't a safe. He did ask, but I suggested that his foreman would be the best man to keep it.'

After they left, Brennan said, 'Leave it to my men to go knocking on doors.'

'But how could he have planned to kill me in the belfry?'

'Fortuitous. Certainly, you were the deadly target. Just coincidence you went up to the belfry. He would have found some other way to get rid of you. The belfry "accident" would have been a perfect cover. You're lucky.'

★★★

Early in the New Year, the coroner found Turetsky's loss of life was 'Death by Misadventure' and instructed that efforts should be made to inform his relatives in Poland. He had been pronounced dead on arrival at the hospital, the postmortem revealing fatal head, thoracic, abdominal, pelvic and spinal injuries.

A report had appeared in the *Wexford Morning Post* under the headline 'Bellringer falls to death', giving the victim's Polish name and related details, and quoting the head of the ringer group's demand that access to the tower should be made safe. The foundry employer was quoted as 'Turetsky was a reliable worker, in the short time he had known him.' A shorter report made the national *Irish Independent*, halfway down page three.

His Polish 'Internal' passport in the name of Aleksander Franciszek Turetsky, Kierowca żurawia listed him as crane driver. Its pages were smothered in authorisations and stamps, and bore a home address as 163b Szafarnia ul, Gdansk. After months of silence Wexford received a reply from Poland, with a curt 'No Known Relatives'. After that – silence. He was buried in the little cemetery just off Rope Walk Lane in The Faythe. There was no church service, but a priest said prayers at the grave side attended by the forge foreman and a few workers.

Anne Butler had telephoned Manie at White's and said to look for a direction stone with a black fist pointing up a hill, with the word 'Forth' chiselled on it. She said that he would be on the right track if he encountered a house in the middle of the way, some distance up the hill. 'Just drive around it and keep going up. You can't miss our place on the right of the road…stables under big trees, an old house set back and a pair of donkeys in stone-walled paddock. The name on the gate is Cnocán. Just park anywhere.'

The day was overcast and dark. On the direction stone, a wag had chalked an exclamation mark after 'Forth'.

There were two prewar cars – one rather grand – in the yard, children's bicycles and a cart gathering ivy. A large candle glimmered in a front window. He'd brought a bottle of Jamesons and a box of fudge. Anne kissed him when she opened the door, pointing to the mistletoe above it, saying 'Welcome. You'll now enjoy peace, fertility, and prosperity, according to our Druids. Michael cut down a sprig yesterday. It grows high up in one of our oak trees. Merry Christmas! My word, that's a fancy car you're driving. And welcome to Forth Mountain. Come in, come in!'

'Now that's a fireplace!' he exclaimed, winking involuntarily, after being introduced to everyone, not least the young children, as 'Marny Merry' from Africa, which immediately conjured up images, in some minds, of a Great White Hunter shouldering an elephant gun. The old lady sitting in a rocking chair by the fire, could have sprung from a Mazawatee tin lid. The brace of Irish wolfhounds that had unfolded themselves to inspect him, settled back before the hearth, completing a scene of Gemütlichkeit.

Anne had briefed the family ahead of Manie's arrival that he occasionally winked involuntarily, and to pay no attention, which meant, of course, that everyone kept their eyes fixed on him, waiting for the first wink, so when it came the two older children giggled.

'Why do you wink?' asked the little girl and Manie replied solemnly that it was the custom in Africa to wink at the family dogs when one visited. 'It's the "doggy" way for saying "hello". This set two of the children to squatting in front of the wolfhounds and winking at them.

'My sister's children spent quite some time decorating the tree, helped by my brother Michael up a ladder for the top bits', she said. 'Excuse the wrapping paper all over the floor – relics from this very early morning.'

'I got a pony blanket and a book!' piped up the young boy from the floor. 'It's all about children who go into secret world through a cupboard in a spare room.'

'We've got a cupboard in the spare room! The floorboards squeak,' said the little girl, grabbing Mani's hand, saying, 'Come and see the dressing table set I got for my doll's house.' Manie felt a sudden overwhelming pang for Christmas past, his mind's eye filled with scenes of his dead wife and the young children on Christmas days in Kruis Street.

'Would you like to see the rest of the house before we sit down for the festivities?' asked Anne, then led him, still clutching his valise, through a connecting passage. 'These are the servants' stairs…quicker. The old Georgian houses grew like Topsy…full of different levels and creaky floorboards. Obviously, this is the billiard room, and next to it the study,' she said, pushing open a door. 'Our father was an old-fashioned family doctor but took a keen interest in natural science as well, Mother too, in her day. He taught us to identify our hilltop lichen and mushroom varieties…I remember our excitement when we spotted a cuckoo – back from Africa in the Spring.'

'Neither married?'

'Michael has a girl in Waterford…spends a lot of off-time there. We have great hopes. She's a pathologist specialising in pulmonary tuberculosis x-ray interpretation – way over my head.' Pity she couldn't make it today…but parents came first, and all that.'

'And you?'

'I was. A wartime marriage after my husband Donal joined

the RAF – like so many other Irish who joined the fight. But the lifetime of a Lancaster crew was, on average, forty-eight days…and one in three chances of survival. I was told Donal's plane was shot down in the drink by a fighter plane while the bomber was heading home…they'd even managed to pass over the French coast. Ghastly thought that he would have been shunned here, had he survived…no Irish pension, as punishment for fighting for the Brits.' Flinging open an upstairs bedroom door, she said, 'This is yours. Apologies, if you're woken up by the peacocks at some ungodly hour.'

She pushed the door to, and flinging her arms about him, pressed her hips against his and kissed him on the mouth again. Her breath hinted of alcohol. Then, just as soon as the embrace started, she pushed him away, saying 'Later, but not now. We had better hurry back.'

It turned out that Ronan, Michael and Anne's brother, with his family, lived in a house a stone's throw away and they were in and out of each other's houses much of the time, hence the presence of the children's bicycles. Michael was a surgeon at the new chest hospital in Waterford and his brother dealt in farm machinery. There was an easy banter between them at the dining table – the children sitting at a table of their own, except for the baby boy who was placed beside his mother, Judy, in a high chair at the adult table. Before everyone had moved through to the dining room, a girl cousin had arrived with an iced Christmas cake. Judy told Manie that the girl was one of the few lucky Irish nurses who had escaped Singapore before the invading Japanese.

The power failed just as Michael was about to carve the turkey, but, wearing a paper hat and unphased, he donned a surgical headlamp instead, while extra candles were brought, and proceeded to slice the turkey and ham. 'It's all hands to the pump,' explained Anne to Manie. 'Our live-in

Mrs Fanning and her daughter are away with cousins for Christmas, so I'm the official disher-out of the stuffing and vegetables. Judy's job is to follow through with the bread sauce, and gravy.' A few buttery crisp onions had been added to the bread sauce. When Manie expressed his pleasure at the taste, 'That was my idea,' said the Singapore girl, pointing at herself and beaming.

The roast had been preceded by Grace, then a creamed chestnut and sherry soup, served with a garnish of truffle. 'I'm the truffle dolloper,' said Judy, as she had followed Ronan bearing the soup tureen from the cavernous kitchen.

Before the turkey and other dishes had emerged in the same manner, glasses were filled with Sauvignon and Michael had stood to wish all, with a special nod to Manie, a Merry Christmas, the little girl and boy chiming in.

When the pudding and sauce was brought in, Ronan said, to Manie, 'Our custom is to tune in to the King's Christmas message on the wireless at three, then we all go for a walk, before it gets too dark, to Skeator Rock nearby. The dogs need a walk too. Skeator's been around for the last five hundred million years and it's both our families' good luck custom to walk around them and give them a pat before coming back to the house. Granny has decided to stay by the fire this year and watch over baby boy.' Just then the power came on again. 'Yes, I know…we Irish listening to the King of England, but old customs die hard. I hope you don't mind. When we get back, we'll have to get the horses in, perhaps you'd like to help? It's going to be cold tonight. Then it's mucking out tomorrow again – always something to do, and we like to condition my brother's children to help with the dirty work.'

'What do you call a boomerang that doesn't come back?' shouted the girl from Singapore…

'A stick!' and Ronan, clutching his paper hat, countered

with, 'Why had the turkey to join the band? – Because he was the only one with drumsticks.!'

At the Skeator rocks, Manie and Ronan stood slightly apart from the rest when Ronan said, 'It's foggy today, but on a clear day you can see the Saltees Islands off Kilmore Quay… You do realise that you're a bit of a Man of Mystery? Our sister-in-law did give us a vague outline, but isn't it a helluva long way to come to investigate an Irish girl's death in South Africa?'

'You're right, but I'm not at liberty to explain further, except to say that there's something more than fishy about the dead girl. I think it'll resolve itself in the early New Year. And I'm not particularly looking forward to the long journey home.'

'That your car?'

'No, a visiting American car dealer leant it to me while he was away in the States over Christmas. We bumped into each other at White's. It's come in very handy.'

'What did you think of the King' speech – you an Afrikaner?'

'Well, he's not your king either, is he, from this year? I was not aware there were so many colonies and dependencies… sixty-one, is it? Not for long, I think. He spoke with dignity – that's one of the enduring qualities I grudgingly admire – maintained even while the Empire sinks beneath the waves.'

On the way back Michael said that the children would be with the party on their ponies, so the next day's Ride Out would be a slow-motion horseback saunter. He and Manie were walking separately from the rest when Michael chose the moment to hint that Manie should tread carefully around Irish resentments regarding oppression; saying that such feelings were deeply ingrained from an ancestry which, in the main, had endured centuries of British Imperial subjugation, often cruel, ending, officially, only in 1922. Then, of course things had got even worse, he said, with a long year's civil war. The Catholic Church had exploited this burning anti-British resentment, poured oil on the fire – not least demonstrated by the wave of big houses belonging to the Anglo-Irish Ascendency being burnt to the ground, in the effort to get rid of anything smacking of British 600-year long subjugation. The process has forged an iron grip, perhaps approaching madness, on the Catholic Irish soul. Catholic because it wasn't enemy British Protestant. It explains the Irishman's revulsion against suppression and why you can expect frequent condemnation of your new government's suppression of your indigenous people. You must understand that.'

'Yes, I experienced that once, on the train coming down. Catholicism in South Africa, on the other hand, is viewed with suspicion by my church, with ministers preaching frequent warnings about "Die Rooms-Katolieke Gevaar" [The Roman Catholic Danger], and Nat politicians cautioning about "Die Swart Gevaar" [Black Danger], accompanied by reminders that "South Africa belongs to the Afrikaner" – a message duplicated in our classrooms.'

In the still of that night, there was a tap on his bedroom door. It was Anne in a dressing gown and nothing else. He got up and drew her inside, shut the door and led her to the bed. At one point, she yelped and shuddered. 'Ships that pass in the night,' she murmured later. Then a peacock screeched outside the window.

Chapter Thirteen

'Hey, hello again, I see you survived Christmas!' he said, raising a glass of milk in greeting. 'Sit down, sit down.' It was Blankenheimer. 'I've frightened away my drinking pal who just got up and went home to his wife and kiddies when I mentioned the start-up cost of local car assembly…said he preferred making horse-drawn ploughs.'

'How did you get here? I was expecting a message to collect you.'

'I got impatient and hired a car after landing at Foynes… that's the beauty of working for Uncle Sam – I could afford to do so. My God! Irish roads! Flying back, we got fogged up in Newfoundland for some days, including Maureen O'Hara.'

'The Hollywood actress?'

'Yup. Routine visit, not a publicity trip – her husband was the pilot. My interest had worn off by the time we landed in Ireland, and all I wanted to do was get here double-quick. I don't drink Irish Coffee and I found the terminus was crammed full of chattering religious types flying off to Fatima, so I felt crowded out – but God Almighty, what mighty beasts of things these flying boats are…sadly on their last huzzah – like Pierce's horsedrawn ploughs.'

'You seem to have lost weight.'

'True. Blame the ulcer. Hippocrates had the same problem.

I've much to report on Tatiana, so see you at the Garda station tomorrow. Nine, okay?'

The smoke lingered below the roof tops and the Slaney bridge was just a cold foggy ghost, when Manie walked along the boardwalk towards The Faythe next morning. Curious, he thought, how the few women he passed walked very quickly, in small steps, and swung their arms from the elbows, not their shoulders.

Blankenheimer had taken back his auto, and was already there when he arrived on foot, describing to Brennan his Christmas visit to Raleigh, saying that the highlight was observing his grandchildren's excitement when the forty-one-foot Christmas tree was lit up in Lichtin Plaza. 'We gave the Christmas Parade the go-by, in favour of the family turkey,' he added, at which point, he presented them both with maple syrup gift packs, saying it was a North Carolina speciality. 'That's all I could pack, fellas!'

'To business – Tatiana, but before that, Turetsky. I can't give you my sources, even to you two, but he did actually leave his employ as a crane driver and joined as a winch hand on a freighter at Gdansk bound for Sweden, then did the same trick, working aboard a freighter from Gothenburg to Le Havre. We couldn't trace how he got here from Le Havre, although the stamps in his passports will tell the rest of the story. I can say that he was a rather nasty "odd-job man" designed to infiltrate, like many others, the neutral West; his true name being,' – here he broke off to consult his notebook – 'Sergei Fedotov.'

'So,' a pause while Manie tapped out his Meerschaum on a wooden bin, filled the bowl with tobacco and lit it, 'who instructed him to bump me off, one wonders?'

'Clearly, it was thought that you were carrying much info that they desperately didn't want revealed…his minder working either in England or here... . Now that's become Brennan's department. Who knows? It could be someone working as a downtown bicycle shop repairman…a trained operative, whoever he or she is, from behind the Iron Curtain, who has, like many others, blended successfully into Ireland's background.

'Bethesda did manage to trace that both your "Theresa" and "Turetsky" were trained and controlled by the slippery Directorate S within the Russian Foreign Intelligence Service headquarters, just off Sanatornaya Alley in the Yasenevo District of South-Western Moscow. There is no association between the two. "Turetsky" was just a trained thug, whereas your "Theresa" was part of the sophisticated GRU Unit 29155, dedicated to undermining and disrupting regimes in Africa – with a particular focus on Angola, Mozambique, South-West Africa and South Africa. Another extensive unit focuses on Europe – my Bethesda masters (I call it Bethesda, but you know what I mean) would deny similar Western wrongdoings, of course, but I speculate that the new Russian boss, Nikita Khrushchev, is likely to experience similar West-inspired headaches in the years ahead. It's a lethal cat-and-mouse game.

'You were right about those O'Brien books – the underlined sentences were the keys to unlocking all those coded messages you brought, once the encryptions were cracked, and mighty difficult they were, too.'

'So, what did they contain? Although I have a feeling, I know the answer…'

'They're the keys to a major insurrection by your downtrodden millions, interlocking, in a minute and integrated mosaic, all strategic targets to attack – police stations, bridges, power lines, dynamite factories. railway signal boxes, etcetera, and highlighting the most vulnerable points to penetrate, in a coordinated schedule. It's a masterpiece of military planning. But there is a flaw. The manuscripts also list contact names, even addresses. Because it's a slow burner – it could take years before it's activated – some of all this will become out of date, but enough will be valid.

'By the way, I think the twisted florins, you came across in those boxes, were merely used to prove secret recognition between cells, in in an extreme emergency – rather like a Masonic handshake. The beauty of the plot is that each stand-alone cell of rebels will know only what part they must play – the coded instructions contained in their particular concealed box. They will neither know the grand plan nor the parts that other cells will play. As for the money you and others found in the hidden boxes: merely working capital for each independent cell. Such moneys would be from illicit diamond trading, including from gems like those found on your Theresa…small size, high value, easy to conceal, and exchangeable for mountains of cash…you know how that well-oiled racket works infinitely better than I, and how fiendishly difficult it is to break.'

Manie had remained silent though all this, as had Brennan, who pushed back his chair and threw open the window to dispel the pungent fug of Manie's Meerschaum, and Blankenheimer's Turkish cheroot. He said, 'This whole business of coded manuscripts buried in remote boxes seems so clumsy in this age of microdots stuck under postage stamps, doesn't it? All a bit like a boyhood adventure yarn.'

'Clumsy perhaps, but fiendishly clever,' the American said. 'It's a sleeper plot designed to lie fallow for many years, until a flashpoint triggers activation – perhaps, in the future, the shooting of a group of unarmed black kids by a trigger-happy cops, or half a million striking mineworkers – like that three years ago, turning nasty – demanding ten shillings a day. Who knows?

'Another thing: who among our "downtrodden masses" are sophisticated enough to decrypt the papers?'

'Manie, aren't you being naive? Your borders are leaky as a sieve and many locals have crept away to gain training or tertiary education overseas including behind the Iron Curtain …not forgetting the host of South African Communist Party members, to which add disillusioned ex-servicemen and anti-apartheid middle-of-the-road sympathizers. Although the Communist Party has closed down, forestalling its being banned, they've just joined the African National Congress, still permitted to function, for the moment.'

This was too much for Manie who exploded with exasperation at being lectured, saying that it was all very well to sit on the sidelines and pontificate, where encountering a black man was a novelty. It was a different matter with untold millions of them in your backyard and the State struggling to find a peaceful solution. 'It is difficult to remember,' he said angrily, 'when you're up to your arse in crocodiles, that you went in there to drain the swamp.'

Placatingly, Brennan interrupted by saying that they were dangerously straying away from the purpose of Manie's visit and pointed out that it had been acknowledged from the onset, that their task, as detectives, was to unravel 'Theresa O'Brien's' identity and decode the Tatiana manuscripts. They were not there to play politics.

'So, there it is…our Russian friends' future de-stabilization scenario for southern Africa, yielding rich pickings for the Ruskies. Bethesda has retained copies of the decrypts, with duplicates having been sent by diplomatic pouch to the American Embassy in Pretoria, leaving it to them to pass on such material to your government, as they see fit.'

'You should have handed the transcripts to me, to take back to Pretoria.'

'Couldn't do. You've been compromised. They know who you are. If they'd knocked you over the head on the way home and found the transcripts, all your and Brennan's impressive detective work would have come to nought; but you'll get the credit, rest assured, along with Brennan's outfit.'

'That still doesn't explain how Tsarist jewels turned up in Theresa O'Brien's clothing.'

'That's your department. But I guess they became just stock in the illicit diamond pipeline – worth billions, as you know, and mostly in cash transaction form; so you won't be surprised to know that the Russian First Chief Directorate, that's their foreign section, has been in on the illicit trade for a very long time.'

'Yes, Pretoria knows most of that, but if we – and I mean the IDB Branch at home – can trace the buyer of the vanished stone taken from the dead girl's clothing, we should be able to unlock some of the network. Assuming the lost gem was a diamond, it could have measured, like the rest in our possession, at least about thirty-five carats. Give or take minor variations in purity and disregarding the important rarity value of proven Tsarist provenance, it must have an intrinsic value of well over £1 million! Who, in 1949, would have that kind of loose change in South Africa, one wonders? So where did that one lost stone go in the IDB pipeline? Hmmm. To a "no-questions-asked" collector perhaps? But even if it – and the other stones we have – were to be broken into smaller pieces and smuggled to Antwerp for cutting and polishing, or perhaps divided up at Antwerp by a dubious processor, someone still must fork out mega-wads of cash first. My job is done here. What are you going to do with Turetsky's body?'

'Bury him under his theoretical name. The Russians won't want him back as he didn't "exist" and we can pretend that we haven't tumbled to their little game. I'll have to square it with the powers that be, otherwise I'll be breaking the law… falsifying the archives.'

Manie was thinking along the same lines concerning the mythical Theresa and suggested to Brennan that Ireland might either repatriate her body or approve her burial in Bloemfontein beneath an "O'Brien" headstone. Internment notices would appear in *The Friend* and *Volksblad* newspapers accompanied by a short article recalling her worthy rock art studies and untimely end.

Brennan said he'd arrange for a similar piece to appear in the *Irish Times*, recalling her tragic death in Africa and her interest in indigenous rock art; all fact, the only falsehood being her name.

After a shivery walk back to White's in the late afternoon, the receptionist handed him a note from Anne, asking him to phone, giving her number. In his room, Esmerelda Wilde stared at him starchily out of her Victorian frame as he flung himself down on the bed. Calling Anne, he explained that his work in Ireland was done, and he'd be travelling home just as soon as he could get a difficult seaplane booking from Portsmouth.

She asked if there would be time for a visit the following day to meet her old friends, explaining that they had just resettled in their old Irish home again, after having forgone their tobacco farm in Rhodesia – in somewhere called East Manicaland: 'Their farm was attacked, the house was burnt to the ground, most of the tobacco crop was destroyed with several of their labourers losing their lives. So now they're back where they started from…a bit shattered…though still land rich but cash poor. I know they'd like to meet an Africa hand. I'll fetch you.'

★★★

The entrance to the Burkes was an elaborate sandstone structure, so weathered away by the centuries that it was difficult to read the chiselled *Ung roy, Ung foy, Ung loy* motto, and the date, *1437*. Rose creepers tangled through the double gates gave evidence that they had hung open for many years. When Anne hooted, a man came out of the gatehouse with a little girl. Anne unwound the window to shout, 'Hello Fiachra, hello, little Aine…just going up to see the Burkes. Got any honey?'

The man shook his head and said, with difficulty, 'T-T-Too e-e-early.'

Anne fiddled in her handbag for a brush, got out of the car and knelt before the little girl, saying, 'What pretty hair you have! It's so difficult to stop it getting tangled, isn't it? Let me help getting the little knots out,' and proceeded to brush little Aine's hair. 'There! Go and look in the mirror to see how pretty you look,' she said, smiling at Fiachra. 'How's the bad leg, Fiachra? I've brought you some special lineament my brother made up for you at the hospital. The doll's for the little one.'

After they waved and drove off, she said, 'Fiachra is an old retainer and was hard done by after the war. He had made the mistake of joining the British Expeditionary Force and was badly wounded during the battle for Arras and invalided out. Getting home, he found his young wife dying of tuberculosis, no income and a young child to care for…no welfare forthcoming from the state, so the Burkes do their best for him by employing him as their permanent head gardener and "gatekeeper". The locals tend to shun anyone who served in France.'

The 'Big House' was out of sight behind trees down the winding gravel drive of Beech trees. 'They were planted by

Adam's ancestor centuries ago – and it shows,' Anne said. 'Don't fall down the ha-ha after we park.'

'The what?'

'It's a steep bank close to where we're going to park. It's a landscaping trick.'

From a distance, though the ivy had overgrown in parts, the house looked impressive; but as they drew closer Manie saw that a slab of façade masonry had fallen off, and the conservatory was choked with overgrown vegetation, as was the enormous rusting greenhouse at the side of the building.

'Hello, and welcome. You've missed the sheep: they're all packed into the barns for a week or so,' the man said, picking up a ragdoll in the hallway. 'Come this way – we've got a good fire going in the library, warmer than the drawing room. Proper introductions in a moment, but I'm Adam,' he said to Manie. pushing away a large dog that came to sniff the stranger. 'No, not that way. The ceiling in the ballroom has damp rot. You never quite know what might fall on you. The children are playing make-believe in the rumpus room, but I dare say they'll discover you when they're called for cake and crumpets. That's all we're getting.'

The women greeted each other as old friends before Anne introduced Manie, who winked nervously and said hello, unduly squeezing Alexandria's hand with too firm a grip.

When settled, Adam said that the estate had fallen steadily into disrepair in his parents' final days during 'The Emergency' while Adam and his family were in Rhodesia, and now, with ferocious death duties to meet, getting the place habitable again was a challenge. Alexandria and Anne had wandered off to the kitchen when Adam suggested Manie took a more comfortable seat and enquired how things were going in South Africa.

Manie replied he was from down south in the Free State,

mentioning the recent miners' strike, but, generally, that things were under control.

'Well, I won't voice an opinion, but I dare say Anne has told you how we lost our farm in Manicaland, so I won't bore you with more details. Ironically, our estate here should have been more at risk – over 270 Big Houses were burned down or blown up during The Troubles – perhaps ours was saved by my parents occasionally hiding a few Shinners in the basement when the police came searching. The village grocer could have been a bit puzzled, at the time, when my mother ordered an abnormally large supply of food – secretly to keep the men in the basement fed. The servants kept mum, thank God.

'But the Manicaland attack was odd, though, because the neighbouring farm (quite a long stretch away) was left untouched. Perhaps the Terrs just picked the wrong farm. We treated our staff well, unlike neighbour Potgieter who was notorious for ill-treating his black labourers.'

'Terrs?'

'Rhodesia-speak for terrorists. Incidents are few, but there are signs that the threat is growing…if our experience is anything to go by. They say the Terrs can be tracked by their footwear – allegedly their soles have a unique zigzag pattern. Frankly I think that's just bull.'

At that moment the women returned, with Alexandria wheeling in a tea trolley. Perhaps sensing iced orange cake, honey and crumpets by osmosis, the children scampered in and settled, cross-legged, on a zebra skin near the fire, after being introduced. Manie noticed that the zebra's black mane was still intact. The conversation drifted along until one of the boys asked if they could be excused, saying they hadn't finished their game.

Alexandria asked if Adam had been discussing the

Potgieters, saying that she and Anne had been skinnering about them in the kitchen. Turning to Manie, Alexandria said that the Potgieters assumed the trappings of royalty – although one could make allowances for the wife, Princess Angela of a tiny European principality; he, however, was just the son of a wealthy fruit farming dynasty in the Cape, who read Law at Oxford and thence assumed an irritating Oxford drawl. He sported a scar on his left cheek, which he claimed was a fencing scar acquired in Austria during his third year's mandatory 'away' for Law studies.

'Journalists had to enter through the tradesmen's entrance. They oozed boodle, entertained lavishly and liked to show off to sundry visiting Austrian nobility. There was one occasion, when he was in his cups, he went to his strong room and brought out a huge diamond – one assumes it was – and said it used to belong to the Tzarevna Tatiana. You know – one of those murdered Russian princesses. We were there for one of her extravagant birthday parties but it was must surely have been a fake. How could a diamond be so big? It was passed around and when someone asked how he acquired it he just winked.'

'Oh?' Manie asked enquiringly, winking involuntarily himself, his mind racing.

'You can never believe these things, can you, but there were faint whisperings of his dabbling in illegal diamond smuggling – in and out of Beira. All jealous lies, perhaps.'

'Are they still there?'

'Very much so, but they do travel a lot, once the tobacco harvest is in, usually late November, early December.'

Daylight saving brought the dark at four o'clock so Anne had to drive back to Forth Mountain, gingerly, along the narrow country roads. When they reached *Cnocán*, they found the premises in darkness except for Mazawatee's room on the first floor, as Mrs Fanning and her daughter were still away and her brother had returned to Waterford.

'Mother's gone up already. She likes to read in bed.'

Anne asked him to help feeding the animals, then perhaps to linger for a scrambled egg supper, suggesting that they had had enough cake to take the edges off their appetites. 'Plenty of wine, though,' she said. 'Excuse me while I just pop up to Mother for a moment.'

'Feeding the animals' was a greater task than Manie had envisaged, starting with replenishing the stable hay racks and the water troughs, in the poorly lit stables, until Anne switched on another courtyard light.

'Offer them half an apple each, here you are, with your hand flat, otherwise you'll lose your fingers,' she said. 'The peacocks forage for insects – they love ants and centipedes, but we supplement their diet with a muesli we make ourselves. They'll be roosting now, up in that tree, out of reach of foxes, but they like to come down and feed well before dawn, so just plonk this into that hollowed out boulder over there beneath the tree…careful you don't stumble over the mounting block!'

Next came the chopping up of meat and bones for the dogs, in the enormous kitchen, which followed them in when feeding time approached. 'They'll be your friends for life if you feed them. I'll fill their water bowls. Put their bowls down there, by the kitchen door. Now…wine?' she said while whisking eggs, pepper and salt in a bowl and searching for a pan, muttering a complaint that her sister-in-law never put things back in their place.

'So that's it. Scrambled egg on toast, Christmas cake and a glass or two of wine, leftovers at the kitchen table.'

After the meal, they took their glasses and the remains of the wine through to the drawing room, where the fire was still smouldering. Manie prodded it into life, adding another log and some pinecones from the basket.

The wine glasses were very big and after a third glass, Anne announced that she was in no fit state to drive him back to the hotel and that he'd have to stay until the morning.

'When do you leave for England?' she asked with a slur.

'Tomorrow evening. I'm catching the mailboat overnight and then the train for Portsmouth to take the flying boat south.'

'You know your bedroom…I'm off,' she said, getting up, then bending and kissing him warmly on the mouth, before walking unsteadily out of the kitchen. Through the door, he could see her climbing up the winding stairs, clutching onto the banisters.

He sat for a while, staring into the fire and realised he had nodded off when a dislodged log dropped noisily. It must have been midnight when he mounted the stairs and fumbled the way to his bedroom to fling himself down on the bed, and fall asleep immediately, unaware that Anne was there. Eventually the cold and her snoring woke him, so, he cast off his shoes and got under the covers beside her and fell asleep again, the movement causing her to stir and turn towards him.

While it was still dark, the screeching of the peacocks woke them and she murmured, 'My God, it took you a long time to come to bed.'

'You do realise you're in my bedroom?'

'Yes, I know. We've got an hour or so before I must go down and prepare breakfast. Mother's an early riser and likes me to take her a tray of morning tea and a cup of warm water. It'll be an opportunity to explain your presence at breakfast.'

After their first time on Christmas night, lovemaking came easily.

Over breakfast, between the porridge, fried eggs and toast, conversation with Mazawatee drifted back to the horrors of the civil war and the brutality of the Black and Tans. Manie's presence seemed to brighten her, and she launched into explaining that they were out-of-work rank and file World War One soldiers, who were ferried in from England to bolster the constabulary, in its attempts to suppress the Irish Republican Army. They acquired their monicker from being issued with a ragtag of very dark green – near black issue and sundry khaki.

'My husband and I sheltered some starving Shinners for a while, so were lucky we weren't raided by those half drunk or wholly mad brutes. Ghastly people.' She said that others weren't so lucky, recalling how they raided houses, shooting people without provocation. Some teenage girls were stopped by them, for example, and dragged along the street by their hair: 'They used to break into those little row houses you see in Wexford, smash things, hit people with rifle butts, shave women's heads and rape some with impunity It was a reign of terror, ruining hundreds of hapless families to this day, like those of Con Lambert, who was shot, along with someone called McCarthy, not far from here. It was even worse in the southwest of the country, too – and in Dublin.'

'Mind you, Mother, there was deliberate brutality on the Shinners' side…all those constabulary killed by the Shinners. I'll be driving Manie to the station later, so I'd like to detour there to see how Mrs Lambert's doing. She's getting on. Very proud…even now – won't accept charity, so we must

166

be very circumspect – she's our Mrs Fanning's late husband's ancient aunt.'

At this point, the two older children ran in and said, 'We've come to muck out.' Manie was soon given a pair of ill-fitting wellies then found himself being led by the hand to the stables, willy nilly. Anne shouted after him that she'd be out shortly but had to wash up first.

After the horses and ponies were led out and tethered in the yard, Manie was handed a stable fork and instructed to seek out the pats in the hay and pitch them into a wheelbarrow. The urinated areas were next, to be raked and spaded out.

'Here I am,' thought Manie, 'who came to investigate a death, shovelling pony shit in the middle of the freezing Irish countryside.'

Anne came out shortly thereafter to help with the horses' stables, then, when the fresh hay had been shaken out and they had all washed up, she announced that it was time to exercise their charges before restabling them.

It was misty on Forth Mountain, and one of Manie's lasting memories of Ireland was the sight of the children and Anne on their mounts, trotting ahead, in the dreamlike fog.

Another was of two bicycling nuns, in the mist, on his way to Mrs Lambert's.

Anne had brought a box of her mother's scones, a brick of butter, some home-made blackberry jam and a sack of coal. 'Never visit an Irish house without bringing something. I know of some cousin who arrives "with his arms hanging down" – that's the expression. No one likes him.'

The Mansfield home was near one end of a cheek-by-jowl terrace of small dwellings, distinguished from the rest by an old patinated doorknocker in the shape of a hand, a Georgian fanlight over the entrance, and the Virginia creeper that had managed to spread from a tub to neighbouring facades. Alongside the vermilion door was a solitary sash window, echoed by another above.

'What about the coal?' Manie asked, when they parked, to which she replied that it would have to be carried through the front door, and out through the back to be emptied into the coal bin. 'Here's some gloves. Just lug it onto the trolley and wheel it in.'

Old Mrs Mansfield was small and frail. His first sight of the ill-lit interior was a staircase and the back door. The large, coloured print over the little parlour fireplace was the portrait of a long-tressed and bearded man's face with penetrating eyes staring out of the frame; the backs of his wounded and bloodied hands were parted, to reveal rays of light emanating from a vermilion heart in his chest, topped by a small cross. The image of the Nazarite was to haunt him long afterwards. Framed family photographs cluttered the mantelpiece. The only other picture was an incongruous view of the Egyptian Pyramids.

There was just room enough for them to fit in the parlour, along with the tea table. Anne explained that Manie was bound for the train but had expressed an interest in the Black & Tans, at which the old woman's face darkened, and said that they had shot her husband in cold blood, leaving her to hate the British ever since.

'I was left with eight children to raise and no breadwinner. As soon as they could, the older ones had to leave school, as young as eleven or twelve, to earn for the household; meaning that they were deprived of opportunities, not like the children in the Big Houses. We were very poor, and even looked down on by the local priesthood. When we went to Mass, we were only allowed through the side entrance, to sit with the other poor. Thus, it has been, even now, years and years after the civil war has ended.' One of her sons had entered the priesthood and wound up teaching in Nubia. 'He sent me that picture,' she said, pointing at the Pyramids. The priesthood was held in high esteem, opening doors to ascent in Catholic rankings. She was obviously very proud of him.

Driving on to the station, Anne said, 'Bloody British! Bloody Catholic Church! They're both to blame for her predicament. The Brits because they subjugated the Irish for centuries, and the Catholics for forbidding contraception.'

They kissed at the station, and she waited for the train pull away. He watched out of the window, until distance and the mist enveloped her.

Chapter Fourteen

'Groundnuts,' his fellow traveller said, by way of introducing himself. They had just settled down after the seaplane had lifted off from Portsmouth, the spray rushing past the portholes had suddenly stopped. 'Overseas Food Corporation. Harrison. We're going as far as Port Bell,' he said, with a gesture that included his wife and two young boys, transfixed by the view out of the portholes. His wife waved a simpering hello. Harrison had the look of a retired military man, as he turned out to be, having served under Mountbatten as a military engineer.

'Marais,' Manie replied, half rising, and shaking his hand. Harrison said that he was taking over the development, as it seemed to have got into a muddle. 'Most of the surplus tractors they sent from the Philippines are useless, I'm told, rusted up, and no one seems to know how to uproot baobab trees. I don't know what I'll find when we get to Kongwa. Are you familiar with the groundnut scheme?'

When Manie confessed that he wasn't, Harrison described it as an area in Tanganyika the size of Yorkshire…'three million acres…and conceived to satisfy Britain's needs for vegetable oils and fats, simultaneously turning a profit for our dead-broke country.'

'Groundnuts…do you mean peanuts?' An image flashed into his mind of Indian peanut vendors on Durban's North Beach, calling, 'Peanuts salted!'

'The very same. Travelling far?'

Manie said, 'To Durban. I'm from the Orange Free State.'

'Ah, the Boers. You certainly gave Kitchener a run for his money. Outstanding guerilla fighters. I've read Denys Reitz's *Kommando* several times. Ah, here's lunch. By Jove, haven't seen a menu like this since before the war. I believe this is the treatment we're going to get, all the way down. Boys! Settle down now.'

On the cover of the menu was a map of Africa, with faraway-sounding names pinpointing the route – Augusta… Alexandria…Khartoum…Port Bell…Lake Naivasha… Victoria Falls.

Lunch every day, was a five-course affair, served on bone china and consumed with the aid of silver cutlery and crystal glasses, and a flourish of Irish linen nappery, allowing time, between courses for Harrison, above the muffled drone of the Bristol-Hercules engines, to expand on his groundnut difficulties. He heard how millions had already been spent, partly on the employing of a 1200-strong 'groundnut army' ex-military staff, deployed to control a projected 32,000 African labourers.

'I'm told the imported Canadian bulldozers are jammed up in Dar Es Salaam, because there's been a big wash-away of the railway line near Kinyasungwe – wherever that is – so the only upcountry access left is by a rutted road, fit more for donkeys. I'm contemplating getting hold of some surplus Sherman tanks, to strip them and fit bulldozer scoops on the front! That's enough of my grumbling. What do you do; been on holiday?'

'I've been visiting Ireland on government work.'

'Oh, Good Lord. The land of my birth. I went to school there at Kilkenny College, in Dublin. Now there's talk of admitting girls, not in my time! A divided nation, if ever there was. Priests still suggesting that Protestant children have tiny little horns behind their ears.'

Post-prandial fullness and the drone of the engines soon lulled most of the passengers into a doze, even the children, until the announcements, preparing the craft to land at Augusta, bestirred them.

On the next day they had landed in Alexandria, allowing Manie and, another solitary traveller, a girl called Katya, with a smile spoiled by gold fillings, to stroll to the barely detectable remains of the Caesareum, where Cleopatra's obelisks once stood. There they sat as the light faded over the Mediterranean. She was joining her father, a lecturer at the Gordon College.in Khartoum. The passengers were quartered in the Italianate Cecil Hotel. That evening, when the girl asked the waiter what 'Nouilles de Cléopâtre' was, he explained solemnly that it was 'Cleopatra's Noodles', a speciality.

And so, luxury again became routine. At Khartoum, there was a stir when a gaunt man was taken off the plane in handcuffs, followed by the Cleopatra's noodles girl.

At Port Bell the Harrison family departed, in oppressive heat. The air conditioning in his hotel room that night didn't work and there were tears in the mosquito net.

'Coffee,' his new companion said, taking over the departed Harrison's seat, offering a hand to shake, as big as a spade. Manie began to think that this introductory manner was a quirk of the colonial British. The fellow was tall and as big-boned as Blankenheimer. 'Arthur Moodie, wife's Ursula,' he said. 'Our coffee is on the north-western slopes of Kilimanjaro. I'm the administrator at the Kilema Cooperative and Ursula's a teacher of Chaga ragamuffins at the local primary.'

'Marais,' said Manie, bemused that in East Africa people mentioned their occupation during introduction. All Manie offered for clarity was that he was from Bloemfontein.

Moodie grunted noncommittally, and added that banana trees were planted alongside, to shade the coffee plants, thus reducing over-proliferation of the coffee 'cherries', but the banana plants were showing signs of developing Panama disease, he said…a big worry, and that inter-cropping with Chinese chives was the answer. 'There's a big hurry to get this going. Enough about that…Ursula's is really the brainy one…collects ancient Chagga artifacts. Very selective…and can speak the lingo.'

They were interrupted by the captain announcing that he was detouring to allow passengers a last look at the snows of Kilimanjaro and that the bar was open, aft. The plane circled to give everyone a good view of its glacial peaks floating above the clouds.

It was a thud, then spray rushing past the portholes that signalled the flying boat's landing on Lake Naivasha for the night. The Moodies invited Manie to join them for dinner at Sparks Hotel. Waiting for the mail to be unloaded, before disembarkation, Moodie remarked that it was the penny ha'penny airmail stamp that was the glue that kept the Empire stuck together. At over six thousand feet, the air was brisk, passengers discovered, when they stepped onto the floating jetty.

As passengers were obliged to disembark in a new country, every landing, passports had begun to accumulate page after page of, often inscrutable, migration stampings.

The sun had not set, so after resolving the muddle of room location and losing his way in corridors hinting of kitchen smells, Manie and Moodie went for a stroll before sundowners and spotted three very young zebras gambolling beneath the distant acacia trees. Away in the lake, hippos grunted.

At sundowners, Moodie said, 'I'll never want to leave Africa,' gesturing at the view before them.

Turning to Manie during dinner, Captain Younghusband said, 'This hotel was founded by a another South African, y'know, when Sparks tired of Big Game hunting.' The detective and the Moodies had been invited to dine with him – a singular courtesy at a time when the captains of BOAC flying boats were saluted by crew and ground staff. 'Sparks and his wife followed some quirky religion.' He said that the Delamere family lived nearby, as did Lord Galbraith Cole with Lady Eleanor. 'Bound to life in a wheelchair towards the end, Cole shot himself. His grave's quite close.' All this meant little to Manie, but he winked involuntarily and looked interested.

Younghusband said that the hotel was turned into a school during the war, then converted into a nursing home for wounded soldiers. 'Now it's back to being an hotel, just in time to face another change, as our flying boat service is stopping at the end of the year. We're being pushed aside by land-based airliners. They're using Mau Mau prisoners to lay a concrete runway nearer Nairobi, in preparation. End of an era. Sad.' He sighed, passing the port after a satisfying meal. 'In Africa, it's no longer *plus ça change*. East Africa's advancing differently, not for the best, perhaps, and its future's changing forever. We all must adapt or vamoose. The British Rubber Company sent me out to restore the rubber plantations left by the Krauts, but no such luck. We couldn't compete with the Far East, and made matters worse by planting in rows, despite the locals advising us otherwise. Now it's coffee, higher up, as you gather.'

'May I ask what your profession is?'

'I'm a detective.'

'Golly. Flying boat's a usual node of transport?'

"I had to get to Ireland in a hurry, to investigate puzzling elements of an Irish girl's death in the Free State.'

'Solved?'

'Yes and no. She fell from a railway bridge. That was obvious. But certain elements about the accident opened a whole can of worms. More I cannot say.'

'Ah. Must be fascinating work.'

'We plod, most of the time. Dull paper-shuffling, knocking on doors, sifting through rubbish, interviewing people who don't want to be interviewed, writing reports.'

That night, monkeys thundered up and down the roof. The farewell dinner he had shared with the Moodies and the Captain had felt rather like the end of the school holidays. Manie set his alarm for five, then climbed under the mosquito net and opened his travel-worn *1984* in bed. He read, '*Parsons, on the other hand, would never be vaporized. The eyeless creature with the quacking voice would never be vaporized. The little beetle-like men who scuttle so nimbly through the labyrinthine corridors of Ministries they, too, would never be vaporized. And the girl with dark hair, the girl from the Fiction Department – she would never be vaporized either.*' He was a slow reader. In his sleepy mind's eye, the girl in the book blurred with the girl who got off at Khartoum.

The January night was humid at the Victoria Falls Hotel the next late afternoon. He had given the high tea a miss, to consider a book in the gift shop for Rentia titled *Northern Rhodesia Stone Age Rock Engravings* when he turned and found Moodie's wife looking at him. 'That's an unusual book for a detective,' she said. 'I ducked in here to avoid someone we know from the plane. The children call her Helga the

Horrible.' When he explained that the book was for a girl, she remarked that his girlfriend sounded interesting, but he might consider adding an ornament to wear, suggesting some silver Tuareg bangles. For Baboki, his gardener, he bought a Mbira – a simple tribal instrument, played with the thumbs – and for Mavis, extravagant soaps. The Bings and his sister he would sort out later in Bloem. Later, he changed his mind, and kept the Mbira for his sister, and decided to find something more practical for Baboki, like a blanket.

On the last leg to Duran the radio operator handed him a message reading WELCOME AWAIT ME MARINE NOT STATION CAUTION DON'T WALK SIMPSON.

Chapter Fifteen

It was sultry. The launch had transported overseas mail and passengers from the seaplane's mooring at Salisbury Island to the Gardiner Street jetty. Down the street, he could see the Post Office clock and heard the distant chiming. There wasn't an Indian or African hotel staffer to be seen, with only the airline crew handling the post and baggage. Several harbour police were standing on the jetty, one armed with a Sten gun.

'Where are the regular baggage handlers; have they gone on strike?' he asked.

'No sir, they're hiding. There's a spot of bother in the Indian quarter. It seems the Zulus are on the rampage, sir, so we have our Indian staff tucked away securely in the hotel. I'll see your baggage gets to the Marine. Best stay indoors.'

Simpson was sitting in the foyer and rose to greet him. 'Welcome back. Good trip?'

'Luxurious both ends but a bit hairy in the middle. Why are you here?'

There's much to tell, but that's for later. Right now, it's a case of all hands to the pump. I've instructions to rope you in and proceed to the Indian business quarter in Victoria Street. I'll wait for you here. It's a real emergency. We're riding in that police van outside.'

★★★

They could hear the screams and Zulu chanting streets away. When they got there, they were helpless to intervene, finding streets on fire, with hundreds of rampaging natives attacking individual Indians, stoning vehicles driven by them, and smashing into Indian stores chanting 'Uzu, Uzu!' (Kill! Kill!) Between them, Simpson and Marais seized one of the rabble-rousers and bundled him into their police van. When asked what he was doing, the assailant, who seemed crazed with skokiaan and dagga, shouted that the time had come 'to rid the country of these foreign monkeys'. Simpson translated that for Manie, from the Zulu.

Whites were not touched; in fact, some white women and men from the more squalid areas of Greyville were seen egging the natives on, so the two detectives arrested the women, more for their safety, and manhandled them into the van. They were drunk, still shouting, 'Hit the Coolies.' More sinister were the native ringleaders seen urging on the mob, which was constantly swelling with panga-wielding crowds pouring in from the shacks of Cato Manor.

As it grew dark, white troops in armoured cars succeeded in pushing through and sealing off the area. A lot of rioters were shot and left lying where they fell, causing the crowds to melt away, but now police radio reports were coming in of indiscriminate killings in outlying districts, not least some children and the rape of Indian women and girls, accompanied by violent looting.

Manie arrived back at the hotel exhausted, for a few hours' sleep, in the early hours, knowing full well that the mayhem he had faced had to be faced again in a few hours' time. It would be the same – or worse. Looking out of his hotel window, he could see distant fires burning across the Bay, accompanied by explosions and the sound of sporadic machine-gun fire and shots. There was no room service.

178

Next day Simpson and he were posted to Clairwood Racecourse, south-west of the city, to help shepherd frightened and bleeding Indian families stumbling out of army lorries into hastily erected army tents and directing the injured to a first-aid field station. The days and evenings blurred into each other. Members of the Natal Indian Congress were handing out food and blankets, a motley collection of strongly patterned native blankets and bedspreads rescued from the shops. It was raining most of the time.

From the day before, the sight haunted him of four weeping Indian women and numerous children huddled in a building which had been set on fire, one of many. An Indian man lay dying on the pavement, his head split open with blood spreading in the gutter.

Manie was stood down on the third afternoon and Simpson got him back to the Marine. Only when he entered the foyer did he realise he was wet through, as he sloshed through the foyer to Reception. Indian staff were nowhere to be seen, and the manager's wife had taken over the switchboard. He booked calls to Rentia and Mavis, his housekeeper, for early the next morning and arranged to meet up with Simpson at the bar later, after he had reported home to see his family safe

Later, while waiting for Simpson to turn up, he had taken a copy of the *Daily News* and sagged into an easy chair in the Library Bar, to read:

HUNDREDS KILLED
Zulus turn on Durban Indians
> *The alleged attack of a young native shoplifter by the*
> *Indian shopkeeper is said to have triggered a brutal*

pogrom of Durban Indians for the last three days. The unrest centred on Durban's Victoria Street heartland of Indian shops. Police and RDLI troops have now restored order there, but outlying unrest continues, as far as Pietermaritzburg.

The Police estimate that, in Durban, 450 natives were shot dead by police and the army and 142 Indians were killed by the marauders. Another 3,000 people were severely injured, 300 Indian buildings were destroyed and more than 2000 structures damaged. In Durban the natives have retreated, but 40,000 Indian refugees have had to be temporarily tented at Clairwood Racecourse, protected by troops and in some other defendable places. A wave of suicides of Indians has been reported, by Dr Naicker of the Natal Indian Congress, caused, he said, by the disintegration of families, economic failure and just plain misery.

Reverend Ngazana Dube, the editor of Ilanga Lase Natal, *suggested that growing resentment among local natives was the underlying cause. He said 'black marketeering' by certain Indians, the Asian civilians' opposition to economic development of the African, and 'shacketeering' by Indian landlords were all serious contributors. To this, he said, frequent social and racial humiliation of Africans by Indians rubbed salt into the wounds, as were the differential treatment of Indians by Whites. It gave the Indians 'not only better rights, but a sense of snobbishness and superiority over the Africans'.*

*(*Ilanga Lase Natal – New Dawn Natal – *is owned by the subsidiary of our Argus Group. – Ed.)*

'Whisky?' asked Simpson, after spotting him.

'Yes. I've already finished one.'

'Anything in it?'

'Just a splash of water.'

'I suggested we should meet up shortly, just to brief and alert you before you head back to Bloem. That American friend of yours sure did open a can of worms,' said Simpson, after returning with tinkling glasses and lowering himself into his easy chair again, that sighed as he sat down. Both men smoked and Marais saw that Simpson's nicotine-stained fingers trembled.

'Christ, all those bodies in Victoria Street,' he said. 'All that wailing of the women!'

Into Manie's mind sprung a phrase he had heard, as a seven-year-old, used by the Dominee to introduce an incomprehensible and endlessly boring sermon, while he sat squirming in church beside his father and young sister – 'there will be weeping and gnashing of teeth!' quoting from the gospel of Matthew. He had envisaged the entire congregation, loudly gnashing their teeth. So vivid was the image, that he twisted about to look at the rows of people behind to see if they were grinding their teeth at that moment.

'Up north,' he heard Simpson saying, 'I saw men crushed by German panzers at El Aleman, and left near the railway line, but this was different. Did you serve up north?'

'No, I was made a Key Worker, guarding Italian prisoners of war in Jagersfontein – and internees like Hendrik Verwoerd. This was my first riot, and I hope my last.'

Simpson grunted and said that, with great secrecy, Pretoria had forwarded sections of the decrypted stuff that Marais had unearthed originally, but relevant only to his region and this had led to further discoveries, including countless boxes of shock and electrical detonators stored a distance away from dynamite sticks, all hidden in a harbour warehouse, behind forgotten crate loads of rusting tins of peas…he heard that they had even found a small mountain of gelignite, some beginning to weep, concealed in a decommissioned steam engine in Germiston, 'and…wait for it, in an abandoned police station in Parktown Johannesburg, along with thousands of AK-47 look-alikes, smuggled in from China, pistols, rifles, machine guns, grenade launchers, and ammunition…and lots more in other places, including a disused cowshed at Irene, near Pretoria.

'All in all, there's enough discovered to blow up Durban harbour, all the power stations, police stations, army headquarters in Pretoria – the lot.'

'Arrests?'

'No. Everything has been immobilised and put back in place in great secrecy…including those aluminium boxes you and others unearthed. A special unit has been formed, within the Security Branch, to straddle the country, and see who comes to claim the stuff. So far, it's been as quiet as a mouse, and I don't think that these anti-Indian riots aren't connected.

'Gelignite is, as you know very well, relatively stable, and there was plenty of evidence that both material types had been stolen from quarries, road-building sites and the mines over several years. Some had been "liberated" in transit, from the manufacturers at Modderfontein and Umbogintwini, down the coast here.

'Although IDB has been the initial funding channel for buying the smuggled arms – as it throws more light on why your fake "Theresa O'Brien" was carrying diamonds and reinforces evidence of strong Russian interference emerging…. I suppose that, now the Russkies have the Bomb, and much of Europe tucked cosily behind the Iron

Curtain, it's pretty clear what the next target is…turmoil and exploitation in Africa.'

'Look. I feel pretty done in, as I'm sure you are and my concentration is wandering. Let's just order some pub grub and call it a day. I'll delay my return to Bloem for a day – and we can meet up at The Three Monkeys again – same as last time – tomorrow, perhaps in the early afternoon? Another whisky?' he asked, looking at the bar menu.

The rest of the conversation, between mouthfuls, dwelt on fishing, an all-consuming new pastime of Simpson's since he had managed to buy a house close to the beach in Durban North. There was talk of standing on the beach at dawn and casting for shad and Stumpies. 'You cast between the second and third wave,' he said. 'They like to feed close to the shore at that time.'

In the hotel bedroom that night, he opened the crumpled pages of his *1984* and read, *'If there was hope, it must lie in the proles, because only there in those swarming disregarded masses, 85 per cent of the population of Oceania, could the force to destroy the Party ever be generated. The Party could not be overthrown from within. Its enemies, if it had any enemies, had no way of coming together or even of identifying one another.'* Then he turned off the light and fell asleep exhausted, thinking of Rentia, and lulled by the distant sounds of the harbour coming through the open window.

He was jangled awake by the switchboard operator saying 'your call to Bloemfontein', followed by a prolonged unanswered ringing, then the operator saying that there was no answer and asking whether he would like to make the trunk call to Clarens. The wait seemed interminable, until he heard the voice of the kitchen maid saying, 'Yus?

Ullo?' then the operator asking for Missus Myburgh and the maid replying, 'The marram is milking. Wait.' Again, an interminable wait until, with a scrabbling noise, Rentia came on the line with, 'Helloo. Who's calling?' then 'At last! You're back! Are you in Bloem?' After explaining he was in Durban, and her expressing excited delight, she said that she would have to cut him short, saying 'Ring me later. Maisie-cow's full to bursting with milk,' then a click, as she rang off.

The Swiss horologist was still there, who, seeing him at breakfast, exclaimed, 'Been away?' for which Manie gave no explanation, except a, 'Yes, for a while.' The turbaned Indian waiters were back, standing among the potted palm trees, their faces inscrutable.

There were no rickshaws beside the hotel so, against advice from the receptionist, he sauntered up to The Three Monkeys. The pedestrian bustle had vanished and there was a Sten-gun-toting policeman standing on the corner of Gardiner and Smith Streets.

'It's my day off. I've ordered the best Ethiopian coffee and – a bit late in the day – croissants again. I've asked for cheese and jam. Take your pick. Okay?' said Simpson. On a wall rack were papers full of riot news and the formation of a Commission of Enquiry. Gesturing at that headline, Simpson said, 'Of course there won't be a single non-European on the panel. Bloody fools. It's all sickening, but I think you and I have exhausted the subject? Now, about the dead Irish girl.'

'She was a very good Russian fake,' said Manie. 'On the surface she was an erudite Irish post-grad student on secondment here; but her clandestine role was to help lay the foundation for future unrest, using IDB connections… but you know all that?'

'Only the bare bones.'

They were interrupted by a pretty girl bringing their coffee, who said smilingly, 'Eat the croissants while they're warm.'

After she left, Manie observed that the older he got, the younger and prettier girls became. 'I wouldn't mind lying on her bare bones.'

'Careful, she's the owner's daughter.'

'Back to the fake Irish girl…she must have been in contact with someone here in the same line of deception… discounting the IDB gangsters she was running away from.'

'Hang on. A thought…I always carry a transcript of the girl's notebook we found on her body – full of archaeological scribbles to puzzle over, but one name stood out because heavily underlined, and it didn't seem to fit in with the rest. Wait…yes, here it is…**Doda Yegolide**. Any ideas?'

'It's Zulu! Unlike you Bloemfontein Charlies, we Banana Boys learned to speak "kitchen Zulu", just to get by. It means "The Golden Man" or "The Gold Man"…Got it! Goldman! Adam Goldman!"

When Manie looked blank, Simpson explained that the security branch had been monitoring Adam Goldman since his return from Palestine, a year after the founding of the State of Israel. During his time in Palestine, he had served in the Palmach, the military wing of the Jewish National Movement and learnt much about guerilla warfare. 'You had no reason to know that Palmach was there to protect Jewish settlers in the vacuum created by a possible British retreat, during the war, leading to Nazification and Arab opportunistic attacks. The link with your dead Theresa O'Brien is worth considering.'

The girl came back again, offering another round of coffee and more croissants. 'They're the last of today's batch.' Only then did Manie notice that the pupil of her right eye was malformed, smudged into a keyhole shape, one side extending into the white. Conversationally, he asked if she worked at the café full-time. She replied that she was on holiday from English Studies at Howard College. Presently she said she was fascinated by acrostic poetry and how this form occasionally occurred in Anglo-Saxon Latin, and had recently resurfaced.

'And what does acrostic mean? Explain to a simple Afrikaner.'

'Easy! It's when words rhyme at the end or beginning or end of each line – like: "Little maidens, when you look, On this little storybook, Reading with attentive eye, Its enticing history, Never think that hours of play, Are your only holiday"…and so on – that's Lewis Carroll, by the way. Excuse me, I have some other customers.'

'Funny,' Manie said. 'With half the town in turmoil aftermath, here's an English late-teenager more concerned with English doggerel. I'll never understand you English – worse than the Irish!'

Returning to the discussion about Goldman, Simpson said that the man had travelled to several Iron Curtain countries, including Poland, with a girl called Eesha Pillay, from Durban. Through the usual sources, we found that they, far from being just 'enlightened' tourists, met up with a Viktor Yastrebov to solicit military aid during the 1947 conference of Marxist-Leninist Communist parties held in Szklarska Poręba…that's in Poland… . It was Yastrebov, high flier in the Comintern, who, soon after, authorised the millions of roubles' worth of arms like Kalashnikovs and Scorpions to be deposited in caches bordering South Africa. 'It's these arms,' he said, 'that were being secreted into the country in dribs and drabs.'

'Well, my job is done and I'm going back to the Free State,' Manie said. 'It's not my job to arrest people. I was instructed to unravel the Theresa O'Brien business and that's been done with your help. I'm not Special Branch and have no desire to join it, but from what you and I have learnt, we whites won't be able to sleep soundly in our beds for very much longer. Everything's going to get very messy, very soon.'

On his way back to the Marine, his route was down West Street, where the pavements boasted blue dividing lines and regularly stamped admonitions of 'Don't Spit!' and 'Moenie Spoeg Nie!' Although these were aimed at Hindu betelnut-chewing pedestrians, none were in Tamil. At the corner of Field Street, the *City Late* was already on sale; and at Gardiner Street he had to wait for the trolleybus, crossing over from Smith Street.

The Minhas were clustering to gossip in the giant old fig trees beside the Post Office and the pigeons were circling. The whole town was beginning to go home. All at once, he felt very alone. On impulse, he dashed to the Indian flower sellers outside the station, bought a handful of carnations, and returned, cutting through Farewell Square to reach the Museum steps just before closing time. An unmarked van was parked at the steps and running up them, he almost collided with labourers carrying down filing cabinets, boxes of books and papers, a large desk, a typewriter and a bottle of vermouth.

It was a macabre moment when he spied Sophia, ashen-faced, sitting in the back seat of a car beside a uniformed policewoman. Sophia saw him and he held up the flowers, then the car moved away. Instinctively, Manie disliked short balding men who sported pencil-thin moustaches, and this plainclothes policeman was one of them, who demanded, 'Who are you? How do you know that woman in the car?'

Manie remembered the moment when Sophia's eyes filled with tears when talking of her father being shot by the Russians, her escape from Soviet-occupied Poland and her help in detailing the Irish girl, Theresa. 'I'm a detective,' said Manie, showing the plainclothes man his identity card. 'I've been investigating the death of a girl who worked with that lady,' (pointedly using the word 'lady') 'and I think your barking up the wrong tree.'

'You'd better come down with us to our offices,' said the security branch man, more as an order than a request. 'Wait in our van until we've finished.' Manie was still holding the carnations. The labourers broke one of the desk legs while loading it into the van; they were a clumsy lot.

The Security Branch was housed in unmarked offices in Baker Street, and the Captain said he and his staff were from Pretoria and operated independently. Manie had discarded the carnations in the van but saw them being clumped together with the museum 'evidence'. He said nothing. It amused him to think that they might be viewed with suspicion. He imagined the Kafkaesque hours wasted by one of his men looking for microdots on the newspaper wrapping.

After phoning Simpson for extra verification, the security man's attitude changed, and Manie suggested that perhaps Pretoria had got hold of out-of-date information and explained he'd got to know Sophia while checking the background of the Irish girl who worked for Sophia, who proved to be a Russian named Vera Yelizaveta Tarasova. 'And that girl is very dead.' He said he could find no evidence that Sophia was implicated in any plot, and that the Irish girl's employment was purely coincidental.

'You realise you've buggered up her current research material, by bringing her stuff here? Your labourers kept dropping stuff and treading on research material.'

'That's the least of my worries. She'll get it all back when we're finished with it,' he said, pulling a brandy bottle out of a drawer and pouring them both a slug.

Manie snorted in disbelief. 'I wish to see her. What's your name?'

'Captain Auf der Heide.' He could hear a black prisoner being beaten and grunting in pain. There were shouts of interrogation by a guard.

The security man sat looking at him, saying nothing, then suddenly got up and disappeared. Returning, he beckoned Manie to follow him into a grubby room that smelt of dehydrated vegetables. Behind a small reinforced-glass panel sat Sophia, beside a female guard, still wearing the same clothes. She brightened when he appeared. Manie had to press a button and speak into a microphone, with Sophia replying in the same manner.

'I had nothing to with all this,' Manie said. 'I arrived back from Ireland a few days ago but was delayed from calling on you by the riots.'

'I don't know why I'm here…they won't tell me anything except to show me a piece of paper and say they were arresting me under section 6 of the Political Terrorism Act. I'm a scientist – not a bloody terrorist! This is like Poland under the Nazis all over again.'

'I think the momparas in Pretoria have got all muddled up,' Manie said, looking steadily at Auf der Heide, 'and the riots have made them jittery. I'll do my best to get you out of here, but no promises. Meanwhile, what do you need – money, toiletries, clothing? Do you have a lawyer? I think you'll have to resign yourself to staying here overnight, but I promise to get things going just as soon as I leave here.'

She asked him to advise the museum director, and her neighbouring flat owner, Mrs Nelson, to take in milk deliveries; lastly to let Father Jankowski know and ask for help. She explained that he was parish priest at St Peter's Catholic Church on the corner of Hospital and Point Roads. It served the Polish community.

It was deep dusk when he emerged from the building and the Hesperides had come out, smoking on street corners. An offer of a lift was not forthcoming and there was no rickshaw in sight. 'What a moeras!' he thought, as he made his way back over the cracked pavements to the Marine, realising that he would have to postpone his return to Bloem yet again. Ordering a taxi from the hotel, he went to see a timid Mrs Nelson, explaining that Sophia had been called away suddenly, and that he had been asked to deliver the message, saying that he had no further details. Mrs Nelson was left pondering Sophia's relationship with this Afrikaner. She had spoken to him through a door protected by a safety chain and defended by a snarling Pekingese. Somewhere in the flat, a canary was chirping.

Next, he went in search of Father Jankowski. The heavy front door of St Peter's was unlocked, and his first sight of the dim interior was a hanging red lamp burning near the tabernacle. He had never entered a Catholic church before, and he felt unsettlingly foreign before the carving of the crucified Christ above the altar, the stained-glass window, now illuminated by an electric light outside, and the Stations of the Cross. Incense smells lingered among the dark wooden pews. At the altar, the solitary figure of a priest was emptying the penny-candle boxes. A few candles still burnt on a rack near the figure of Mary, a circle of stars about her head. When Manie approached him, the priest said, 'I'm afraid it's a bit too late for Confession.'

'No, no, are you Father Jankowski?' On a grunting nod, Manie said, 'I've been asked by one of your parishioners for your help,' and went on to describe Sophia's dire need for intercession and that of a sympathetic lawyer. The priest said he would follow it up promptly, and he'd demand to see Sophia, though he might be prevented. Father Jankowski had a high domed forehead and sympathetic eyes. Inexplicably, Manie's mind flashed back to Mazawatee's description of the brutal Black & Tans, and the sound of a black man being beaten at Baker Street.

He was no Cleopas on the road to Emaus, but disillusionment in his pro-fascist masters stole into his heart at that moment and settled there.

Explaining that he had to leave for Bloem the next day, he gave the priest his home number and asked to be kept informed.

'Where's the Swiss man?' Manie asked the head waiter, whom he came to know as Rajesh.

'I'm told he was removed, sir.'

'Removed?'

'Some policemen removed him away, sir.'

'Hadn't he paid his bill?'

'I don't think so, sir. Not that. The Marine would never disgrace a man publicly, like that; I believe it was political, sir.'

'At this rate there'll be no one left.'

'Sir?'

'Nothing. Is your family is safe?'

'They are safe, sir.'

'What's on Special, Rajesh?'

'Well after soup, Minestrone with Parmesan cheese and pesto, we have Grilled Escalopes of Veal on special, with Rosti Potato, Asparagus Tips and Wild Mushroom Cream, sir; but would you not like to peruse the menu? There is much else.'

'No, that's fine.'

'Hello Rajesh,' came a familiar voice. 'Good heavens, the "Our Man from Bloemfontein"! What a pleasant surprise! Gillian my wife and I are treating ourselves to a slap-up meal…it's our escape, far from the madding crowd…' It was the Minister from the Durban-bound train he had encountered before he left for Ireland. 'Are you dining alone?' He glanced at his wife. 'Well then why not join us?' It was an invitation Manie could hardly refuse. 'Rajesh!' gestured the Minister, and after joining them, he apologised and asked to be reminded of Manie's name. Devilishly, Manie winked involuntarily and identified himself as Detective Sergeant Marais.

There was a momentary freeze, until the minister, who turned out to be a Canon Irvine, broke the ice by saying, 'Why, that's fascinating! What challenging work you must do.'

Manie wondered what his church Predikant would say. He remembered one of his endless sermons which started with 'He who sups with the Devil should have a very long spoon!'

'Awful business, the riots. It's a case of the subjugated persecuting the suppressed – rather like squealing pigs attacking each other in a truck on the way to the abattoir, still jostling for position. Such animosity can only end when South Africa is free of Apartheid,' said the minister, then started when his wife kicked his shin, under the table.

Manie ignored the mention of Apartheid, but said he had witnessed, at first hand, the brutality of the riots and the aftermath of dead bodies strewing the streets, a sight he hoped never to see again, whereupon the minister retold of his church's role in providing first aid, food and tents to those rendered homeless, in the aftermath, in conjunction with members of the Indian Congress, the Red Cross and others until Irvine's wife interrupted and suggested they should talk about something else over dinner, with her saying she was a potter. 'When Bridget switches on her electric kiln all the streetlights dim on the Berea. It chews electricity!' The rest of the conversation focussed on potters' wheels, off-centre wobbles, biscuit-ware, slipware and glazing until Manie excused himself.

After he had left, the minister asked his wife why she had kicked him, and she pointed out that, being a policeman and an Afrikaner, he was probably inwardly proud of the Nationalist government's sweeping into power and glorified in the elevation of Afrikanerdom. Little could she know of the inner turmoil with which Manie was troubled.

He booked early calls at Reception then escaped to his third-floor suite. In bed, he opened his copy of *1984* book-marked with a trolley-bus ticket, and read, '*The Party told you to reject the evidence of your eyes and ears. It was their final, most essential command. His heart sank as he thought of the enormous power arrayed against him…*' After a few pages, Manie turned out the light.

He had flung open the windows on entering and now listened in the dark to the night-time harbour sounds floating in from across the bay. Dutifully, he thought of Rentia, yet his mind soon drifted to the encounter with 'Mazawatee', and her description of the Black-and-Tans' mindless brutality and Mrs Mansfield, downtrodden by the past regime, in her cheek-by-jowl cottage, where the coal had to be brought in through the front door.

Chapter Sixteen

'I see your thumb has healed,' he said to the waiter in the Phoenix restaurant, as he plonked down the mandatory pea and barley soup with hefezoft and butter on the side. In Bloemfontein it was hot, and the waiter was sweating. 'Thank you,' he said. 'Good Christmas?'

'Yes, in a manner of speaking.'

He borrowed a copy of *Die Volksblad* from the rack, while waiting for Lore Herzog, his Super, to arrive, and read,

Death for Auschwitz Garrison

Cracow, Poland. 7th January 1949

The Supreme National Tribunal concluded in Cracow yesterday. Of the forty people indicted, 23 (including the second Auschwitz commandant, Arthur Liebehenschel, political department head Maximilian Grabner, and women's camp director Maria Mandel) were sentenced to death, and six others to life imprisonment.

Another story on the same pages was headlined, *"Sex is immoral'* with the sub, ***Prohibition of Mixed Marriages Act,***

***Act becomes Law**. The legislation now prohibits marriage between Whites and 'Non-whites.*

Further legislation, according to Prime Minister Dr Verwoerd speaking in Parliament yesterday, will be a population registration Act and a so-called Immorality Act' which will require all individuals living in this country to register as a member of one of four officially defined racial groups. It will prohibit extramarital sexual relationships between those classified as white on the one hand and those classified as non-White (Blacks, Coloureds, and in due course, Asians) on the other.

Although there was loud condemnation for the passing of the Act by a minority group within the United Party, voiced, most vociferously, by Helen Suzman, the Parliamentary Member for Houghton, there was majority support for the legislation. Suzman forecast that the Act would trigger untold misery.

At time of going to press, response from Non-European quarter has been muted, with strongest opposition to date coming from the English churches. The Anglican Bishop of the Orange Free State, Bishop Robert Carey, for example, protested that Marriage was a matter for God and the churches, not the state.

He put the paper down and caught sight of himself in one of the mirrors between the dark wooden panels and saw the face of a tired, careworn forty-something man. In a far corner, munching away steadily and saying little, sat three Supreme Court of Appeal judges. Manie recognised two of them. 'Well at least it's only three, not five, so the case is only of middling importance,' he thought.

Herzog weaved between to the tables and wheezed

with an overweight sigh as he sat down, followed, almost immediately, by their favourite waitress, Elsa. All the girls were required to dress in dirndls, and the costume suited her particularly well, in her mieder, laced tight to the body, but with a décolletage blouse, tight pleated skirt, below the knee socks and soft flat shoes.

They ordered the usual Schweinshaxen, with sauerkraut, braised cabbage and potato dumplings set off by a big dab of coarse mustard, side plates of green salad, and the inevitable thimble of schnapps to accompany lidded tankards of dark beer.

'I'm going to miss these meals,' said Manie.

'How come?'

'I'm resigning.'

'What?' Herzog asked, with such surprise that he dropped his butter knife on the plate with a crash.

'How come? You're due for a promotion. Pretoria thinks highly of you.'

'I'm going to marry again and go farming near Ceres.'

What he didn't mention was that his overseas trip had opened his mind and he was now sickened by the coming harsh subjection of the bulk of the population. Widespread arrests were already taking place across the country as a direct result of his investigations and a sampling of what had happened to Sophia and the noise of black prisoners being beaten now revolted him. He knew what would happen, particularly to the blacks. He heard that some prisoners had already been drugged and dumped at sea. While recognising that a threatened massive insurrection had to be put down, he did not want to be party to the brutal means that would be employed. It was the Black & Tans all over again for the benefit of a few privileged beings.

'Can you fix up my pension?'

'Because you're in favour they'll probably up your rank for a better retirement package. I'll see what I can do. Who's the girl?'

'Rentia Myburgh. She farms near Clarens…lost her husband in an accident some years ago. She's up here now and tomorrow we'll be talking to the pastor about the rigmarole of a marriage in the Moederkerk.'

'Clarens! My God, that's in the gramadoelas.'

'Not really. Its rich soil just begs to be farmed, the scenery is majestic, our forefathers trekked and fought there and Rentia is the best thing since sliced bread. She's up here in Bloem at the moment. We're due for a meeting, in an hour, with the Moederkerk Pastor to discuss wedding details. I'd prefer to just steal away and get married by a magistrate, but Rentia demands otherwise.'

'But you know nothing about farming!'

'Not so. My sister and I grew up on a farm called Waaifontein near Winburg – that's not so far from Clarens. We used to run around kaalvoet with the piccanins until we developed veldsores and had to wear shoes for the first time. Our pa farmed potatoes, mielies and sheep – so we absorbed "agriculture" through the skin. I remember we used to climb the windpump for the view until Pa stopped us. My Sussie called it the windbloem. So you see, I'm a plaasboetie at heart.

'Rentia'll continue the little dairy business which she knows well, although I'll lend a hand, whenever, but I'll concentrate on crops – mielies, sunflowers for oil, peanuts – they call them "groundnuts" in East Africa – and sorghum – that's a fancy new name for kaffircorn.'

'Juss!' Herzog exclaimed at Manie's sudden change of direction, and asked what he would do about his Bloemfontein house. Manie said his sister would probably move into it from De Aar upon early retirement: meanwhile he'd rent it out.

'I must ask you for another favour: Lungelo.'

"What about him? You mean Izambane?'

'The same. He's good and served me well, but he's like a fish out of water, because the local Basutos dislike the Zulus…yes, I know, that's why he's stationed here, to remain unbiased – but could he be transferred closer to his family in Zululand? I know he wishes it.'

'You going soft on the Kaffirs?'

'No, but I got to know him better while in the Drakensberg. We would have drowned if he hadn't stood fast, preventing our being swept away. It was during that time he said his family was struggling.'

'I'll look into it.'

Baths in old Bloemfontein homes of any consequence were wide, deep and of enamelled cast iron, copious enough to accommodate a hefty-framed Free State farmer, or Manie and Rentia's bathing together. There was nothing fancy about the honest-to god brass taps either, nothing to impede their full-throated spluttering and gushing delivery, and to fill the bathroom with steam.

'What are you going to do about Baboki, your garden-boy? We can hardly employ him in Clarens,' Rentia asked among splashings. She lay cradled in his arms. 'Here, soap me.'

'And where else? You'll have to stand.'

'Not yet.'

'It's a long time since we made love under the stars in the Berg, isn't it? And the world has changed. The Bings'll take him over…apparently their old retainer is about to be pensioned off, so his transfer couldn't have come at a better time. Their gardener is going blind. Marianne said he keeps on mistaking her plants for weeds and pulling them out. Knowing the Bings, they'll see he's taken care of.'

'And Mavis? You can't leave her in the lurch either. She's a motherly soul and you must see that her whole life has been centred about you for so many years.'

'I don't know. You two seem to get on very well. She may well have plans, but would you consider her as a housekeeper in Clarens – or would that disturb your long-term servants? She's a practical soul and perhaps you could part-time employ her in the museum?'

'Why are you really leaving the police? The real reason.'

'The truth? In Ireland I encountered evidence of what violent suppression of the subjugated did. Untold misery and burning resentment that led to a bloody revolution and civil war. Our government is about to do the same thing – and I want nothing to do with it.'

Rentia remained silent for a long while, then he turned on the taps again with his toes, and another cloud of steam and water splurged from the faucets while Rentia started to chatter about bridesmaids, dresses, invitations, friends and distant relatives of both parties requiring invitations, not least Manie's offspring and broods. The wedding date had been set for a month hence and Manie thought uneasily about the cost, that seemed to rise by the minute, until she revealed that a doting and wealthy uncle had offered to cover most of the expenses, as Rentia's parents had died some years ago. All Manie had envisaged was a very quiet wedding – even perhaps in the tiny chapel above van Reenen's Pass, which seats only eight people, and yet here there was talk of it turning into a society wedding – complete with the railing up from Cape Town of Cornelius Carstens and his Orkes to play at the reception, as suggested by the uncle.

'Make love to me now,' she said suddenly. Their daughter was conceived that night.

The heavens opened in the wee hours, accompanied by flashes of lightning which lit up the curtains and followed almost immediately by peals of thunder that commenced with crackling, tearing sounds like giant linen sheets being torn asunder. They lay cradled in each's arms in the big brass Victorian bedstead listening to the roar of the rain.

Both frightened dogs had wormed their way underneath the bed.

Manie realised that, for the first time in many years, he felt deeply content. As the storm grumbled, his mind drifted back to his declaiming lines of Lennox in an agonisingly schoolchild performance of an abbreviated *Macbeth*, while a stagehand wound the wind machine and rattled a thin sheet of metal simulating thunder. The lines came back as he lay there – '*The night has been unruly. Where we lay, Our chimneys were blown down and, as they say, Lamentings heard I' th' air, strange screams of death, And prophesying with accents terrible, Of dire combustion and confused events new hatched to the woeful time…*' He chuckled inwardly as he remembered the bemused faces of an indulgent parental audience, in that remote little school in the Free State, before the cramp of 'Afrikaanse Kultuur' took hold. The teacher was bewitched by Shakespeare.

It was Saturday, and the phone rang during breakfast. It was Father Jankowski who said, 'I have very bad news. You had asked me to keep you informed about the release of Sophia Vitali-Kluczynski from detention. This was refused and during her transfer to a small detention centre near Pinetown, she fell down concrete steps and knocked her head very badly, so I was told. She was taken to Addington Hospital but died of related injuries…Hello?'

'Fucking police!' Manie shouted down the phone, startling not only the priest in Durban but Rentia and Mavis. His dogs sprang up and scampered out of the room barking.

Jankowski said that a special Mass would be said, and he understood that his small Polish flock would help with the cost of her burial at Stellawood Cemetery, in due course. Manie had no idea of what a Mass was but thanked him sadly and said he would respond later, after thinking it over.

Coffee from the percolator, the smell, the taste, sugared, warm and milky, marked a restful conclusion of Saturday breakfasts in the Marais household ever since his wife was alive, with the weekend stretching ahead, but spoiled, on this occasion, by the sudden news of Sophia's death in custody. It was overlapped when the phone jangled again. It was an operator from the Bloemfontein exchange asking if would accept a call from Bethany Mission Station.

It was Pastor Roentsch. The line was bad and full of crackles, the pastor's voice sounding very far away.

'Is that you, Detective Inspector? Can you help? I've had word that they're going to uproot my congregation and cart them off to the Wilderness of East Griqualand. This is insanity, Inspector. These people have lived here for generations…this area is their ancestral home…I'm told the expulsion police are going to come today.

'You're my last resort, Inspector! Bloody Native Lands Act!'

'I'll come as quickly as I can and see what I can do. Probably not much. It'll take an hour and a half to reach you.'

On hearing of Manie's mission, Rentia insisted on

accompanying him, so they set off on the untarred road towards Reddersburg, churning up dust in their wake, until they took the corrugated spur to Bethany. Manie drove on the wrong side of the road to lessen the juddering of the corrugations on the car's suspension and arrived at the mission, well ahead of the enforcement squad's arrival.

'Just look at that sky. Not a cloud and so azure blue,' she said.

'That's what I love about Highveld skies. You don't get such rich blues in European skies – at least the ones I've seen. Something about air molecules.'

'A beautiful day for the threat of such ugly work,' said the pastor who came out to join to them. 'See, over there, they've already positioned a bulldozer some distance away up the hill. The driver's the son of a local farmer. When I went to speak to him, he refused to explain why he was there. An unfriendly man. Please come in for tea. Hannah!' he shouted. 'Visitors!'

The Mission Station was strangely deserted. 'I've warned everyone that there's trouble ahead and that they had better gather their possessions, just in case the worst happens. Have you managed to speak to your authorities, Manie?'

'I have, but our police say it's out of their hands. The Removal Force is controlled from Pretoria, and all our local police knew was that they had been alerted…that's all.'

Hannah had taken Rentia aside and said to the men, 'I want to talk woman-talk,' and Manie heard their low voices discussing the coming wedding, of bridesmaids and the accommodation of the relatives.

'Oh God, here they come,' exclaimed Roentsch as the sound of army trucks approaching grew louder and louder. They stopped near the largest hillside settlement. Armed personnel with police dogs, some blacks, some whites, headed for the settlement with loudhailer commands being shouted

202

in Xhosa, Tswana and Afrikaans. As the squad entered the dwellings, there were raised voices of commands and protests, accompanied by the barking and snarling of dogs.

'We'd better get up there quickly,' said the pastor and they raced up the hill.

Out of breath, Manie shouted to the man with the loud hailer, 'Who's in charge?' and winking involuntarily

'I am. Who the fuck are you?'

At that moment, he saw a grey-haired old man being manhandled out of a hut and went to stop the attack when a shot rang out. Manie felt a violent burning and stinging at his sternum and ribs then an abnormal warmth in his chest. Looking down, he saw blood gushing uncontrollably. With hands clutched to stop the flow, his legs gave way. Thus crumpled, he sensed he was drifting towards a bright welcoming light.

Then there was nothing.

Momentarily, all action at the settlement froze, as if in a Victorian *tableau vivant*, except for the dogs and children, until a Griqua shouted, 'They have shot the white man who tried to help us.'

'You've shot a police detective, you bloody fool!' Roentsch screamed. 'Get you men to help me carry him down to the mission. Quick, goddam you brutes!'

They had heard the shot, but staying back at the house, they first realised what had happened when the two women saw Roentsch and the others carrying Manie's limp body, bleeding like a stuck pig, into the refectory, where he was laid out on its table. They rushed in, to discover Roentsch stuffing loose material into the wound.

Up the hill, the shouting, barking and cracking of sjamboks went on, but were dulled to the little group around the refectory table. Hannah raced to the mission house to phone for the doctor in Reddersburg, only to learn that he was away.

It was agreed for all three to race Manie to the Emergency Ward at Bloemfontein General, forty-five miles away, in Manie's car, while blood seeped onto Rentia's lap in the back seat. The urgency distracted Rentia from the full calamity until halfway there when she broke down and wept uncontrollably. Despite that, trivial thoughts raced through her mind among the more tragic ones of a destroyed love – that she would have to tell her uncle to cancel the Nico Carstens booking and send out notes cancelling the wedding.

There was no hope, of course and Manie was pronounced Dead On Arrival.

The clock in the tall NG Church belfry at Clarens was striking three as people began to arrive.

One of Manie's sons had done well by developing a stud farm near Nottingham Road. He and his wife had flown up in their Beechcraft, with their two boys, the day before, with Rentia's uncle fetching them from the Die Uys Huis airstrip. Christopher Marais was partially crippled from a riding accident and relied heavily on a stick. They had never met Rentia, although their trails had crossed.

Manie's sister, Nerene, had come up by train to Bloem from De Aar, where she had been met at the station by Manie's brother Jannie and wife Marliese. They had motored across from Koffiefontein with Etienne Le Roux and wife Sandra, to complete, together, the journey to Clarens. It was a tight squeeze.

Looking up at the weathervane crowned by a north-eastern-swivelled rooster, Etienne observed, by way of breaking the silence among the small group, that it was a good Afrikaans one, as the letter for 'eastwards' was 'O' (for 'Oos').

A small cluster of Sothos stood a little distance away.

'I wonder who they are,' Jannie murmured.

'I believe they're a Sotho choir who'll sing a hymn; but they're not allowed into the church, being black, so this could be interesting. I'm told the dominee has been asked to keep his otherwise mind-numbing oration short, so I can say something. Pastor Roentsch from the Mission Station will, too, and possibly Rentia, if she's up to it. I think Nerene may stand beside her.

'Lore Herzog's in uniform, and oh my God…look at all those other policemen over there…like stuffed shirts. At least Rousseau and his wife aren't dressed up like the Gestapo.'

Rentia and Nerene had smothered Manie's coffin with local wildflowers. Despite the dominee's protest, Mavis was seated with the rest of the family. After the dominee's set piece, ending with biblical quotations, Etienne went up and said among comforting words, 'I didn't know Manie very well, but I expressed a wish to speak. We live in Koffiefontein, and I am a writer. Last week, I heard that my novel *Seven Days at the Silbersteins* had been banned, and labelled as "undesirable and pro-Communist", according to a notice in the *Government Gazette* confirmed by my receiving an official letter to that effect.

'This is the deteriorating state of things Rentia's Manie rebelled against. With a senior policeman's special knowledge, he could see that our government was rapidly lurching towards Nazism…he expressed as such to Rentia days before his tragic death, attempting to protect a very old black man from totally unnecessary police brutality…and suffering the tragic consequence.

'Manie's death is not in vain. His decision was to leave

the police force, disillusioned that this arm of the State was now obliged to kowtow to a mad ideology, dreamed up by an academic in one of Stellenbosch University's ivory towers. May his soul go marching on.'

He returned to his seat. When Pastor Roentsch got up to go to the rostrum, there was a muttering of voices and two families got up and left the church, one of the men saying loudly, 'That's enough! That's enough!' pushing aside, as he left, members of the small choir now gathered in the vestibule.

The Pastor said that he blamed himself for calling on Manie for assistance when he received word that his entire flock was to be uprooted and dumped far away in some Griqualand East gramadoelas. If he hadn't made that call, Manie would be here sitting beside Rentia. 'But instead,' he said, 'he and Rentia rushed to the assistance of me and the mission folk and died as a result. I came across a phrase in a poem by an Anglicised American poet, T S Eliot, which encapsulates what I have struggled to put into words. He wrote "the time of death is every moment which shall fructify in the lives of others". Manie's death was a noble one, and his motives will be cherished in the hearts of we who are left. He was shot by the removal police simply because he was attempting to protect a fellow human… . Why our government has chosen to uproot my Griqua flock is a subject for another day, save to say that there will be a Day of Reckoning, mark my words.'

Rentia was too overcome to speak, but Nerene, his sister, spoke of the brother and sister's early days on the Waaifontein farm, of running wild and free, of climbing the creaking and groaning windpump and putting their mouths to the water gushing into the cattle pond, of Manie's kindness, as a young child, to the piccanins on their farm. Their father had been cross when he discovered that Manie had given away several toys to them, after her brother had learnt that they had little to play with; except for a few miniature cattle they had made from clay. 'Once, I heard him saying to one of them, handing the child a toy car, "Here, you can brrroom-brrroom with this one." Life was simpler then. We would watch, for hours, black veld ants scurrying, in and about their antiholes on the hot, bare earth.' She talked of their shared love of music, most notably, in their teenage years of the Great Masters, inspired by their mother, an accomplished violinist, playing on the more primitive harmonium while they crouched at her feet and umped the foot pedals, one at a time.

'As children, one of our favourites was the hymn "Nearer my God to Thee", which, after our dominee's final prayer, the little choir at the entrance of the church is going to sing in Sotho. They've been rehearsing it for days.' The singing went on as the undertakers shouldered the coffin and walked between them, out of the vestibule, followed by Rentia and the rest of close family, to await the rest of the congregation.

Manie was buried beside a hillock on Rentia's farm Vergenoegfontein. Some months later, after the earth had settled, Rentia planted a Cellicia Emteenus Africana tree on the grave which, in the years that followed, grew mightily, so that its roots cradled Manie's coffin in an earthly embrace. A family of black-collared barbets came to settle in its branches.

Rentia never married again. On some good days – and there are many good days in Arica – she and their young daughter, Sarie, would picnic there. She would talk about the old days, when Boer women and children had hidden in the caves to escape Kitchener's concentration camps during the Boer War; but, more frequently, she would recall times when she and Manie had looked up at the stars in the Drakensberg.

Sometimes she would reflect on more ancient times, when the San people had painted images of strange half-human creatures and animals on the cave walls and overhangs, and of the dinosaur bipeds which had left their footprints in the Clarens sandstone, 180 million years before.

THE END

Epilogue

If you went to Vergenoegfontein today, you would see wide fields behind the milking shed, of mielies, sunflowers and sorghum, which Rentia's uncle had planted. Though elderly, he was a strong man and had settled on her farm to develop the fields, following Manie's intentions.

Mavis was accepted by the Clarens community 'as long as she knew her place', and only once did someone remark nastily about her crinkly hair.

She dwelt on the farm and split her time between ruling over the kitchen staff and doing clerical work at the little museum.

Roentsch and his wife Hannah were obliged to close the mission station after his Griqua flock had been forcibly removed, so the couple returned to a devastated West Berlin. They never returned to Africa.

Lungelo was transferred home near Gingindlovu and was pensioned off after a boulder crushed his foot. His first wife had given him two daughters and his second, three sons. By the time Lungelo was a Kehla and could wear an isisico head-ring, his daughters were of marriageable age. Both were pretty, domestically well trained and good at beadwork, so it was not surprising that their suitors had to pay a Labola bride-price of ten cattle each. His sons were umfaans, at the time, so their job was to look after his herd, which continued to multiply, a source of great pride. Two of the sons eventually joined the railways, but the first-born went on to study at Adam's Mission then Agricultural Economics and Agronomy at Fort Hare, where he got caught up in the in the civil rights movement.

Graham Greene wrote *The Human Factor* after he returned to England from Africa. In part, it exposes the hypocrisy of the West's relations with South Africa under Apartheid. In the introduction from the 1982 edition of his novel he wrote, 'They simply could not let South Africa succumb to black power and Communism.'

Anne Butler, of Forth Mountain, lost her life in a boating accident on the River Sur. She had been trying to rescue an overwintering greylag goose that had become entangled in drift netting when her boat overturned. 'Mazawatee' died soon after.

Nerene, Manie's sister, settled into his Kruis Street house, and gave piano lessons. In the evenings she struggled to compose preludes, inspired by Sotho chants, after discovering a clavichord gathering cobwebs in Haarburgers music shop. On still nights, her new neighbours could hear its faint, often hesitant, twangy sounds.

Robin Bing became so anti-Apartheid in his occasional articles that his Argus Group masters saw fit to reassign him to the *Cape Argus*. After his wife, Marianne, died, he moved to London and spent the rest of his working life subbing for *The Times*.

Etienne Le Roux joined Die Sestigers, a circle of liberal Afrikaans writers which included Andre Brink, John M Coetzee, Breyten Breytenbach and poet Ingrid Jonker. After the fall of Apartheid, Nelson Mandela began his inaugural Presidential address to Parliament on 24th May 1994 by quoting from her poem 'The Child is Not Dead'.

The gemstone, lost from Theresa O'Brien's clothing, landed up in Rhodesia with the pretentious Potgieters, and was smuggled via Beira to Antwerp, where a 'bent' diamond cutter broke up the stone into 'saleable' smaller gems. The remaining stones in Manie's possession were returned to the Russian Ambassador in Pretoria. Then they vanished again, never to be listed in the present-day Kremlin Armoury, which houses the State's jewellery.

Glossary

A

abba – (Xhosa/Zulu) The act of carrying a child on your back.

Afrikaans. A dialect of Dutch. German, French, Malay, Khoi and Xhosa words were absorbed over the centuries, giving Afrikaans its unique character. It was only recognised as an official language in 1925.

Afrikaner. One whose home language is Afrikaans.

Afrikander. (Dutch) An African breed of cattle with curved, long horns. Derived from a breed herded by the Khoikhoi (Hottentot) and encountered by Dutch settlers in the Cape, in 1652.

B

babushka – (Russian) Grandmother or elderly woman; also refers to a headscarf tied under the chin.
bakkie – (Afrikaans) Pickup truck comprising a driver's cab and an open back to carry sundry loads.
blink-klippe – (Afrikaans) 'Blink' is to glitter. 'klippe' 'pebbles'. Thus 'glittering pebbles'.

boerewors – (Afrikaans) A traditional sausage made of beef, pork, or lamb and seasoned with spices.

boet – (Afrikaans) Brother or mate (informal term of address).

braai – (Afrikaans) Short for '**braaivleis**'. Meat grilled on an open fire.

céad míle fáilte – (Gaelic) A hundred thousand welcomes.

D

da – (Russian) Yes.

Doda Yegolide – mysterious words that appear in Theresa's scribblings. Resolved in the novel.

Dominee – (Afrikaans) Minister or pastor of the Dutch Reformed Church.

dorp – (Afrikaans) Small village.

dziękuję – (Polish) Thank you.

do widzenia – (Polish) Goodbye.

E

eish – (Zulu) An expression of surprise, frustration, or dismay.

F

fontein – (Dutch / Afrikaans) A natural Spring. Significantly, often used in South African place names.

G

gogga – (Afrikaans) Bug or insect (word often used by maids of children).

gramadoelas – (Afrikaans) Remote or 'in the 'middle of

nowhere'. The word first appeared in the writings of Herman Chares Bosman.

H

Haloo! – A local variation of 'Hello!'
hoekie – (Afrikaans) Small corner or nook.
howzit – (South African English, derived from Afrikaans & Zulu influence) 'How is it?' or 'How are you?'

I

indaba – (Zulu) Meeting or discussion (can refer to a gathering of leaders). Commonly used by English speakers.

J

jislaaik – (Afrikaans) 'Wow!' or an exclamation of surprise/shock.

K

kaffirs – (Offensive term) Derogatory term for black Africans, included for historical context only. Originated from Arabic slave-trader's word for 'infidels'.
kiaatwood – (South African English) A type of African hardwood (Pterocarpus angolensis), known for its rich colour and durability.
kleuringe – (Afrikaans) A dated and now offensive term historically used to refer to people of mixed ancestry in South Africa.
koppie – (Afrikaans) A small hill or rocky outcrop, common in the South African landscape.

Kromdraai – (Afrikaans) A crooked turn. A place name.

L

lekker – (Afrikaans) Nice, good, or tasty (commonly used to express enjoyment).
lucerne – (South African English) Alfalfa, a type of forage crop.

M

maas – (Zulu) Fermented milk similar to yogurt.
Mfecane – (Zulu) Historical term referring to a period of widespread chaos and disturbance in Southern Africa during the 1820s and 1830s.
mielie-fields – (Afrikaans) Corn or maize fields.
Mzansi – (Zulu/Xhosa) A popular name for South Africa (meaning 'south').

N

Namaqua Fig – A type of fig tree (Ficus ilicina) native to southern Africa.
Sutra Placer at Nezametnoya – (Russian) Old Russia's only source of gem-quality sapphires.
nie – (Afrikaans) No.
nyet – (Russian) No.

O

opsaal – (Afrikaans) To saddle up (a horse). A Boer rallying cry during the Boer War and again as South Africa left the Commonwealth at the beginning of Apartheid. Mythical brand name of a local brandy in the novel.

outspanning – (English adopted from Afrikaans 'uitspan') Unyoking oxen and allowing them to rest and graze near a natural source of water.

P

Piccanin – Young black boy. Nowadays regarded as a pejorative in South Africa. Seventeenth-century origination: from Spanish pequeño or Portuguese pequeño 'little', pequenino 'tiny'.
Piet (Maritz**) Retief** – (Dutch/Afrikaans) Name of a Voortrekker leaders who, with his delegation, was massacred by the Zulus on the orders of Zulu Chief Dingaan. Now a town of that name. Pietermaritzburg city also named after him.
proszę – (Polish) Please.
przepraszam – (Polish) Sorry or excuse me.

R

Romanov – (Russian) Former Russian Imperial dynasty 1613 – 1917. Came to prominence when Anastasia married Ivan the Terrible.

S

Salam-u-'Alaikum – (Arabic) 'Peace be upon you' (greeting).
Schaaplaats – (Afrikaans/Dutch) Place name near Clarens mentioned in the novel. Location of San rock art also fossils.
shisa nyama – (Zulu) 'Hot meat' or 'grilled meat'.
skelm or skellum – (Afrikaans) Crook or sly person. From Dutch derived from old High German 'skelmo'.
sláinte – (Gaelic) Health (used as a toast when drinking).

slán – (Gaelic) Goodbye.

spasibo – (Russian) Thank you.

spruit – (Afrikaans) A small stream or seasonal watercourse.

sustertjie – (Afrikaans) 'Little sister, used as a term of endearment.

T

taal – (Afrikaans) Language (specifically the Afrikaans language).

tafel – (Afrikaans) Table.

tannie – (Afrikaans) Aunt or an older woman (term of respect).

taoiseach – (Gaelic) Prime minister of Ireland.

thula – (Zulu) Be quiet or hush.

tickeys – small silver South African coins.

tokoloshe – (Zulu) An evil spirit in Zulu mythology. Summoned by malevolent people to cause trouble.

totsiens – (Afrikaans) A shortening of 'tot wedersiens'. Goodbye.

tovarishch – (Russian) Comrade.

trek – (Afrikaans) 'Pull'. Commonly, twelve to eighteen oxen, coupled together in 'spans' (pairs), were employed to pull the wagons during the 'Great Trek' into the interior, away from British rule. Nowadays 'trek' is in common use and can apply to any long and arduous journey – such as an expeditionary walk in Nepal.

Trek-Boer – (Afrikaans) Migrating farmer in the eighteenth and nineteenth centuries. (See above.)

tronk – (Afrikaans) Prison or jail.

tsarist – (Russian) Relating to the Russian Tsars or the system of government before the Russian Revolution of 1917.

tsotsi – (Sesotho or Pedi slang) Gangster or thug from a Black township.

tuisnywerheid – (Afrikaans) Home industry or cottage industry.

U

ubuntu – (Zulu) 'Humanity'.
uitlander – (Afrikaans) Foreigner or outsider.
uitspan – (Afrikaans) To 'unharness' or 'to rest', often used for stopping to rest on journey.
uisce beatha – (Gaelic) Whiskey (literally 'water of life').
umfaan – (Zulu) Boy.
u**mfazi** – (Zulu) Woman or wife.
umkhukhu – (Zulu) Shack or informal dwelling.
umkhulu – (Zulu) Grandfather.
umlungu – (Zulu) White person. Can be derogatory. Originates from description of Whites shipwrecked off the Pondoland coast. Sea foam.
umuthi – (Zulu) Traditional medicine.

V

vasbyt – (Afrikaans) To persevere or endure hardship (literally bite tight').
veld – (Afrikaans from the Dutch 'veldt') Field, although, in South Africa, rather 'open grassland'.
veldskoene – (Afrikaans) simple leather shoes, good for walking in the veld.
Vereeniging – (Afrikaans) Place name. (means 'union' or 'association').
verkrampte – (Afrikaans) Conservative or narrow-minded person 'cramped'.
verlig – (Afrikaans) Enlightened or liberal.
veroggend – (Afrikaans) In the morning.

vlei – (Afrikaans) Marsh or wetland.

vleis – (Afrikaans) Meat.

voetsek – (Afrikaans) 'Go away' or 'get lost' (often used harshly).

volk – (Afrikaans) People or folk.

voortrekker – (Afrikaans) Pioneer (specifically those who participated in the Great Trek). One who 'goes before'.

vrou – (Afrikaans) wife.

Vrystaat – (Afrikaans) Free State (one of South Africa's provinces).

vuka – (Zulu) Wake up.

W

wag-'n-bietjie – (Afrikaans) 'Wait a little (also a thorny bush that catches the clothes of passers-by).

winkels vir naturelle – (Afrikaans) 'Shops for natives' (Afrikaans phrase).

witam – (Polish) Welcome.

witblits – (Afrikaans) Strong homemade alcohol (literally 'white lightning').

witbooi – (Afrikaans) 'White boy'. (Can be derogatory. Can refer to a mixed race pale-skinned boy.)

wurra wurra wurra – (Afrikaans) A description boring 'waffle'.

Y

yebo – (Zulu) Yes. I agree.

Z

zol – (Afrikaans slang) Hand-rolled cigarette (often

containing cannabis, called 'dagga' in South Africa. Indigenous in some parts).

Zulu. Refers to an indigenous language as well as the race. The ancestors of the Zulus migrated from the Congo basin to Southeastern Africa (mainly Natal). Scattered Zulu 'tribelets' were consolidated by Chief Shaka, but later subjugated after their defeat by the British under Lord Chelmsford. They remain the largest indigenous group.

Notes

Apartheid

While 1949 wasn't the official start of apartheid ('apartness'), it was a crucial year for its development. In 1949, the National Party government in South Africa, which had come to power in 1948, began implementing policies that would form the foundation of apartheid. Specifically, the Prohibition of Mixed Marriages Act was passed in July 1949, preventing marriages between white people and people of other racial groups. Additionally, the ANC (African National Congress) adopted its Programme of Action in December 1949, marking a shift towards more militant resistance against apartheid.

During the years that followed, evermore draconian measures were introduced, during which time some three and a half million blacks were uprooted and forced into so-called 'homelands', otherwise known as 'Bantustans'. Classifications of ethnographic and linguistic groupings were arbitrary. It was an efficient device to prevent Blacks, resident Asiatics and local Chinese from participation in the administration of the country.

During this time, Chinese South Africans experienced a complex and evolving situation. Initially classified as 'non-white', they faced discrimination similar to other non-white groups, but their experiences were also shaped by their relatively small population size and diplomatic ties with the Republic of China (Taiwan). This led to a unique trajectory where they were sometimes granted 'honorary white' status, allowing them to bypass some of the more stringent apartheid laws.

The Coloured (mixed race) population in South Africa was, roughly, well over three million, thus comprising more than eight per cent of the total population. The government classified individuals as 'Coloured' based on their mixed-race heritage, a status that reflected their diverse genetic background. Like the Asiatics (local Indians), they suffered from similar restrictions and severe discrimination.

Indian South Africans, while facing discrimination and various restrictions, also experienced complexities in their relationship with the African population and the ruling white minority. Pre-1949, Indian activists like Mohandas Gandhi focused on the rights of Indian people, but later, movements like the Three Doctors' Pact sought to unite all non-Europeans in a broader struggle against apartheid. Although Indians were granted some privileges denied to Africans, they were also subjected to discriminatory laws and policies, including restrictions on movement, voting, and land ownership.

Sources: South African History Online, Wikipedia, and personal observation

Detention under the 90-Day Act

In 1949, the law did not allow for indefinite detention without charge, unlike the later 90-Day Act of 1963, which did. Although detainees, such as Sophia, detained for assumed political offences, would typically be held until formal charges were brought, they were not subjected to the extended periods without charge that characterised later Apartheid legislation. Even in 1949, however, individuals arrested for alleged political offences had only a limited right to legal representation, the process often obstructed by police or state officials.

Bail before court appearance was theoretically possible, though heavily restricted in political cases. The police could oppose bail, and magistrates often sided with the state's security arguments, making it challenging for such detainees to secure it.

Russian interference

From the early Apartheid years, the African National Conference became increasingly influenced by the South African Communist Party (SACP), which enjoyed close political ties to the Soviet Union. Following the SACP and ANC's formation of MK* in 1961, SACP members such as Arthur Goldreich made several tours of the Soviet Union and Warsaw Pact member states to solicit military aid. The Soviet Union became the largest contributor of war materiel and arms to MK. It suppled an estimated 36 million rubles' worth of military equipment, including pistols, rifles, machine guns, grenade launchers, and ammunition. By 1982 an estimated 90% of MK's equipment was of Soviet origin. The remainder came from other Warsaw Pact member states or sympathetic revolutionary movements; for example, MK received ex-Portuguese Uzi and Sterling submachine guns from the People's Armed Forces of Liberation of Angola (FAPLA) during the mid-1970s. The People's Liberation

Army of Namibia (PLAN) also donated some arms and ammunition to MK.MK used these weapons during its economic sabotage activities inside South Africa, as well as in semi-conventional military operations in Angola and elsewhere.

MK cadres were frequently sent to the Soviet Union, and to a lesser extent East Germany, to receive military training on these weapons abroad. However, the Soviet Union, East Germany, and Cuba also sent military instructors to help train MK cadres in friendly African nations where the ANC operated in exile, such as Angola, Tanzania, Uganda, and Ethiopia. MK stored most of its equipment in large arms depots located in neighbouring states around South Africa and operated various smuggling routes to bring this materiel to its domestic insurgent cells. The materiel was secreted across the border in small quantities and the cached.

Source – Matthew Graham, 2010. "Cold War in Southern Africa", Africa Spectrum, Institute of African Affairs, GIGA German Institute of Global and Area Studies, Hamburg, vol. 45(1), pages 131–139.

*uMkhonto weSizwe (Zulu for 'Spear of the Nation'), abbreviated to MK.

Illicit Diamond Trade

Illicit Diamond Buying (IDB) in Apartheid-Era South Africa

In South Africa, Illicit Diamond Buying (IDB) referred to the unlawful purchase or sale of rough diamonds outside the state-controlled, monopolised distribution system — most notably run by De Beers. It was not the same as the later phenomenon of 'blood diamonds', which refers to gems mined in war zones and sold to finance rebel movements, a problem that gained prominence in West Africa decades after apartheid began. In the 1940s, IDB was already a long-standing issue in the country's diamond fields, rooted in theft, smuggling, and corruption within a highly protected industry.

The illicit trade had existed since the first diamond rush of the late 1860s, when surface diggings made theft easy and smuggling networks quickly took shape. Early laws, such as the Trade in Diamonds Consolidation Act of 1882, made it a serious crime for anyone other than a licensed dealer to possess or trade in uncut diamonds, with penalties of up to fifteen years' imprisonment. By the early twentieth century, magistrates were routinely handing down minimum sentences of five years' hard labour, with no option of a fine.

By the mid-twentieth century, the scale of IDB was immense. It was estimated that around £10 million worth of diamonds were being smuggled out of South Africa each year. To counter this, De Beers created the International Diamond Security Organisation (IDSO), led by former MI5 chief Sir Percy Sillitoe. The IDSO's work extended far beyond South Africa, targeting smuggling routes that linked Kimberley to major diamond trading hubs such as Antwerp, Paris, and Beirut.

One of the enforcement tactics used during this period was the so-called 'trapping system'. Undercover operatives, often posing as illicit buyers, would approach those suspected of possessing stolen stones. If a suspect agreed to sell, the deal would be used as evidence for arrest and conviction. While effective from a policing standpoint, such entrapment would be highly controversial today, and it was a key part of the IDSO's anti-smuggling campaign.

The fight against IDB also shaped everyday life for mine workers, especially Black and Coloured labourers. Mining companies introduced 'closed compounds' — walled barracks where workers lived under guard for the duration of their contracts. These compounds, championed by Cecil Rhodes in the late nineteenth century, were designed to prevent diamonds from leaving the mine site and became a model for Apartheid's wider system of labour control. Workers leaving the compounds were subjected to strict searches, and the mere suspicion of IDB could be used to justify surveillance and restrictions.

The penalties for those convicted of IDB were severe. In addition to lengthy prison sentences and heavy fines, offenders could be sent to notorious institutions such as Cape Town's Breakwater Prison, where conditions were brutal and chains were sometimes used for months at a time. Within the prison system, however, 'IDB men' often enjoyed a certain status, sometimes boasting of hidden caches of diamonds awaiting them on release.

In apartheid-era South Africa, IDB was more than an economic crime – it was a focal point where monopoly control, global smuggling networks, and systemic racial oppression intersected. For the state and mining companies, it was a threat to be eliminated through strict laws, specialised security organisations, and coercive labour systems. For those involved, it could be a means of survival, profit, or quiet defiance in a society built on exclusion and control.

Source: Historical note based on research compiled by Morgan Morgan with AI assistance for the Diamond Fields Advertiser *(DFA), Kimberley, South Africa, 2025.*

Previous novels by William Paterson

The Kirkwood Trilogy which comprises

The Snake in the Signal Box
What Happened at Yonder
The Girl in the Summerhouse

The first two are set in then-named Natal Province of South Africa, between both World Wars, and the final novel in the trilogy is set during World War II.

The second edition of *The Snake in the Signal Box* carries a foreword by Thomas Pakenham, author of *The Scramble for Africa.*

The third novel, *The Girl in the Summerhouse,* carries a foreword by Former Justice Albie Sachs, after whom The Albie Award was named by Alma and George Clooney.

All three novels are available worldwide as paperbacks and eBooks.